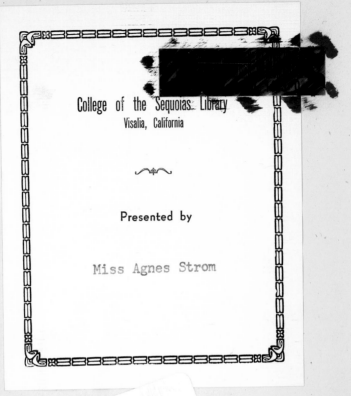

THE SUDDEN GUEST.

By Christopher La Farge

HOXSIE SELLS HIS ACRES

EACH TO THE OTHER

POEMS AND PORTRAITS

THE WILSONS

EAST BY SOUTHWEST

THE SUDDEN GUEST

MESA VERDE

CHRISTOPHER LA FARGE

The Sudden Guest

"................. conscience,
the sudden guest, ... worst of witches,
that makes the moon grow dark, and then the gravestones
move restlessly, and send their dead to haunt us!"

PUSHKIN

COWARD-McCANN, INC.   NEW YORK

To my brother

Francis W. La Farge

for friendship rendered

THE SUDDEN GUEST

I

PROBABLY another false alarm, thought Miss Leckton, and she brusquely turned off the radio. Nevertheless, it was a depressing sort of day, the air both moist and warm. She rose from the morris chair in her library, and went over to look at the aneroid barometer on the wall by the fireplace. It read 29.80. Not low enough, in September, to account for the depression in the air, nor was the air enough, surely, to explain the depression she felt, the sense of thickness in the lungs as though the act of breathing was a difficulty. She could have understood that if the wind had blown from the southwest, one of those smoky storms that make one feel as though one were going to come down with jaundice. I trust it's not my heart, she said to herself. Then she dismissed that as pure nonsense. There was nothing in the world the matter with her. Though sixty is no longer young.

Miss Leckton walked to the door and went into the living room. There has never been an autumn, she thought, when I have had so few flowers in the house. What with the awful drought this summer and no proper servants to help her, the flowers were scarce and poor and their arrangement a chore. The calendulas and cosmos were pretty, but the marigolds were few and wilted quickly. The chrysanthemums weren't out yet, and such dahlias as flowered were clumsy and over-large for her vases. The roses were not in bloom. If we get another hurricane, she thought, there'll be no flowers at all.

3

None at all. It was a very unpleasant thought. She walked to one of the south windows and looked out at the afternoon.

The lawn fell gently from the house to the herbaceous border to the south. The border itself was protected by a low hedge of yew, still ragged and with gaps in it. It had not yet grown together, having been planted since the hurricane of 1938. Beyond the yew hedge, the land fell sharply to the rocks of Olneys Point. The tide was high and ebbing, and the two great rocks, The Ewe and The Lamb, showed off-shore only their weed-brown tops in the salt water of the ocean. The wind, Miss Leckton noted, was northerly. North-east, about, and fresh. The waves it created made a white and decorative pattern of broken surf around the rocks. The sky was overcast, the light grey but fairly bright. In the distance she could see the black remnant of Motherledge Lighthouse swept by the passing waves.

The trouble was, she must make up her mind—now. She turned from the window and looked at the clock on the mantelpiece. Three-forty. Either she was going to make preparations for the hurricane—it was to come again, again, her inner thoughts said—or she was not. There'd be only a little more daylight and no one to help her but George Potter, with the somewhat problematical assistance of Mrs. Kluger. She and George would probably have it all to do. There was so much to do, if you once started. So much easier to disbelieve, to say that the really ominous warning on the radio was calamity-howling, that there couldn't be another hurricane, now, in 1944. So much to do. So many decisions to make. And one was alone to make them, nobody to ask, nobody with whom to discuss. Even Leah, Leah was gone. She threw back her head, a little defiantly, and she said aloud, "And a good thing too." But there was still the decision to make, and it seemed to her then that it was almost as though she had to decide, she, Carrel Leckton, alone, whether or not there was to be a hurricane. Again.

She was seized rather suddenly with a sense of anger. Why did this have to happen to her? Wasn't it enough to be in the middle of a terrible war, without having nature rise up

4

in revolution against your security? Life was hard enough as it was. One could get no proper servants, or if one acquired them (at fabulous wages!), they left on a moment's notice and with no possible consideration. There were no deliveries to Olneys Point now—literally none, not even milk. If she hadn't had George Potter and the car, she could not have opened the house at all this season, much less survived in it. And now George's wife was nearly useless with grief over the son who had been killed in Italy. Or, anyway, reported missing in action. Curious that a Negro couple should have had only one child. Usually they bred so very prolifically. She shuddered slightly and dismissed the thought. If there were to be another hurricane, she would prefer to move George and his wife into the house, make them leave the tenement over the garage. But would that cause trouble with Mrs. Kluger? She might not like having them there, sharing the servants' bathroom with her. It was all so difficult!

The anger grew. It might be just alarmist stuff on the radio, just a scheme to get you to listen to the commercials. There had been false alarms before. Several of them. People expected hurricanes in 1939, being still frightened. It was fantastic to have another one so soon, in 1944. And here she was, alone, to meet it and cope with it—if it came. Five days before she was to move back to New York. A strange cook-general, whom you hadn't had for above a month, a native, more or less, of unknown temper; a Negro chauffeur, old and faithful, to be sure, but getting much too independent, with a wife made undependable by grief. Why couldn't Ella Potter take her loss quietly? Was she the only person in the world who had ever suffered a loss? It was all too much, too much. The lights would fail, the water system would fail, the cellar possibly flood again, the telephone would go out. Even the car—that last link with life—might again have something happen to it. And here she was, all alone, to decide everything.

As her anger faded, turning now into a depression of spirit, a sense of facing a load too heavy to lift unaided, there

5

flashed (but briefly) through Carrel Leckton's mind an image of recollection that she, accustomed in that capacity, had undertaken to forget or to bury so deep it might not be exhumed. The recollection took the shape of herself, standing in the door of her own house here, the wind tearing at her skirt and hair, and saying to those people, "No. Not here. You'll find a quite good, safe spot at Cottrellton. No. Not here. I am sorry"; and the image of herself moved with the wind inside the house and shut the door, with Catherine's help, against the force of the gale.

She had not wanted them. Not then. Then there was Catherine Lovatt, the waitress, and Anna—Anna Mulvey, the cook, and George and George's wife, Ella, and their boy, Desmond—he must have been about fifteen then, and so useful, too. No, no. There were plenty of people then. It was all quite different. She had neither needed nor wanted all the others. Leah was there then, for part of the day, anyway. Leah. That, at least, was one thing she did not now have to cope with. No. It had been a question then of getting rid of people. This time, thank goodness, there was no Herbert Golotz to get rid of. Or try to get rid of. You could never entirely rid yourself of that sort of man, there was no way to communicate to such as he that he was ... her mind checked at the words 'not wanted' as she thought, He's dead. That's all over and done now. All over and done. The point was, really, that at least she had only herself and the house and Mrs. Kluger and the Potters to think of. She would know—this time—how to cope with an invasion. That old doorbell was gone now, too. One learnt by experience. One is not strong for nothing. One was still vigorous at sixty. It was a matter of decision.

She looked out the window now with a more seeing eye. The light was beginning to fail quite perceptibly. The wind seemed about the same. A gale. Half a gale, more accurately. Turning, she looked at the clock again. It was nearly four o'clock. She had stood here, doing nothing, for almost twenty minutes. Then she spoke aloud.

Unconsciously, when she did so, her words took the form

6

of a decision past the realm of her power. "We shall have the storm," she said. Her mind heard the words: they sounded as though she were declaring in favor of a dance or wine for dinner and the declaration were quite decisive; and she amended her words, saying, "We ought to get ready. I must speak to George." She was aware of a curious sense of relief, compounded in part of the act of decision, in part of a realization that there was really not so much to do, that there was time to do it. It was all very different from 1938, when she had been busy with a lot of other decisions, problems, personalities, and the storm had broken on them while they were still scarcely aware of what had smitten them. There had been Herbert Golotz to get rid of, Leah to battle, those people—what was their name? oh, yes, La Perche, La Perche and his wife—to send packing. How astonishingly importunate such people could be! Perhaps their importunity was really the callousness of ignorance, an incapacity to realize that one might not be welcome in someone else's house, all of a sudden, just because the wind blew. The woman was a pale little thing, looked more foreign than he did. He had had red hair. Grover La Perche. From Lonsdale. Funny how one remembered such trifles!

Miss Leckton went back into the library and turned on the radio. It became audible at the end of a five-minute broadcast of local news, and there was the repetition of the storm warning.

"The storm is expected to strike the coast of southern New England some time after eight o'clock this evening. The time will depend on the acceleration of the storm's rate of progress, if any. There is a possibility that the center will still head out to sea and not strike the shore line at all, but this is not now expected by the Weather Bureau. The storm is now estimated to be . . ." There was a loud crackling noise of static that drowned out the words momentarily and the voice resumed, ". . . and east of Atlantic City. Hurricane warnings have been hoisted all along the coast from Hatteras to Maine and the Coast Guard is busy evacuating persons in seaside resorts in the danger areas. That's the news at this

7

moment, brought to you ..." the static again interrupted, "... of Seventy-six Monmouth Street, Cranston's leading store. Further bulletins on the progress of the storm will be broadcast as received. Attention, please! You have a date with fascinating glamour when ..." Miss Leckton switched the machine off.

"They have no sense of propriety," she said aloud.

She picked up the telephone and she called Cottrellton 72-J. After it had rung several times, Ella Potter's voice answered.

"Miss Leckton's garage," it said.

The phrase annoyed Miss Leckton as usual. She had told Ella over and over again that it sounded like a commercial garage. But Negroes, she thought, are like that, you can't teach them some things, and they can be almost as stubborn as the Irish.

"Ella," she said. "Do you know where George is?"

"Yes, ma'am," Ella said. "He's putting the car away all safe and he's fixing up the garage doors so they won't blow off in this hurricane like the last time."

In spite of herself, Miss Leckton heard herself saying, "Oh, we may not get this storm. All right, Ella. Ask him to come over and see me, will you?"

"Yes, ma'am," said Ella.

Miss Leckton hung up.

How stupid of me! she thought. Why did I say that we might not get this storm? Now perhaps Ella would take no precautions in fixing up the tenement windows—although George seemed to have made up his mind pretty independently. Still, it was up to her to act, and not depend on the vagaries of a somewhat hysterical colored woman. She called the garage again.

She interrupted Ella's formal opening to say, "Listen, Ella. There does seem to be a real possibility that there will be another bad storm some time this evening. Have you and George fixed your windows and shutters securely?"

"Yes, Miss Leckton," Ella said. "We've already done all that. We took the canvas chairs off the lawn and put them

8

in the garage, we did. George, he closed up the tool shed and he has run a rope to that young pine tree, to hold it steady, like. Everything's all right here. You want me to do anything else over here?"

"No, thank you," said Miss Leckton. "Just send George. If I think of anything further, I'll call you. Thank you."

"It's lucky I got all my washing in yesterday," Ella said. "Not like 1938. That was a Wednesday. And I had more help then."

"Yes," said Miss Leckton quickly. If she did not interrupt, Ella would start in about her son. "All right. That's good, Ella. Get George now."

"Yes, ma'am. I did that. He was right downstairs. He'll be right over. Please not to keep him too long, Miss Leckton."

"No," said Miss Leckton. "Thank you." She hung up again.

The thing to do was to go now and see Mrs. Kluger. How extraordinary people were! Imagine Ella remembering that the 1938 hurricane came on a Wednesday! Of course, that meant washing on the line to her. She was a happy and a useful woman then. Not all nervous and wrapped up in her own griefs. In normal circumstances, she could have seized the opportunity to tell Ella how badly the wash was being done. But nowadays one did better to let that sort of complaint go unsaid. Actually, one was fairly lucky to have someone to do the laundry at home.

She went out into the hallway. Through the side-lights of the south door one could see the angry ocean. But it was still just a storm and not too bad at that. The grey of the ocean and of the sky created the illusion that the grass of her lawn was green and fresh. It was not, after the summer's drought.

She went through the dining room. The silver would have to be put in the office cupboards, it would be safer there. The dining-room windows had held before, but one could never be sure a second time. After all, the windows on the south and east of the living room had blown in. Oh, thought Miss Leckton, may that not happen again!

9

She went through the swing door into the pantry, and through that into the kitchen. No one there. She walked to the foot of the back stairs that came out into the corner of the kitchen, and she called up them.

"Oh, Mrs. Kluger!"

"I'm coming down in jest a minute," called Mrs. Kluger's strong and rasping voice.

It's high time, thought Miss Leckton. Well past four o'clock. It would be tea-time soon.

This was the first good chance she had had to look at the storm to the westward. The waves were rolling far up the sand of Cato's Beach, and the whole long crescent of its sandy shore was white with the spray or reflected the grey of the sky in its shining wet surface. There were even small whitecaps on Ten Acre Pond, which lay north of the beach and behind what was left of the sand dunes. They had been so tall, so beautiful, those dunes, before the hurricane. Now they were short and rounded, and the beach grass was just beginning to grow back on them. God alone knew how much would be left of them if there came another hurricane. Beyond the dunes, the soft greens and browns and yellows of the marsh grass were rippling together. It would have been beautiful if it hadn't had an overtone of fear to it. It looked too much as it had looked before—it was too reminiscent.

Rubbish! thought Miss Leckton then, as she heard Mrs. Kluger's feet on the wooden treads of the stairs. Rubbish! It looks like this every time there's a September storm. The thing may go out to sea. The radio was scarcely infallible. She was conscious that much of her sense of depression had lifted. There was now something to do.

The noise of Mrs. Kluger's big feet on the stairs stopped, and Miss Leckton could hear them begin to ascend again. She did not like to be kept waiting.

"What's the matter, Mrs. Kluger?" she said.

"I jest forgot to turn off my radio," said Mrs. Kluger's voice. "Burn out my tubes."

The heavy steps ascended, and then Miss Leckton could hear her cook's progress on the floor above. Time was fleeting by. There was much to be done. She walked over to the west window again and looked at the waves on the distant beach. It was necessary to do something, to occupy one's mind. Otherwise one would become too vexed and that was something that might prove disastrous. The day was past when it was safe to let oneself be vexed with servants—and show it.

Presently Mrs. Kluger came down into the kitchen.

She was a large woman with heavy legs and ankles and big feet and an enormous bosom. Her face was amiable and her cheeks were covered with a brilliant orange make-up that was unevenly applied and made a shocking contrast to her white hair. She wore a flowered cotton house-dress of a predominantly pink color that clashed with the rouge on her cheeks. Her movements were slow and heavy, but competent.

"Burn out a tube," said Mrs. Kluger, "and it takes them three weeks to replace it at that store in Cottrellton. Folger's."

"Yes," said Miss Leckton impatiently. "Yes, yes. Mrs. Kluger, it sounds now as though there were some possibility that we might get the edge of that storm here."

"Edge?" Mrs. Kluger said. "Sounds like the whole business was going to land right on top of us. According to my radio."

"It is possible," Miss Leckton said. It was extraordinary how much this woman could annoy her. Yet she did her work well, and was far from a bad cook. "At all events, I suppose it best to be prepared. I though I'd get you to give me a hand in putting things ready."

"Always best to be ready," Mrs. Kluger said. "Now in the last storm, in 1938, my daughter was to Matunuck, expecting her first, and we did get nervous. But we were lucky. We were far from water, and we had a lot of canned goods in the house, and were all right, only thing happened was part of the roof blew off of the barn. To tell you the truth, I could wish my daughter wasn't living to Chog's Cove now. It's low and the wells and cellars there tends to flood easy. And her husband in the navy and nobody knows where, and my husband departed. That was in 1940, he was a railroad man. He certainly scurried around in the 1938 storm."

11

"Yes," said Miss Leckton. "Now the first thing is food . . ."

"Sure," Mrs. Kluger interrupted her. "I been all over that. I got everything arranged handy." She walked to the big closet that projected onto the kitchen porch to the north. "Everything's in the larder," she said. She opened the door and proudly waved Miss Leckton to inspect it.

Miss Leckton looked. There was no gainsaying it, everything was in perfect order, spotlessly clean.

"Now you'll see," said Mrs. Kluger. "Here is sterno and its stand, plenty of sterno, you want something hot quick. That electric range, that's bound to go out first thing, they always do. And plenty soup and here's some beans, they're nourishing. There's everything right here, ready to hand. I did it after lunch."

It was as she said, Miss Leckton admitted. Everything was in order, there was plenty for an emergency. Or—the thought flicked through her mind—there was plenty for her and for Mrs. Kluger, and even for the Potters, for several days, provided they didn't have to feed a lot of other people. But that couldn't happen again. No. Not again. She could deal with that now.

"Instant coffee," said Mrs. Kluger. "Enough sugar, but God knows that's scarce anyway, makes it hard to whip up a tasty dessert, don't it? Tea here, some of your China tea, though you only got about a half pound left, Miss Leckton, and some of my orange pekoe. Bacon. Eggs in the icebox, and that'll go out too, for sure, but they come in when George Potter come with them today, and they'll keep. A dozen eggs. We should have ordered more maybe, but they might spoil, no refrigerator. Clam chowder, three cans of it. Consommé, tomato soup, and a couple cans condensed milk, been here a long time, seems like. You'll be O.K."

It seemed a little odd to Miss Leckton, this cheerful detachment of Mrs. Kluger. She spoke of it as though she were wholly uninvolved, as though Miss Leckton were to face the storm, and its aftermath of disruption and scarcity, quite alone. It was a little disturbing.

"That's excellent," Miss Leckton said. "A beautiful job,

Mrs. Kluger. Now there are other things to do. I shall put away the silver in the dining room. When George Potter comes, I shall get him to take down the pictures from the living room and the dining room and put them in the office. In the meantime, perhaps you'll take the books from the tables in the living room, near the windows, and move them into the library. Just put them in the corners, on the floor by the big bookcase. The north side. And any ornaments, bring them in and put them on the desk in the office. And then we'll all move the furniture a little away from the windows. One never knows. Water does leak so terribly in these storms."

She was careful to avoid any mention of danger. She didn't want to alarm this woman.

"Can't tell what'll happen," said Mrs. Kluger. "You're real near the water. Sometimes a window will give right up, jest blow right out. Happens plenty of times."

"Oh, I don't anticipate that," said Miss Leckton.

"Might as well figure on the worst," said Mrs. Kluger. "I'll get right after it. You got enough sheets, we could cover the furniture in the dining room and living room? Keeps the salt off."

"Yes, that might be good, if we have time," Miss Leckton said.

"Plenty of time," Mrs. Kluger said. "You going to want your tea, ain't you? Pretty soon?"

"We could omit that today."

"No need," said Mrs. Kluger. "Tea is a good thing. Takes but a minute." She went to the electric range and turned on one of the coils. She filled the kettle and set it on the stove. "Pity this thing is electric," she said. "You'd ought to have a kerosene range for emergencies."

"I suppose I should," said Miss Leckton.

"After last time," Mrs. Kluger said. "Now I'll get after the books and so forth."

She turned from the range and began to walk toward the pantry. As she did so, the door to the kitchen porch was opened by George Potter.

He came in quickly, shutting the door behind him, but even in that brief moment while the door was opened, Miss Leckton could hear the roar of the wind and the steady pounding reverberations of surf on rocks and the sibilant suck and crash of waves breaking on Cato's Beach. These sounds had been but an undercurrent before; now they rose to a new intensity. Even when George had closed the door she could still hear the storm more clearly than before, and it alarmed her, her heart beat a little faster. Without greeting him, she turned to the window. There was still plenty of light, she noticed, and as she looked she calmed down again. It was blowing very stiff, almost a full gale now, but no more. It was not an uncommon storm for the season. When she turned back, George stood there smiling, his hat in his hand, his face wet with the moisture of sea spray.

"Evening," he said. "That's a *real* storm."

"You're wet," said Mrs. Kluger. "You'd ought to have worn a raincoat. You cold?"

"No," said George. "No. It's warm out. Too warm altogether, for a September storm. I guess we're going to get this hurricane, Miss Leckton."

She found herself with a sudden and passionate desire to deny this prediction. It was as though, now, George and Mrs. Kluger had imposed the storm on her, so that her original decision was being taken away from her, nullified, as it were, by their sureness in their own opinions. It was so strong, this feeling, that it took her a second to control it.

"It's possible," she said. "I want you to help me here, George. Take down the pictures in the living room and the dining room, put them in the office. You might do the same thing in the guest room too, but I'll do the upstairs sitting room myself. They are all small pictures there, my own things. I'd rather put them away myself."

"Yes," said George. "But before I start, I just thought I'd inquire about Mrs. Kluger's car."

"What about it?" said Miss Leckton sharply.

"There's room in the garage," George said. "I made room. It's outside now, back of the tool shed. It's out of the wind, but this salt spray isn't going to do it no good, not if it sets there long. I want to nail up the garage doors, way they won't blow off like last time." He turned to Mrs. Kluger. "You want me to put it in there? Won't take but a minute."

"Why, thank you, Mr. Potter," she said. "That's real kind of you. But no. Jest leave it where it is."

"You'd better let him put it up," said Miss Leckton. She stopped herself then, for she had almost gone on to say why, to tell what had happened to her car before. That would have been a mistake.

"Thanks," Mrs. Kluger said. "But I'll tell you, Miss Leckton. I'm going home after I've got you your supper and washed up. I won't feel easy here, with my daughter and her children, and one jest an infant, in that place at Chog's Cove."

"You're leaving?" said Miss Leckton. She couldn't believe it, couldn't take it in. She was assailed by a whole host of feelings she was quite unable to sort out, to analyze. One should not feel this way, she thought. It was confusion mixed with a lot of other emotions she couldn't—or was it, did not want?—to name. What difference did it make whether Mrs. Kluger stayed or went? If she left, it was one less person to cope with.

It was quite obvious that Mrs. Kluger, when she spoke, answered to the tone of Miss Leckton's question.

"I'm sorry if it bothers you," she said. "I thought it all out. You got Mr. Potter here and his wife, and to tell you the truth, this seems to me a sort of a poor place to ride out a hurricane, with the sea so near and all. Right around you, almost."

"It's quite safe," Miss Leckton said. "Quite safe."

"Yes," said Mrs. Kluger. "But I'd be too upset here, thinking about my daughter. It isn't like the old days when there were lots of hands to help out in a hard time. Her man's gone to the war and there's no one to look after her, and her neighbors are all in the same sort of fix, let alone they got no gas to waste. She lives out on the Seldom Brook road, a mile from the village, near the marsh inlet. It flooded the last time, Peggy Arnold told me, she had it then. Cellar full of water and you could keep your feet dry, if you was spry, by hopping from chair to chair on the ground floor. If there had been enough chairs, Peggy said." She laughed.

"And if you go," said Miss Leckton, "when will you return?"

"As soon as may be," Mrs. Kluger said. "In the morning if all's well and the roads ain't blocked. Or flooded. I'll leave everything here for you, all ready. I can get back at noon anyways, barring a disaster."

"I should prefer that you stayed," said Miss Leckton. "Here we are isolated. Your daughter is right near a village." She spoke as calmly as she could.

"No," said Mrs. Kluger. She moved to the range and turned a switch from high heat to low, for the kettle had begun to boil. "No. I'm sorry. I'm going to leave about eight o'clock, after you've had your supper." She glanced out the window. "If I can," she added with a laugh.

Miss Leckton could find nothing to say. She felt anger rising up within her strongly, and she was afraid of herself, of the words that might come tumbling out if she once began to speak. It was impossible for her to agree, to say the simple phrases, 'Very well,' or 'All right.'

"Then I guess I'll just put a piece of canvas over the hood of your car," said George. "Something to keep the wet off your magneto and wires."

That was too much for Miss Leckton.

"No," she said. "There are other things I want done here. Many things. We have wasted enough time already. I say, we have wasted enough time."

"Thank you, Mr. Potter," said Mrs. Kluger. "It can wait. That car's been out of doors in all weathers. Starts good."

"You can begin on the pictures, George," Miss Leckton said. She turned and left with an unnecessary vigor, going through the swing door into the pantry so rapidly that the door banged loudly against the dresser behind it. As it swung to, she was aware that she had cut a ridiculous figure for a woman of her age and position, but that it had been beyond her to prevent herself from behaving so. By the time she had reached the dining room, she was in control of herself again, and she started at once collecting the silver. She set her expression to one of absorbed concentration on her work. It gave to her long face a mask-like appearance.

The office was a narrow room that lay north of the dining room and was half its width, the pantry and the back stairs occupying the rest of the space to the west wall of the house. It was entered by a door to the right of the dining-room fireplace, and it contained high cupboards on both its long walls, with an ugly flat-topped desk at its single window. Through that window one could look over the high privet hedge, see part of the roof of the garage-tenement, and the heavy and distant growth of maples and oaks which covered the rise of land to the north, beyond the low ground and Ten Acre Creek.

Each time she entered the office, her hands full of an assortment of silverware, she looked at the view to the north. It had a particular fascination, for it made her more conscious than usual of how islanded she was, though that very fact had often seemed to her the most desirable characteristic of the place. South of Olneys Point was the sea. To the west of her lay Cato's Beach with its curving sand dunes, the shallow water of Ten Acre Pond, the autumn richness of its marshland. To the north, the land dropped slowly to the banks of Ten Acre Creek, a sallywinder flowing with the tide through a beautifully patterned low area of marsh grass. Ten Acre Creek turned south and flowed to the sea at Plover Point, broadening into a miniature bay there, and thus bounded Olneys Point to the east. Beyond the marshland and the creek, the land rose sharply, the deep greens and browns of the marsh giving way to the olive greens of huckleberry and blueberry, the high grey-green of shad bush, and these, as one went higher, replaced by alders and swamp maples and a few tupelo trees, a few clumps of birch, and the rather clumsy forms of the wind-beaten black oaks. The road from the house led north, over a stout wooden bridge, and began to climb to the high ground as it swung slowly to

17

the eastward between the trees, toward the village of Cottrellton, six miles distant.

When she had put away the last of the silver, she stopped her work for a moment and looked out the office window. It was then that she noticed how quiet the room was—and, noting that, became aware that the wind had shifted, that it was blowing no longer from the north at all, for the window had ceased to rattle and the sounds of the storm had diminished sensibly in volume. It was at the moment when she fully realized this change that George came in, carrying a portrait of her father.

"The storm has abated," Miss Leckton said.

"Will I put them in the lower cupboards or just lean them against them?" George asked her.

"Lean them against them," Miss Leckton answered. "The wind has dropped."

"It's shifted, Miss Leckton," George said.

"Shifted where?"

"To the east," said George.

"But it's dropped?"

"No. It's blowing harder. It's blowing real hard."

"To the east," Miss Leckton said.

It made her feel quite poorly for a moment, a sense of weakness all over, a slight sense of dizziness that came and passed. Odd, she thought. I'm not usually dizzy. It must be the black coffee at lunch-time. She said no more to George, but got on with her work. As she went into the dining room, she listened. It was true. The storm was higher, noisier, a gale now.

Soon enough, the work here was done. The pictures were all neatly stacked, the silver locked away. George and Mrs. Kluger had moved the furniture away from the windows in the south and east walls. There was no more for her to do but move the little things in the upstairs rooms.

"I'll get you your tea," said Mrs. Kluger. "It will do you good."

Miss Leckton felt that there was no use in telling Mrs. Kluger that she didn't need good done to her, that she was quite all right, quite able to cope with considerably more than this demanded, but she did want her tea, and her legs felt tired.

"Very well," she said. "In the library."

"Right away," said Mrs. Kluger, and she dropped the last of the sheets over the sofa on the east wall of the living room, and then walked in her heavy but purposeful fashion toward the kitchen.

"I'll go outside now and close up the shutters," said George. "I'll just nail them in a bit, too. I better do it while we still got light."

"Yes," said Miss Leckton. She surveyed the living room. It was in good shape now. It would be all right if only the windows held. But that was not an event to anticipate, to think about. "Can you do the upstairs windows from the outside?"

"I can do the east windows from the porch roof. Yes, Miss Leckton. I'll have to do the others from inside. I'll do them right off before the wind shifts to the southward."

He seems very convinced, thought Miss Leckton, that it will shift. It was stupid to be so sure. Obstinate. Just because that was what had happened in 1938. Stupid.

"And we'd better collect newspapers here, and upstairs," said Miss Leckton. "In case we get the real storm. For window leaks."

"Yes," said George. "I'll do those shutters now. And I'll collect that paper. And then I'll just slip a canvas over Mrs. Kluger's car."

"If you must," said Miss Leckton. She could hear her annoyance in her own voice. "But please to do the important things first. After all, I don't consider it important that Mrs. Kluger should be assisted to desert me at this juncture."

"No," said George. "I'll just do those shutters now." He left the room.

Miss Leckton found herself wondering, as she went into the library, how long it was, how many years, since George had stopped saying 'Ma'am' to her. Quite a long while. Though his manners were good, in spite of it.

19

She sat down in the morris chair. In a moment Mrs. Kluger would bring the tea, and she could have that. It would taste good. It would give her a chance both to rest and to think. To be alone. She became aware of the fact— a novel one, never before experienced or, at least, consciously noted—that she didn't want to be alone. Not at all. Nor to think. One's thoughts were disturbed today, out of control. One remembered such odd things. Like the color of that La Perche man's hair. Five years back. No, six.

She waited impatiently, not for her tea, but for Mrs. Kluger's appearance. Curious, that was.

II

MISS LECKTON had just reached out to turn on the radio (in reluctant preference to her own thoughts) when she saw Mrs. Kluger coming through the door with the tray. She was surprised that she hadn't heard the woman's heavy footsteps, until she realized that the noise of the gale had risen sufficiently to penetrate within the house. Listening to it now, she could hear its components: the battering pound of surf on the rocks, the onrushing noise of waves cut and slashed by the flat and sharp-edged layers of the shore ledges, the forever eager but empty voice of high wind, sounding as though it hastened to fill a void of infinite capacity and appetite. Out of the total composition, she missed acutely, after all these years, the cruel whistle, the ghost-cry of wind tearing at the leaves of trees. It was a notable lack. This was a land of gales. One learnt their voice.

But when Mrs. Kluger had set the tea tray on the little table by Miss Leckton's chair, there was nothing her mistress could think of to say that would detain her—either for a moment's company or for the sake of further argument about the threatened desertion. Indeed, there was no comfort at all to be had from Mrs. Kluger's presence, since it was so obviously temporary; and this fact continued to annoy as well as trouble Miss Leckton while she poured herself a cup of tea. Yet the tea itself comforted her, its heat and its taste were good, the simple, accustomed act was reassuring.

In the midst of turmoil and war and the vagaries of life in 1944, one could still drink tea at five o'clock, in one's library, surrounded by books, the many ornaments, the furniture —the symbols of a continuity of family. Continuity. It was a pity she had thought of that. It reminded her of the inertia she had not been able to overcome, as a result of which this place would go to Leah, if she did not change her will. To Leah. To become, in time perhaps, the Golotz place, that had always been—well, for ninety years at least—the Leckton place. It was something she would have to consider again, very seriously. If not to Leah, to whom else? She had no other relative so close. Leah might remarry some day. There was always that possibility. If only, Miss Leckton thought, I had not been so angry with cousin Ellett Pursey! To alter the will would mean now that she must get all the papers away from him, choosing a new lawyer, probably a stranger —or else have to face Ellett again with the change. He would not approve. He had stood up for Leah. It was very awkward. What business is it of his, she cried to herself, how I dispose of my own property? It was not his business, not at all. It was quite simple to be tolerant and kindly when neither the tolerance nor the kindliness came out of your pocket day by day. And yet ...

She looked out the east window. The day was almost over, the light was dim now, yellowish grey. One could not see very clearly; the screening of the porch that lay on the east side of the house made vision more obscure. Yet one could see—mostly, perhaps, by knowledge?—the smooth stretch of the lawn falling toward the violently troubled water of the miniature bay that lay within the thin and sandy arm of Plover Point. If one did not know, one would not ever guess that trees had once been on the lawn—the great, tall elms, perfect, symmetrical, the symbols of the established, the orderly. They had been planted by her grandfather in 1861, she remembered to have been told, the year of Fort Sumter. She made a rapid calculation. They were seventy-seven years old when the hurricane toppled them, one after the other, ruthlessly. All nine of them.

Miss Leckton was suddenly assailed (not for the first time) with a sense of guilt that she had not replanted the elms. She wondered now whether her failure to do this had come from the same insecurity concerning the future of the place. One does not plant trees so hopefully at fifty-five years old as one does when young, when one can look forward with assurance to seeing the young saplings become fine, full trees. Unless, of course, one were planting them for someone else, for another generation. In brief, for Leah. Why, she asked herself, should I plant trees for a niece who flouted me, who deserted me, who . . . what else? Thinking about this, conjuring up the revolt, the disobedience of Leah, was unpleasant. It shook you. It was like walking on marshy ground that quaked unpleasantly under your tread. It roused again the emotions that had racked her in that first great storm. She didn't want to think about them. It was not a time for that, with the dark closing in, the wind rising and rising, the house empty . . . or almost empty . . . but that, she thought, setting down her empty teacup, that was good, wasn't it? No one, this time, to confuse you, invade you, trespass on you. But the house would be empty. Or she could get the Potters over. Could she?

It was too unpleasant to think about, too disturbing. There was the upstairs to secure, the candles to check and leave handy, the electric torches to see to. Food, thought Miss Leckton. That was done. Pictures, furniture, books, done downstairs. Shutters: George was doing them. She rose and walked through to the living room. The shutters were closed; so also in the dining room. He was probably doing the upstairs shutters now, leaving those on the porch to the last. She had better go upstairs.

She paused in the library long enough to ring for Mrs. Kluger and to switch on the electric light. Then she looked at the barometer and set its brass index hand to the present reading: 29.68. Low, yes. But not out of the way for a line storm in September. The clock on the little French inlaid desk between the north windows of the library said twenty-five minutes past five. She must remember that. Call it half

23

past five. One could see how far the glass had dropped at six —if at all. It had read . . . she could not remember the former reading, around quarter to four. The index had said 30.05 when she had set it just now. It had been several days since she had moved it. It didn't matter. The glass had dropped, of course. Half past five. One would look again at six o'clock.

Miss Leckton went out to the hall (it led in a pleasant ten-foot width from north door to south door) and climbed the stairs to the upper floor. She entered her bedroom, which lay over the library and was of the same size. She had to switch on the lights because George had closed the shutters here on the north windows and the east window. There was no furniture under the east window and the foot of the bed did not quite reach to its jamb, so there was little harm to anticipate from there—if the shutters held, and the window held. It had held before. There was some comfort in that. The branch of the elm had pierced the glass, but with a remarkable cleanness, and it had been possible to stuff a towel successfully around it. Not even one mullion of the sash had been cracked. Astonishing, when one considered how the porch below had been utterly crushed. Well, there were no elms for Leah (if Leah got the place) but at least there were no trees to crash against the house, either. One could take comfort from that. Had this been, perhaps unconsciously, in the back of her mind? She dismissed the idea at once and peremptorily. I have never, she said to herself, anticipated disaster. I am not that sort of person. Though there had been some unexpected thoughts that had come to the surface this afternoon. Very unexpected. Like the La Perche man's hair. Why did this continue to recur? It was silly.

The windows in the upstairs sitting room were shuttered too, she discovered, as she continued her tour. She moved the chairs from the neighborhood of the two south windows, pulled the little table away from the east window. Then she took down the framed photographs of her father and mother, of Grandfather Leckton, of the family groups, the pencil sketch of Dora and herself when they were young

24

women, and she put them face down in a neat pile near the fireplace, behind the round table. It took her a minute or two to decide about the other pictures; they were less important. Was it worth while to be so forehanded? Well, it would only take a moment. The water-color of Venice, the small group of photographs, Uncle Gerald and his first wife, the three engravings of Raphael's Hours. Then she went to the linen cupboard in the hall and got another sheet and returned to cover the heavy curling-backed settee. That would do it. Probably she was just giving herself a lot of trouble for nothing. But it was an awfully nice room, she was attached to it. It had the same sense of people having lived in it, of all the pictures, furniture, having accumulated. Too much of it, perhaps. Too much, certainly, for modern tastes, but not for hers. It has, she thought, that lovely sense of continuity. As she heard the word, she said aloud, "I must look to the guest room." It was good to be active at a time like this.

She went out into the hall again, crossed it and opened the guest-room door. She was met with a blast of air that almost tore the door from her hands, and with the rush of air came a terrific noise, as though the storm had leaped into the room and was raging there. It was terrifying. She wanted to slam the door and run, cry for help, find someone. But then she saw George. As suddenly as the terror had come, it vanished. She moved swiftly into the room and slammed the door. At once the pressure of the wind, the sense of the gale's presence, abated perceptibly.

George was pulling the shutters closed on the first of the two south windows. She did not attempt to speak to him, the room was too noisy. The heavy brocaded bedspreads on the two beds had blown back and were billowing up and down as though some small animals were terrified beneath them. The cover on the square table had blown off and was fluttering on the floor, the pictures were flapping (although one could not hear any noise attributable to them) against the red and salmon-colored wallpaper. There were no little ornaments or vases to be seen anywhere; only the large Dresden china clock, with the little cherubs seated on top of the barrel (whose end made the clock's face), still decorated the shelf of the fluted mantelpiece. The air smelt strongly of salt water and seaweed. While she noted all this, her skirt moving in the wind, the sound suddenly diminished and the room became still. Turning, she saw George had finished that pair of shutters, had closed the double-hung window and was latching it shut.

"How are the shutters, George?" Miss Leckton asked.

"Fine," he said. "Fine, Miss Leckton. Those new catches I put on them work just fine. They'll hold good. I hadn't but one to nail up, one on the dining room. I put all them little vases and whatnots in the bathroom on account of the wind is more to the southward now, I was afraid something might get broke."

"Good," said Miss Leckton.

"I'll just go ahead," said George. "Some things still to do and the light's going."

"I put two torches in the front hall," she said.

She could not hear his reply, for he had opened the second of the south windows and the wind entered again, its voice both loud and tangible. She watched as George leaned out, unlatched each leaf of the shutter, struggled with it, pulled it closed, and latched and hooked it into place. He was quick about it. It was lucky there was a man to do it, the job required strength. She remembered that. Presently George shut the window and latched it, and one could hear again. It was odd: the diminution of the sound of the storm did not seem to make it more distant or less alarming.

As George straightened up, she spoke to him without considering at all what she was going to say. It was as though the inability to communicate over the importunate noise of the gale made speech necessary now, and the rapidity with which one seized the chance to speak was the measure of one's control over a destiny. This was quite ridiculous, of course, but she was forced to admit that this was what she had felt at the moment. The storm generated its own pressures.

"I don't at all like the idea of being alone here after Mrs. Kluger leaves," she said.

That was not the way to have expressed it. It sounded as though she was afraid, and even if that had been true, she did not propose to show fear before a Negro servant; nor, for that matter, before herself. She had meant to say, she was afraid for the house, the contents of it; but it seemed impossible to phrase that accurately at such speed.

"Yes," said George. He straightened up and went over to the west window and unlatched it. "I been thinking about that, Miss Leckton. I been thinking you better put a few things into a bag and let me drive you right now to the Maple Inn in Cottrellton. You be better off there."

Before she could agree or protest, he had opened the lower sash and was leaning out the west window, busy with the shutters. There was, this time, hardly any rush of wind into the room, only a slight stirring of air, and although one could hear the gale cutting past the house, and the tremendous sound of surf on Cato's Beach, it was definitely outside the house, something she could hear as a spectator and not with the sense of participation in the gale that had seized her as the south windows were opened.

It is possible that Miss Leckton might have entertained the idea of moving out, at least temporarily, had the storm again come into the room with her. As it was, her natural resistance to such an idea, which contained the odious suggestions of retreat from danger and the abandonment of one's home, was instantaneous and unchecked. It seemed to her quite impossible to retreat—thus denying all the codes of her life and of her education—and the house suddenly represented a safety that was wholly inconsistent with its exposure to the storm. She knew it was inconsistent, but equally strong was the force of the idea of the house, the home, as the place of safety, the symbol of security. This time, when George closed the window, she was ready to speak and had thought of what to say. Indeed, she delayed speaking long enough to move back toward the door to the hall, so as to switch on the electric ceiling light. The room had become very dark as the last of the shutters was closed.

"That is quite out of the question," she said. "My place is here. This is where I belong. I would not consider it responsible to leave at such a moment. In no circumstances will I leave." That sounded too positive, so she amended it, adding, "Unless, of course, it becomes utterly necessary."

"Might be too late, by then," said George.

"I do not want to discuss it," Miss Leckton replied.

"You remember . . ." said George, but he interrupted himself. "You want me to close up the bathroom shutters?"

"Yes," she said. "I'll help you to move the ornaments."

She went to the door of the bathroom and opened it. On the floor were neatly stacked the vases, the books, the ornaments, the blotter and penholder and the rest of the desk's paraphernalia. Glancing back, she saw George busy in straightening the bedspreads, putting the table cover in place again. Whatever one might say of him, he was a good workman, obedient. This was an excellent moment to make the next move.

She started the job of replacing the ornaments for the mantelpiece. In a moment George joined her.

"Will I put these pictures on the bed?" he asked.

"Yes," she said. "Face down. And George, I think it would be a good idea if you and Ella were to move over here after Mrs. Kluger goes. At least until we are sure there is going to be no hurricane, or until it has blown itself out."

"Yes, Miss Leckton," said George. "I expect that is a good idea, all right, only I'm mighty afraid it ain't going to work out so good."

"How's that?" she said rather sharply. "Why not? There's plenty of room."

"Plenty of room, that's true enough," George said. "It's just that I doubt if Ella is going to want to come over here."

"And why is that, if I may ask?"

"She got her mind set to be in her own room when the hurricane comes, Miss Leckton."

There it was again, thought Miss Leckton: the absolute

28

assurance of the storm's arrival; the imposition of the storm, as it were, at any price.

"That's just nonsense," she said. "Tell her she has to come."

"I doubt she'd listen to me," said George. "She's got her mind set now."

"She'll listen to me, then," said Miss Leckton. "I'll call her."

"Yes," said George. "You can try that."

The ornaments were replaced, the bathroom was clear of all but its own furnishings. She looked at it with satisfaction; the sight of all the pretty gold-labelled bottles and jars, the neat white face towels and bath towels, monogrammed and perfectly folded, the thick and soft bath mat on the edge of the tub, the charming hooked rug on the floor, the Currier and Ives prints of the Darktown Fire Brigade, so very amusing, could give her a satisfaction that was simultaneous with her deep annoyance with Ella, with George's futility as a husband.

"And why," she asked, "is Ella so set on staying at home?"

As she waited for George to reply, she knew that the whole matter of Ella's presence in the house—which indeed implied George's presence as well—was becoming of too great importance to her; and that it had also a quality of familiarity, as though she were reliving an experience, whether real or imagined or dreamed she could not at the moment decide: she was too anxious to hear his answer, as though it held, somehow, the answer to something she was forced to unriddle. Overlaid on this curiosity was a resentment against it, a sense of having yielded ground, lost caste, in finding oneself enmeshed in so powerful a curiosity about something so essentially trivial as Ella Potter's decisions and wishes, the answer to a question posed to an inferior. It was she who should be giving answers. Her world had always, since her maturity, revolved around her decisions, her answers; her questions had been, it occurred to her, the method of arriving at a discipline: they were Socratic in essence, demanding but one reply already foreshadowed in the question itself, as responsibility always dictated.

But George did not answer her question. "She's got certain reasons," he said, and repeated the phrase as though pleased with its sound. "Yes, certain reasons. You call her up, Miss Leckton, she ain't going to listen to me. I'll just go along now and finish." He went into the bathroom and closed the door behind him.

It was entirely proper of him to close the door: it was an obvious protection to the contents of the bathroom. Yet it annoyed her more than she could say, this abrupt termination of the discussion, this avoidance of the question (that key question which was to unlock something now remotely obscured in her present aggravation of mood), this insistence on getting on with the job. And there would be something indecent about pursuing him into the bathroom. Well... there were still things to do. That was so. She would do them and then she would call Ella. In no circumstances would she go over there. No. Although the garage-tenement was hers, not the Potters', yet she was aware of a barrier there, as though she had unwillingly surrendered it to them and they could—it was so ridiculous!—bar her from it. They could not, of course. Yet one would be in an awkward position, refused of co-operation by Ella on the doorstep the woman undoubtedly thought of as her own, yet which in fact belonged to Miss Leckton. One should not, she thought, encourage servants to such a sense of possession, even though to do so made them faithful in an era of faithlessness. Desmond had been born there. It must all have something to do with Desmond.

She went out into the hall, closing the door to the guest room behind her. At the far end of the hall, the stairs went up to the garret. She hesitated a moment: there was so much stuff stored there. But it was quite useless to try to do anything about that now. If the roof leaked, then it leaked and that was that. There was no purpose to be served by moving all those heavy objects about, perhaps into a position where the water would fall on them. It had come through the roof in 1938 in the most peculiar and arbitrary places, and if

there were to be such leaks from this storm, they would have
to wait to be discovered. It would, at least, require a hurricane to make the garret wet. She was lucky, all things considered, to live in such a sound, well-built house. The
thought not only confirmed her in her determination to
stay where she was, but made George's suggestion of flight
to Cottrellton appear in a properly ridiculous light.

She went through the other two rooms—the sitting room
and her bedroom—once more, glancing over the arrangement of furniture, checking her work, and switching off the
lights of each room. No use to waste electricity. Then she
went downstairs again. At the foot of the stairs was Mrs.
Kluger, apparently waiting.

"Oh, there you are," said Mrs. Kluger. "I didn't know
where you'd got to."

It seemed to Miss Leckton a most inept remark, so she
felt no need to answer it.

"Where would you like your supper?" Mrs. Kluger asked
her. "Since we put the dining room away. On a tray? In
the liberry?"

Miss Leckton considered this. It would be better, no
doubt of it, to have a tray in the 'liberry,' more comfortable
and more pleasant than the now sheeted dining room,
stripped of its ornaments. Yet it was probable that Mrs.
Kluger had suggested this not with any idea of her employer's comfort (of body or mind), but rather because it
would mean that the woman could get her work done more
quickly and thus desert the ship at an earlier hour. However, it did seem best to eat in the library.

"Very well," said Miss Leckton. "In the library. At seven."
She mentioned the usual time in order to forestall any possible suggestion that she eat earlier than her accustomed
hour.

"O.K.," said Mrs. Kluger. "Pity it's so warm tonight. Else
I'd build you a nice fire, makes it cosy." She smiled at Miss
Leckton and turned to go her heavy-footed way back to the
kitchen.

There was one thing about it, thought Miss Leckton: of

31

all the rooms on the ground floor, the library was the furthest from the kitchen. She wondered if Mrs. Kluger had realized *that* when she suggested a tray. Still thinking about this, she entered the library.

It was dark now, but one could still see a little through the unshuttered windows. Peering out to the east, she could see that the storm was still about as it had been, there was no serious change. This, indeed, might be all there was going to be. The spell of her own activities was still strong upon her, and it made her optimistic. She switched on the light by her morris chair, the standing lamp by the desk. The room seemed cheerful—but more than that, it seemed immutable and full of comfort.

The clock on the desk said five minutes past six. It reminded her to look at the barometer. It had fallen, but only a very short distance. It registered 29.65. That wasn't much of a drop, in a gale, in—how long was it?—oh, yes, forty minutes. She reset the brass index hand. She would take the reading at seven, when her supper came in. Meanwhile, the thing to do was to call up Ella. It was too ridiculous about her not coming over. She lifted the receiver and called the garage.

"Miss Leckton's garage," said Ella's voice after a moment's ringing of the bell.

"Ella," said Miss Leckton. "I want you to shut up your place over there and come here for the night. I'd like you to be here about half past seven o'clock. Bring what you and George will need."

There was an appreciable pause before Ella answered her.

"Where were you thinking we'd sleep?" Ella said.

"In the kitchen wing," Miss Leckton answered, making her voice brisk and authoritative. "Mrs. Kluger feels she has to go to Chog's Cove to stay with her daughter and her grandchildren. It seems quite mad to me, but there it is. It will be better if you and George are here." She paused a moment, but as there was no reply from Ella, she continued, "The barometer is fairly steady and not very low, and I think there's a fair chance the storm is headed out to sea, but even so, we'd better be prepared."

"Yes, Miss Leckton," said Ella. "It's good to be prepared. That's so. But I guess I'll just stay where I am, if you don't mind."

"I do mind," said Miss Leckton promptly. "I wish you here."

"Yes, ma'am," said Ella. "But I guess I pretty well decided to stay right here."

"But that's ridiculous," Miss Leckton said. "It's ridiculous. That place . . ." She caught herself up sharply. She had been about to say that nothing could happen to the garage, that it was far less likely to be damaged than the house. As she was trying to decide what to say next, she saw one leaf of the shutters close on the east window, the figure of George dimly moving past the narrowed aperture to get at the other one. It gave her, in conjunction with Ella's refusal to come over, a curious sense of being shut in, almost locked in, abandoned without help or hope of escape. But she made an effort to curb this feeling, and spoke firmly into the telephone.

"Now Ella," she said. "It really is ridiculous. It will be far better for you to be here with me, for that will mean you and I and George will all be here together. If you insist on staying there, George will feel he has to be there with you. Do you wish me to be quite alone here?"

"Oh, no, Miss Leckton," Ella said. "Oh, no, ma'am. I told George he was to be there at the house with you as much as you needed him. I don't mind being alone. I just couldn't leave here."

"Why?" cried Miss Leckton. "Why?"

"Well, you see," said Ella, her voice gentle and patient, as though she were talking to a child, "I couldn't leave Desmond's things all alone in a storm, could I? I wouldn't feel right, Miss Leckton. No, I wouldn't feel right."

"Good God!" Miss Leckton said. "I never heard anything so ridiculous! Now listen to me, Ella . . ."

She gathered herself together, shifting in her chair as she

33

prepared to overwhelm this obstinate woman. But as she did so, she turned her head and saw George outside the more westerly of the north windows, struggling with the catch of the left-hand leaf of the still open shutters there. She could see only his head and shoulders, but the effort of his exertion was clear even with so poor a view, in so dim a light. Turning her head further, she saw that he had already closed the shutters of the other north window.

It seemed to her then that she could not bear this: could not stand having that pair of shutters closed up too. Through that window one could see the narrow foreshortened shape of the two dormer windows of the garage-tenement, and the dusk already made visible the warm light that came from them. If Ella refused . . . if she were as stubborn as she could be . . . if she, Carrel Leckton, were left alone, at her age, to face this new storm . . . and shut in . . . no! no!

"Hold on," she cried into the telephone, and she put the instrument hastily on the floor and rose to her feet and almost ran to the window. As she reached it, the first leaf came shut.

She rapped her knuckles on the glass, calling out, "No, George, no! Do *not* close it! Do *not* close it!"

But it was at once obvious that he was unable to hear her voice, to hear the rapping on the glass, and that he was wholly concentrated on the task of closing the last leaf. In desperation she opened the lower sash. It was sticky, it came hard, opening a few inches at a time in response to her jerky movements. The noise of the storm filled the room, it was a high sound now; it gave her the sense already that one's voice would vanish into it and be lost.

She put her head near the opening and she called, at the top of her lungs, "George, George!"

He did not hear her. He was occupied in tearing the tendrils of the Virginia creeper away from the clasp of the shutter, away from its edge and the slats of it.

Miss Leckton realized, somewhere within her, that this had now gone far past its essential importance, that she was being driven by some interior force over which she had

34

little or no control, and to which she was yielding herself in an emotion that was extraordinarily pleasant. And as she reached that point of realization, she heard herself screaming.

It was so odd and unusual a thing to have done—even this scream that recorded itself mostly as an effort of the throat and lungs, whose high sound was scarcely audible except as an echo of relief in her ears—that she found herself making a conscious effort to stop; but the only effect she had was to transmute the scream into words that were equally ineffective. "George! George! George!" she had cried out. She was on the point of screaming again—against the storm, against the inevitable—when George unexpectedly looked up and saw her, and she caught his eye, and saw in it the reflection of alarm. Like a cold cup of water in the face, it shocked her, this image of her own loss of control seen in the face of an inferior; and as she calmed, she realized, with a surge of shame that made the blood rush to her head, that all she would have had to do would have been to lean out the window and touch him on the shoulder: he was as close to her as that.

In control of herself now—except for the sensation of hot blushing in her cheeks—she beckoned to him. He came close to her, reaching up on tiptoes, his head above the sill and turned sidewise. She bent down till her lips were near his ear and she shouted slowly (but so loudly that he drew back a little), saying, "I think I'll leave the window open. Leave the shutters open. Open, George."

He nodded his head at her and withdrew. Miss Leckton closed the window and watched him, in the new and not altogether comforting quiet of the room, as he opened the left-hand leaf, latched it back against the wall, and walked away in the direction of the tool shed, his body leaning back at a stiff angle against the force of the wind.

The shutters were open. That had been accomplished. There was both accomplishment and a sense of defeat in the fact. She felt shaken and insecure. She sat down rather heavily in her chair and picked up the telephone. It did not respond.

She jiggled the receiver hook angrily. After a moment a voice said, "Number, please."

"Never mind," Miss Leckton said, and she hung up and replaced the telephone on the stand beside her chair.

She did not feel up to calling Ella back. Not yet. She did not know what to say to the woman. The whole business seemed different, the shutters had done something to her. She would do better to wait a while, collect herself.

At that moment, and with a suddenness of surprise that made her whole body twitch a little, the telephone rang, loudly and persistently, ring on ring.

III

IT was probably Ella, thought Miss Leckton, calling up to say she ... well, calling up. But it didn't sound like a local ring. Anyway, the telephone was still working, that was something. She picked up the whole instrument (it was the old-fashioned kind) and set it on her lap, unhooked the receiver. It continued to make the loud rattle of its impulse to ring after she had it to her ear, and she made a grimace of distaste and held the receiver off from her.

"Hello," she said. "Yes. Hello. Hello!"

The rattling sound ceased, and the unmistakable voice of an operator said, "Cottrellton 72-R?"

"That's right," Miss Leckton said.

"Miss Carrrel Leckton, please. Miami calling."

"Where?" said Miss Leckton.

"Miss Carrel Leckton, please, Miami calling," the operator repeated, her voice dispassionate and a little bored.

"This is Miss Leckton."

"One minute, please," said the operator. After a brief pause, she said, "Go ahead, Miami. There's your party. Go ahead, please."

There was a series of clicking noises.

"Hello?" said Miss Leckton. "Hello."

The voice that answered her then was altogether different. It was warm and clear. It was so clear that it seemed impossible it should be coming from Miami, during a gale.

37

"Is that you, Aunt Carrel?" the voice said.

"Leah!" cried Miss Leckton. "Leah! Where are you?"

She realized that this was not what she had meant to say, that she knew perfectly where Leah was, that it was the astonishment of hearing Leah's voice that had upset her, coming on top of the incident at the north window.

Leah's next words, however, proved that the intention of what she had said had been understood.

"I know," said Leah, that extraordinary warmth in her voice, sounding so like her mother, Dora. "I know, Aunt Carrel. It's been a long time. It's just that I was worried about you and this hurricane. How are things there?"

"Oh," Miss Leckton said. She pulled herself together with an effort, resisting the voice and its warmth, resisting her own temporary weakness, reverting to the comfort, the solidity, of an old attitude. "Quite all right, thank you. We are merely having a good blow at the moment. The glass is not too low. Everything is quite all right here."

"Who is with you?" Leah asked.

"I have plenty of help," Miss Leckton answered.

"I wondered," said Leah.

"Of course, in these times one can hardly expect the sort of staff one could have in peacetime," Miss Leckton went on, rather rapidly but firmly. "It's really fantastic, the whole servant problem. It was hard enough to keep people here in the old days, or even just before the war. I don't know what's come to them. They seem to find this isolated, though it has never seemed so to me. They get to Cottrellton quite regularly. There is a moving picture there now."

"But you have someone? The Potters are there?"

She is so persistent, thought Miss Leckton. Considering that she left me, that she ran away the moment she was able to, I cannot see what business it would be of hers if I chose to live here entirely alone. Nor what *she* would do about it. It was curious, Miss Leckton was beginning to enjoy herself, her poise had been restored. It was not exactly that she was grateful for the call, but that she was happy to be able to restore, by any means, her own inner control.

38

"The Potters are here, of course," she said.

"I was so sorry to hear about Desmond," Leah said. "Poor Ella! Will you tell her again from me, please, how much I have thought of her? I wrote her."

"So she said," Miss Leckton answered. She was not going to involve herself in promises concerning Desmond and Ella at a moment when Ella was behaving like a hysterical fool. "You are still stationed at Miami, Leah?"

"Yes," said Leah. "Still here. In the meteorological branch now, here at the field. That's why I called up. The reports come in to us. It looks as though you'll get the storm soon now. The hurricane. I was worried about you."

"Very good of you to call up," said Miss Leckton. "I think it quite possible the hurricane may go out to sea. As it did in 1939. The radio is getting very undependable these days. They are trying to be as sensational as the evening papers, I expect."

"I wouldn't count on it," said Leah. "The reports are fairly accurate here. Have you got the house ready, just in case?"

"My dear Leah," said Miss Leckton. She leaned back in her chair, more comfortably, almost smiling. "I cannot understand this sudden interest in my welfare, the welfare of Olneys Point. Nor do I entirely understand why you should presume that no one is capable of taking precautions except yourself. From a considerable distance. As a member of the Women's Army Corps, stationed in Florida, what did you think you'd be able to do? That you couldn't have done here?"

There was a pause. Miss Leckton was very pleased with the way she had phrased that last question. It made up for the moments lately when she had found herself saying things she did not exactly intend.

"I don't think the storm will get to you—at least the real part of it—until quite late," said Leah, her voice sounding still warm but less confident; as though the original impulse that had moved her to call up, thought Miss Leckton, had failed her now. "Somewhere between ten and twelve. I

39

thought you might like to be warned, that's all. I know you don't like the radio. I'm glad you've done something about it."

"Your five minutes are up," said the operator's voice. "Please conclude your conversation as quickly as possible."

"All right," said Leah. "Good-bye, Aunt Carrel. I didn't mean to upset you."

"You haven't upset me at all," said Miss Leckton. "On the contrary. Good-bye, Leah. Thank you for calling."

"If you could send me the little oval picture of Mother, the one in the silver frame that used to be in my room," said Leah, "I'd be very grateful."

"All the contents, all of them, of this house, were left in my charge," said Miss Leckton. "You know that, Leah."

"Oh, yes," said Leah. "I was only asking you. It would be nice to have here. It's entirely up to you, of course. Good-bye."

"I'll give it some consideration," said Miss Leckton, but she realized as she said it that the wire had changed its tone. "Hello?" she said. There was no answer. Miss Leckton hung up and replaced the telephone on the stand.

Probably there was the answer, she thought. It seemed a tortuous way of extracting a picture from your aunt, to call her up and warn her about a storm. She smiled. I don't think she got any change out of me, she said to herself. It was pretty late in the day for Leah to be concerned now. If she sent Leah the picture—it wasn't one she herself particularly valued—what sort of gratitude could she expect, and how would it be expressed? It was pretty late in the day for that.

The phrase stuck in her mind and she repeated it, so that it took on a more literal meaning. The clock on the desk said twenty minutes past six. It gave her rather a shock to realize that it was only fifteen minutes since she had looked at the barometer and set it; and yet within that time she had talked to Ella, she had ... she coughed ... stopped George from closing the shutters, and she had talked to Leah. From Miami. It seemed much longer a span of time than that. The relative quality of time was a recurring phenom-

enon. It seemed only about half an hour since she had decided to prepare for the possible coming of the storm. Seen
as a whole, the time had fled past. Seen as a part, it seemed
endless.

There was nothing further to do now until supper. Except
to wash up. She felt her hair with her hands. Very untidy.
The wind from the guest-room windows—the room that had
been Leah's—had probably disarranged it. She rose and went
to the fireplace and looked at herself in the heavy gold-framed
mirror over it. The glass of the two side panels was foxed
with dampness, but the central panel was clear. It's clear, she
thought, but it's cold. People nowadays didn't know how
to make a proper mirror. Since the panel had been repaired
and renewed, one could see oneself in it, right enough, but
it certainly made one look horrible.

She patted her hair as she examined her image. It would
be better for her when her hair had gone white altogether;
this grey mixed in with the dark brown was so unbecoming.
On the whole, one looked less of a hag with white hair.
Mamma's hair, she thought, went quite white at forty-five,
and was most becoming. She herself must take after the
Lecktons, not the Purseys. But even in this mirror, she felt
she didn't really look her age. Perhaps fifty, or a little more.
Fifty-five. Upstairs, she would look better, younger. Particularly when she got her hair neater.

She turned from the mirror and started for the door to
the hall. The thought crossed her mind—not lingering there,
not making an impression, really, and vanishing again—that
she didn't quite know for whom she was making herself look
neat. Well—against the storm, perhaps.

Upstairs in her bedroom she had a moment of hesitation
concerning her clothes. She looked at herself in the long
mirror on the bathroom door. The dark green cloth skirt,
the grey blouse, the green jersey, the brown oxfords on her
feet—a sensible costume for an emergency. Yet it would be
a fine gesture to change, to put on the purple velveteen tea-
gown, the one with Mamma's lace collar, and appear in it
when Mrs. Kluger brought her tray. The woman would

41

thus see that her employer gave little or no importance to this storm. She had a sudden and remarkably clear image of herself seated in her chair, the gown lying softly over her knees, the wide sleeves falling down as her hands and arms rested graciously and at ease on the arms of the chair, a picture of confidence and repose. As she would have liked to look for Maude Cleever, if Maude had come again. Yet as the image appeared, it destroyed itself, as though some force within her made her see, uncomfortably, that it was nonsense, that that was not the way she sat or posed; and she found herself embarrassed, conscious of a relic of an adolescence that seemed tremendously distant and removed. She had never posed. Why should she start now? I believe in being frank and direct, she thought; and it is idiotic to dress up for a woman like Mrs. Kluger. There had never been a chance to dress up for Maude Cleever.

Looking at herself again in the glass, she was pleased by her appearance—except for her hair. Her figure was good—of medium height, still slim. She moved a little, shifting her weight from foot to foot, turning her body a little, first this way, then that, She moved as a young person moves—well, not exactly young, but not as old people move. Perhaps this was vanity, but why not a little vanity, now and then, if it was reasonably justified? Her mind was once again crossed by the thought she had had before: for whom, this appearance, this vigor? It was not pleasant, the answer seemed like the thin cover over a deep of unpleasantness, and she dismissed it, and entered the bathroom.

Putting her rings neatly and carefully on the glass shelf, she washed her hands and her face. Then she brushed her hair—how pleasant it was to have it short, free of those masses of hairpins! She rearranged it, with comb and fingers, put back the four bobby pins that were all she now wore. I need a new permanent, she thought. When would it be possible to have one? She would have to wait until she was settled again in New York. Well, that would be all right. It was a little long, the wave had grown out a bit, but it was not too bad. Should one dye the grey? No, that always made

one look older, oddly enough. I shall look my age, she
thought, with the satisfaction of one who is aware that she
does not appear as old as she has years upon her. She replaced
her rings—the sapphire surrounded by brilliants in the old-
fashioned setting, the topaz with the Pursey crest cut into it,
that her mother had used as a seal for her letters. She
switched off the bathroom light, got a clean handkerchief
from the sachet in her bureau, looked fleetingly again at
her image in the mirror over the dressing table, and left her
room, turning out the light there too.

She paused a moment in the hall to listen. She could
detect no increase in the intensity of the storm. The shutters rattled, the house was full of the sound of wind and
surf, but softened and subdued. The only real discomfort
was that it was so close, so warm. The air had that heavy
quality she had noticed earlier; it was difficult, actually difficult, to breathe a full breath. It would be better, doubtless,
if she took off even this thin jersey when she got to the
library. Have it handy, but take it off. It would be pleasant
to open a window. Perhaps she could open the unshuttered
window a little, it might give some relief from this sense of
oppression. She moved to the stairs and started down them,
hesitated and stopped. The picture of Dora, in the silver
frame. It was in the drawer of the guest-room dressing table,
the lower drawer, at the back, done up in black paper.

It was not that Miss Leckton really had decided to send
it to Leah, for she had not. She had an impulse, merely, to
see it again, to try to discover why Leah particularly wanted
that one. It was far from the best picture of Dora. It had
been taken in 1916, a year before her marriage.

The simple recollection of that made Miss Leckton flush
with annoyance—after all these years. What an astonishing
thing it was, that both the mother and the daughter should
have chosen to marry Jews! Out of all the people of their
own world, the Leckton world, the world of New York and
Rhode Island, of Philadelphia too, if you wished, through
Grandmother Pursey, born a Wegener—to choose a Jew from

43

Louisiana, a Jew from England! Less extraordinary for Leah, of course, for the blood was there, yet that did not explain it. After all, Leah was only eleven when her parents died in the plane crash at Baton Rouge in 1930. And Sam Davids had been an Episcopalian, a southerner, not at all a Jewish sort of a Jew. Though even so, the marriage had terribly upset Mamma, and would unquestionably have equally upset Papa, had he lived to witness it. Perhaps if he had lived, had added his voice to hers and to Mamma's, Dora could have been dissuaded. Well, it was done now. Dora and her husband dead. Papa and Mamma dead. Herbert Golotz dead. And Leah a widow. Childless, by the grace of God. There was always the hope that she would marry again, someone of her own class. Though the record seemed against it. It was upsetting. This was a queer day. Everything, anything, seemed to upset one. It was the oppression of the air.

For no reason at all, she recalled the remark that Birac had made in 1938 when she had wanted to get rid of that creature, Harry Frosten, get him out of the house, off the place, at any cost.

"You live on a peninsula," Birac had said, "and the good God has now turned it temporarily into an island."

It was extraordinarily like what Mrs. Kluger had said: "A poor place to ride out a hurricane, with the sea so near and all. Right around you almost."

A peninsula. It was a disturbing conception now, where it would never have been in the least disturbing before the 1938 storm. It was as though, at this moment, the physical properties of the place had also a moral value; as though one were on a peninsula of life, as it were, and a storm—the war, the increasing years, the whole breaking up of the established social fabric one had grown up with—threatened to turn it into an island. Such an island as had isolated her before, with all those people; when it was—or, more properly, became apparent that it was—impossible to turn that awful Frosten out of doors, to tell him to be off, to go about his business, to leave the property. Not only had that been im-

44

possible, but one had even had to harbor him in one's house. The peninsula (the physical one) had indeed become an island.

Miss Leckton shrugged her shoulders and continued on down the stairs and into the library. The tea tray had been cleared away, she observed. She glanced at the clock: it was six-thirty-five. Twenty-five minutes to dinner. It occurred to her, as she slipped off the light jersey and folded it over the back of her morris chair, that it would be remarkably pleasant now to have a glass of sherry. But the sherry was in one of the locked cupboards of the office, and against it were now stacked the pictures from the other rooms. It was too hot, too oppressive, to make so much effort as would be required to get the bottle out. Nor could she ask Mrs. Kluger to do it. It did not do to let servants have access, even temporarily, to one's cupboards.

She seated herself. This, she thought, is one of the moments when one should do some knitting. Knitting had always annoyed her, as had embroidery. She had done all the knitting anyone could ever be expected to do in the last war. There was hardly time to read—and she did not feel she could keep her mind on a book or a magazine.

She was acutely conscious of the need to do something, not because she wanted to be active for activity's sake, but because her mind was so full of so many thoughts and they seemed so unpleasant. They were right below the surface: if one sat still, they would emerge, inevitably. Every time she had stopped to think this evening, it had been disagreeable. Something to do with the storm and the heavy, sticky air. Oh yes, she thought gratefully, the window.

She rose and went to the unshuttered north window. Again with considerable effort she raised it about six inches. Through the aperture came a slight movement of air, but with the air (which lacked freshness) came also a marked increase in the sound of the gale. Somehow that sound had increased, not in volume, but in unpleasantness, as though the fact that it came from the darkness had added to its impact. There was always something a little menacing about a storm at night; but in the old days, its effect had been to make the house seem a place of safe haven, of refuge, its comfort and security augmented. That was not true now. This storm (which might increase in scale) was too much an echo of the storm of 1938, it was too potentially destructive, and, cloaked in darkness, it seemed to come at you with an element of frightening surprise. Reluctantly, she pushed the window shut, and as she did so she found it necessary to whisper, "There, that will give a bit of fresh air to the room." She could see the light clearly shining from the windows of the garage-tenement; the illumination fell on the tops of the lilac bushes and made their ceaseless toss and sway quite easily visible. But even so, the light was comforting. Comforting *and* annoying, as one thought of Ella—but still comforting. She returned to her chair.

Twenty minutes to supper. One could, of course, go out and see Mrs. Kluger. Would it do any good? No. No good. I am not, thought Miss Leckton, going to plead with the woman. I shall not put myself in that position. She is not worth it. Not worth it at all. How curious that she was engaging her mind with a proposition of how to retain people in the house, to get more people in it, when before her effort had been the very opposite! Golotz, Frosten, those La Perche people. Even Mrs. Cleever—at first. And Leah. Well, in a way, Leah.

In spite of herself she found herself thinking about Leah. It was not what she wanted to do: it seemed then impossible to avoid it, as though this were one of too many thoughts crowded into the insufficient area of her mind, and it had to come out, come to the surface, relieve that pressure within her. Half in relief, half in reluctance, she began to think about her niece, but although she tried to confine her thinking to Leah as a child, as an adolescent, growing up in this house and in her apartment in New York—in fact, on those phases of Leah's youth which most showed forth Leah's final and fundamental ingratitude—she was not able to do so.

46

Beyond control, she found herself seeing again, in sharp if occasionally detached images, the day of September 21st, 1938. The day of the first hurricane, the day of Leah's desertion.

IV

THE day had begun badly, inauspiciously, and the reason for this had seemed to Miss Leckton to have been Leah's fault: a combination of the girl's habit of early rising, with her almost morbid interest in the radio and the news. Leah had been aware, because Miss Leckton had often reminded her of it, that the house was not in any sense soundproof. On the contrary, it had an annoying quality of being sound-conducting, and if a noise were made in Leah's room (at the southwest corner of the second floor), it could penetrate easily into her own room at the northeast corner, in spite of the hallway and the walls that lay between. Miss Leckton's hearing, too, was uncommonly (and in this instance, troublesomely) acute.

She had waked to hear a man's voice bleating in Leah's room. She glanced at the travelling clock by her bedside. It said six-fifty-five. What an unconscionable hour to play the radio! The girl must have had it on very loudly—in spite of all that her aunt had done to persuade her not to have the thing yelling through the house—for it was almost possible to hear what the voice was saying. Miss Leckton knew that she would not be able to go to sleep again with that noise in her ears—if indeed she should be able to go to sleep again at all—and so she rose and put on her slippers and her wine-red flannel dressing gown and went out into the hallway and across to Leah's room.

48

Here, naturally, the sound was much louder: so much so that Miss Leckton said to herself, "Is the girl deaf?" She knocked on the door and entered without waiting for any response.

The room was deserted, the bed empty. The radio was on loudly, the light glowing behind its golden dial panel. The shades were up, and the early morning light, blue and soft, filled the room. From the bathroom came the sounds, faintly over the voice of the radio speaker, of splashing. Leah was in her bath. Beyond intention or wish, Miss Leckton found herself listening to the radio.

"That means, of course, Dr. Benes, the president. It means Hodza, the premier, who, you will remember, spoke so bravely over this network in what seems now a long, long time ago, although it can be counted in hours, and several other members. It does not however—this is important to note—include the entire cabinet. It does not include Czech popular opinion ..."

"Leah!" said Miss Leckton. "Leah!"

There was no answer. She closed the door behind her, so that at least this awful noise might not further permeate the house, and she moved to the radio.

"We know therefore," continued the voice, "that it is deliberate German propaganda to constantly keep before the world the imminence of war unless they have their way and that pressure has evidently frightened Monsieur Daladier and Prime Minister Chamberlain to the point where they have lost all sense of decency. With regard to their statements to Hitler ..."

Miss Leckton turned the nearest knob and the voice dropped to a whisper, the contrast of sound so sudden and violent that she found herself straining forward to hear the rest of what was being said.

"In other words," whispered the voice, "we don't have here any settlement of the European problem. What we have is a rushing into a series of difficulties which may be greater than those which Mr. Chamberlain hopes to avoid. Good morning."

Miss Leckton turned the knob again until the radio had clicked off.

"Nonsense!" she said to herself. "Sensationalism." Then she walked to the bathroom door, which was not quite shut, and knocked on it.

"Leah!" she said.

"Hello," said Leah's voice. "That you, Aunt Carrel? You're up early."

"I am up because I was waked by that awful noise. The radio."

"Oh, I'm sorry," said Leah.

"What good does it do to be sorry?" cried Miss Leckton. "You know how the sound carries in this house. You knew that."

"Oh, dear," said Leah. "It's just this terrific news. It's so terrible. I had to hear Kaltenborn. Columbia had the news releases first."

"I do not see that there is anything in the news to warrant your having your bath with the door closed and the radio full on," said Miss Leckton.

Without further word she turned and left Leah's room and walked back to her own. When she got there, she didn't know what to do. She was far too upset, too annoyed, to be able to go to sleep again. Breakfast would not be ready for another hour. If there was someone up, Anna or Catherine, it might be possible to get some coffee. Her morning was now spoiled, at all events. She hated to be forced to bounce out of bed like this, at such an hour, and it was hard to be made angry at the same time. How extraordinarily thoughtless of Leah! Kaltenborn, indeed!

As she made her way out into the hall again and downstairs toward the kitchen, she went on thinking about this. What was it the man had said? Oh, yes. "The pressure has frightened Daladier and Chamberlain to the point where they have lost all sense of decency." Rubbish! What could they do? It was fantastic, ridiculous, wholly unrealistic to expect France and England to go to war to save the Sudetenland from doing what the majority of its inhabitants wished.

50

Whatever you might say about Hitler, he had unified Germany, had pulled it up from the bog of despair, the slough of despond, made it strong, virile. One might not like all that he had done, nor approve all the ways he did it. He had been rather awful about the poor Jews, to be sure, but they had probably brought it on their own heads. Give them an inch and they took an ell. There was nothing for Leah to get excited about, though, now. This was entirely a question of the Germans of the Sudetenland and the Germans of Germany. It might be a little hard on Czechoslovakia, but some people acted about it—people like Leah, who was young and excitable, people like Kaltenborn—as if it were the end of the world. The only thing that was really important was not to have another war. And in particular, to be sure the United States didn't get drawn into it, if there were one. But there would be no war.

Thinking about this now, as she sat in the evening of a September day in 1944 and relived a morning of 1938, Miss Leckton recalled that she had felt quite exhilarated by the time she had reached the kitchen. Such exhilaration was out of all reason, for certainly she had been annoyed, deeply annoyed at Leah for disturbing her last hour of sleep. Nevertheless, she recalled the sensation now with astonishing clarity—so clearly indeed that it gave her a synthetic sense of well-being at the moment—and she wondered briefly what had caused it. Perhaps it was the sense of busy responsibility: Leah to correct and improve and control, the cook to speak to (she should, properly, be up and about at this hour), the day to plan, the waitress to talk to about flowers, about the packing they would begin on Friday, George Potter to see about the place, about putting the rose-beds properly away this year—all the many, slightly urgent duties of a full life. Even the time of day—now that she was up, for whatever reason—was a contributor, for the early morning of a day to be looked forward to, is in itself pleasant. One was planning, arranging; there was as yet none of the frustration of plans failed of execution. She remembered now, too, what she had been thinking about at the moment: how she should

51

go about the task of impressing on Leah that it was not proper to behave so thoughtlessly; that one could not so indulge one's hobbies at others' expense; that, after all, seen in its broadest aspect, Leah was a guest in her aunt's house. "It is not that this is not your home," she would say, "but that you must not forget that it is your home through a singular set of circumstances." That was good.

Miss Leckton found her mind now drifting into a reconstruction of what she had thought about Leah, and from that into an extension of what she would have said—should have said. It had all the beautiful clarity, the pointed reference, the subtle and polite directness of the imagined conversation. But as she did this, her well-being faded into a sense of discomfort, of malaise, the sort of feeling that assails you when you first begin to wake from the release of sleep, to a day that contains a positive sadness; the filmy realization of sorrow or discomfort, even of pain, sensed if not yet clearly discerned. Coming on top of her mood of well-being, imaginatively generated, it was disturbing. She tried to fight it off, to return to the enclosure of the past experience, and, failing in that, to attribute this still somewhat nebulous malaise of the spirit to the storm, to the weather. But that seemed wrong, it did not explain it, and she was conscious that the explanation lay deeper, in life itself, her life, the circumstances in which she lived. Yet so unpleasant to her was such self-investigation at that moment that she made a gigantic effort to recapture the thread of her recollections, falling back upon the action of her movements, where her reconstructed intentions had so oddly betrayed her into discomfort. The kitchen door. The kitchen door. That was it!

On that distant morning, she had been about to go through the swing door into the kitchen; and mentally she now did so.

Anna Mulvey, dressed in a cotton flannel wrapper of a violent blue color, had been standing by the electric range. Her hair was in paper curlers, which gave to her rather ugly face a positively comic appearance. How really amusing! Miss Leckton thought. Imagine a woman of her position, single, ugly, at least sixty years old, still taking trouble enough to put her coarse black hair into curlers! For whom? Oh, of course, it was Wednesday, and tomorrow was the day out for the servants. Anna was beautifying herself for the benefit of the village of Cottrellton. It was a delicious idea.

"Good morning, Anna," she said.

"Oh-my-God!" cried Anna, turning around with great suddenness. "Oh, it's you, Miss Leckton. You gave me a start, surely."

"I'm sorry if I startled you," Miss Leckton said. She hoped that the amusement she felt within her had not betrayed itself in her voice, which she had made as sweet as possible. "Is Catherine up?"

"She's dressed already," Anna said. "She'll be down in a minute. Will I call her, now?"

"No, thank you. Is that coffee you are making?"

"Yes, ma'am."

"Ask Catherine to bring me up a cup when it is ready, will you? I was awakened and I shan't try to get to sleep again. I hope the radio did not wake you too."

"What radio would that be now?" asked Anna.

It was impossible, of course, that Anna hadn't heard Leah's radio, since the servants' rooms lay immediately beyond the girl's bathroom. Nevertheless, Miss Leckton felt she could not make a reply to Anna's question, much as she would have liked to rid herself of her own sense of the outrage that this early waking had worked on her.

"Did you really hear nothing?" she said.

"Ah, we make so much noise ourselves," said Anna, "what with this and with that, we'd hear no radio at this hour."

"Very well," Miss Leckton said. "Tell Catherine about the coffee, please."

"Yes, ma'am," said Anna.

Miss Leckton returned to the front of the house, making her way toward the stairs. When she got to the foot of them, opposite the living-room door, she decided to take a look at the weather. She went along the hall to the library. It had its usual slightly unaired, musty smell, thickened by

53

the taint of tobacco smoke from Leah's cigarettes. Even though they were thrown out of the ash trays into the fireplace each night, that scent of stale tobacco always hung on disagreeably. It reminded Miss Leckton of the days when her father had been alive and had smoked cigars here; they had left a far more obnoxious smell. She found herself divided between a sensation of real relief that she had not to be greeted by this cigar smell (which had had a persistence beyond the morning airing by the servants) and a sorrow that those days were gone. Life had been so much more simple then: there were some decent, fixed standards for living. One knew where one was, socially, politically. The issues of goodness and badness seemed now, in retrospect, clear-cut as opposed to the confused ones of today. One no longer knew where one stood—where one should stand. Or, if one did know, if one made up one's mind firmly, one was likely to be called names by the younger generation. Well, at all events, she must put a stop to Leah's smoking in here. After all, it was her room, the room in which she spent most of her day, and every evening. Leah could smoke in the dining room, her own bedroom. Perhaps in the living room. But if she wished to avail herself of the comfort, the good atmosphere of this room, she would have to make up her mind to stop smoking in here. The girl smoked too much, anyway. She was only nineteen years old. It was ridiculous indulgence.

Miss Leckton walked to the east window and looked out. She could see the water within the soft and lovely curve of Plover Point, the shine of daylight on Thin Pond just east of it. The wind was fresh, from the northeast. The day was overcast, but thinly so; one could see the blur of the risen sun through the clouds. The morning light, blue and soft and fresh, silhouetted the drooping boughs of the elms, made their many leaves into serrated spear points hung on the long dark wires of the branches' ends, swaying in the breeze. It would be a decent day. These clouds would likely clear off around eleven.

She turned away, walked to the barometer and tapped it,

and as she did so, remembered, for the hundredth time, that her father had always told her one must not tap an aneroid barometer. It read 29.90. Neither low nor high, for the season. September 21st. No, quite average. Then she went upstairs to her bed and got into it again after she had brushed her hair and changed her dressing gown to the pretty quilted green bed-jacket that Leah had given her for her birthday, last April. She had only just settled comfortably, the two pillows nicely propped behind her, when there was a knock on the door.

"Come in," Miss Leckton said.

Catherine Lovatt came in, carrying a little, brown-lacquer Japanese tray, with a cup, a silver set of coffee pot, cream jug, and pretty little sugar bowl full to the brim with the square lumps of sugar Miss Leckton liked.

"Good morning," said Catherine, as she put the tray on the table by Miss Leckton's bed.

It was an entirely civil greeting, but that was all you could say of it. Catherine had been a tight-lipped woman, always: correct, well-trained, stiff, withdrawn, lacking any of the ease or the easy charm of the usual Irish. Her dark brown hair was pulled rather severely into a neat coil on the back of her head. Her long upper lip was stiff and unsmiling, her lips were thin and straight and wide. She had a large chin, with a dimple in the middle of it, but the dimple gave her face neither animation nor sensibility.

"Good morning," said Miss Leckton. "Thank you, Catherine. I woke early."

"Yes, madam," said Catherine. "Is there anything else I can do?"

"No, thank you," Miss Leckton said.

"Thank you," said Catherine, and she left the room swiftly, closing the door softly behind her.

It was typical of her, Miss Leckton thought. You got nothing from the woman except the routine replies, although they were always correct—except on the occasions when Catherine protested (as she had each autumn for four years now) at the lateness of Miss Leckton's return to New York.

55

Nevertheless, she had stayed on. Good pay, prompt pay, not too much work, thought Miss Leckton. A cold fish. Well, it made no difference as long as she did her work well. The thing to do with servants was to be civil to them, exacting as to standards of work, exact as to hours off and days off, prompt in pay—and keep the whole relationship decent but distant. It would be, she reflected, a nuisance to have servants as friends. That was the trouble with George Potter: her mother had spoiled him; it was so easy to spoil a Negro. These women, Anna and Catherine, they were not spoiled. It was troublesome to run a house as it should be run: to lock up the linen and the supplies, the wines and liquors, the china tea; to lock up one's papers and accounts, one's letters, always. But it was the way to do it. It was horrible to think of one's servants prying about among papers and accounts, one's cheque book, and it was obviously grossly improper to subject them to temptation by leaving around those small things they might pilfer or consume for themselves. After all, when one considered their background, one could hardly expect them to have the same sort of standards as oneself. She remembered the maid her mother had had to discharge —goodness, it must be over thirty years ago now—because she had been drinking Papa's gin now and then.

She thought of these things while she drank her coffee. They gave her a sense of satisfaction, reaffirming a pleasant consciousness of her own importance as head of her house, with much to do, much responsibility to assume. Thinking of that, her mind took up the problem of what she should say to Leah about the radio, about smoking in the library. It would be well, she decided, to do both together, and this morning. The girl had been acting very oddly of late. Indeed, ever since Leah had returned from her stay at Stockbridge this summer, she had been—was upset too strong a word? Disturbed, nervous, restless. That was probably a result, a delayed result, of that business with Herbert Golotz last winter. At all events, she had put down her foot about *that*. The man, however well-dressed and apparently genteel, with his English accent, was a Jew. It was ridiculous to think of a

56

marriage. Very likely Golotz had imagined that Leah had a great deal more money than she had. What she did have, in trust from her mother and father, she couldn't touch at all until she was twenty-one, and that was eighteen months off. Even then, she could not touch the principal until she was twenty-five. Mr. Golotz would hardly wait so long, she imagined. Anyway, she had sent him packing. It could hardly be that. More likely to be the inevitable instability of a young girl growing up.

Usually when Miss Leckton had had her morning coffee, she would feel particularly well. This morning that sensation of well-being failed her, and she was unable to attribute a reason to it other than that of having been waked too early —a not entirely satisfactory answer. Perhaps it was the weather. It seemed uncommonly warm for the time of year; not warm as one thought of warmth in summer, but a sort of pervading heaviness in the air that made one unpleasantly aware of its warmth.

While she lay in bed thinking of this, she heard the telephone ring in the library below her. It rang several times and then ceased. By lying very still and straining to hear, Miss Leckton was able to make out that someone was answering it, though she could not be sure at first whose voice it was. Then she heard, quite comprehensibly, the phrase "That's right," and she knew it was Leah. For some time there was silence, and then the silence was broken at frequent intervals by the voice of Leah saying "Yes" over and over again, rather tonelessly. Whether the tonelessness, the detachment of the girl's voice, was caused by the muting of ceiling and floor and grass carpet, Miss Leckton couldn't be sure. After a while there was no further response and it was evident that the long call was over. Miss Leckton dismissed it from her mind and decided to get up and dress. She had more important things to do than to speculate on Leah's telephone calls; for whatever interest there might be in it, it was quite simple to ask Leah what it had been. After all, it was her duty—her mind shied off the word 'privilege'—to know such matters in her own house, just as she felt it her duty to look over all letters that came to the house, to see who was corresponding with the girl. If one did not know such matters, how could one act intelligently toward one's niece and ward?

When she had dressed, she went downstairs to breakfast in the dining room. Leah was already there, seated at the round mahogany table, smoking a cigarette and reading attentively from a small piece of white paper. One glance, taking in Leah's empty plate, crumpled napkin (a habit Miss Leckton deplored), and coffee cup half empty, told her that the girl was all but finished breakfast. The cigarette reminded her that this would be a good moment to speak about smoking in the library.

"Good morning, Aunt Carrel," Leah said, putting the slip of paper face down on the table.

"You are finished," Miss Leckton said.

"Almost," said Leah. She picked up her coffee cup and drank from it.

Miss Leckton rang the silver bell that was by her place, and sat down. Her half-grapefruit was on her plate, and it looked cool and inviting.

"Don't hurry away," Miss Leckton said, as Leah put down her empty cup. "I have several things I wish to talk to you about." She spread her napkin on her lap and began to eat the neatly separated flesh of the grapefruit.

"All right," said Leah.

There was something in Leah's voice, a tone of depression, of sadness, of something not usual, that attracted her aunt's attention and she looked up at Leah, examining the girl's face more carefully. Leah looked pale, and paleness did not become her. She was not a really pretty girl, though she had rather nice features, and she needed her usual high color to make what looks she had effective. Pallid, as she was now, her skin was in too great contrast to her almost black hair, her heavy eyebrows. The slightly olive quality of her skin appeared to resist the summer tan that seemed so usual nowadays. Looking at her, Miss Leckton was nevertheless aware of Leah's youth: it proclaimed itself in the

58

softness of her face, her young figure, so slim and so mature at once, and in the uncomfortable fact that only in youth could one afford to look so pale and yet not look haggard. Well, there were plenty of perfectly natural explanations for the pallor of a young woman.

"You look none too well," said Miss Leckton.

"Oh," said Leah.

"You are, I believe, smoking too much."

"Perhaps I am," Leah said.

On any other day, Miss Leckton would have said that Leah sounded listless, which would have been the proper word to apply to a girl at such a juncture. But as she framed the thought in her mind, something rejected it. It was not listlessness; it was more like someone withdrawn, who was either not listening to you, or was preparing something in her mind that fully occupied her; as though the withdrawal were in preparation for an effort. It was not as clear an analysis as that in Miss Leckton's mind, yet she knew at once that the girl was not paying her the attention she expected always to receive, and the reason for the lack of attention both annoyed and baffled her. Her annoyance spurred her to approach her subject more rapidly, less thoughtfully, than was usual to her.

"That reminds me," Miss Leckton said. "I want to ask you not to smoke in the library."

"Oh," said Leah. After a pause she added, "Very well."

This ready compliance almost put Miss Leckton off her stroke, but not quite.

"You see," she said, "there should be one room where I, who do not smoke, can be comparatively free from the smell of stale tobacco. The library is, rather particularly, my room. I mind the smell of last night's tobacco there when I come down in the mornings. It clings offensively even after the room has been aired. This morning, on my way back from the kitchen, after I'd been there to ask for coffee earlier than usual—much earlier than usual—it was particularly offensive."

"I'm sorry you were waked," said Leah. "That was careless of me."

59

"Yes," said Miss Leckton. Evidently Leah had been made to feel her mistake, her carelessness, more thoroughly by the morning visit to her room than Miss Leckton had hoped for. The girl in her bath had sounded cheerful and entirely unrepentant. It was hard to tell what would affect young people, engrossed in themselves to the exclusion of the comfort or convenience of their elders, no matter how great the sacrifice of time—and indeed of money—that those elders made. "If you wish to smoke here, or in your own room, that will be quite all right. Or in the living room, if you do not leave the ash trays filled with cigarette ends. But in the library, no. If you want to come in there to read, if you feel the need of my poor company of an evening, you will have to forego your tobacco."

"Very well," said Leah.

Again the reply was surprising to Miss Leckton. She had expected at least some argument from Leah. However, one should be thankful for small favors. Obviously, it had been a good moment to have brought this up. She rang for her coffee and eggs.

"Was it you who answered the telephone, around half past seven, Leah?"

The girl looked down at the paper on the table and then she looked up at her aunt.

"Yes, it was."

"An early hour for a call," said Miss Leckton.

"Yes," said Leah. "It was a telegram."

"For me?"

"No, Aunt Carrel. It was for me."

Miss Leckton opened her mouth to ask what the telegram was about—one never found out anything without asking—when Catherine came into the room with the rest of the breakfast on a tray. While Catherine was serving her, Miss Leckton decided not to ask Leah too flatly about the telegram. It was obvious that Leah should tell her what the wire was about, that she owed that to her aunt. Very well, then. Why should Miss Leckton put herself into the position of having to ask that sort of question, when the answer was

60

her due? Meanwhile, there was the question of the bedroom in New York: this would be a good moment to broach that.

As soon as Catherine had left the room, Miss Leckton poured herself some coffee and began to eat her egg. In a moment she spoke.

"Leah," she said, "I have had a letter, it came yesterday, saying that all the repainting has been done in the apartment. Quite a triumph, considering the painters' strike, don't you think?"

"Yes," said Leah.

"I suppose you will not mind—this is really the first time I've had a chance to talk to you about it—I've had your bedroom repainted."

"Oh, no," said Leah.

"And I had the color changed," said Miss Leckton, eying Leah closely to see how she took this news.

"You didn't!" cried Leah, her face suddenly full of animation, though certainly not the animation of pleasure.

That's better, thought Miss Leckton. That's got her out of her daydreams.

"Yes," Miss Leckton said. "I had grown tired of the yellow paint. I found some very pretty green wallpaper, with a charming pattern of small bouquets of bright flowers, and as I was in New York, alone, in that awful heat, and no way to consult with you, and the apartment people half-crazed trying to get the decorators to work, I seized the opportunity and went ahead."

Miss Leckton took the final bite of her egg and toast, and sat back to observe Leah.

"Well," said Leah. "I must say, Aunt Carrel . . ." Then her voice trailed off into silence. She sat so, for a moment more, her hands folded in her lap, her eyes downcast to her folded hands. Then she drew in her breath and rather slowly puffed it out again, like a smoker blowing rings. "Aunt Carrel," she said, "you wanted to know, I'm sure, what was in this telegram. I'm sure I should tell you, for otherwise everything else that we have been talking about would simply seem silly."

"Well!" said Miss Leckton. She was prepared to ask upon what possible grounds Leah could find the conversation silly, but Leah continued, interrupting her thoughts as well as her speech.

"It was from Herbert," she said. "He wants me to marry him at once. He's coming here today."

V

FOR the moment, Miss Leckton found herself speechless. It was impossible for her to make up her mind which of these two shocking propositions she should answer first. Leah, however, gave her plenty of time. The girl merely sat there, her face unnaturally pale, and looked steadily at her aunt.

"Well!" said Miss Leckton, finding her voice at last. "This is certainly unexpected."

Leah said nothing; she dropped her gaze from her aunt's face to the hands in her lap.

"I suppose," said Miss Leckton, "that you wired him not to come?"

"No," said Leah. "I didn't."

"And why not?" Miss Leckton inquired, her voice sharp with annoyance.

"He is taking the eight o'clock train. There wouldn't have been time," Leah said. "Even if there had been time, I shouldn't have done that."

"That is surprising," said Miss Leckton. "I had thought all that nonsense was over and done with, Leah. That we had settled that at Christmastime."

"Settled?" said Leah.

"I told you then, and I told him," Miss Leckton said. "It wouldn't do. I told him I didn't want him about. That there was really no use his pursuing you further. You and I,

Leah, have been all over this many times. I thought you had agreed with me. I see no good purpose that we can serve by going over it again."

"No," said Leah. "No purpose."

"Then why is he coming? Why this sudden appearance? After all, you haven't seen him since January."

Leah looked up at Miss Leckton then and said, "Oh, no. I've seen him since then. Often."

"You have?" Miss Leckton cried out. "You have? Then you have been seeing him behind my back. Against my wishes. Against my express wishes."

"I have been seeing him," said Leah.

"Why?" said Miss Leckton. "I must ask you, why?"

"Because I love him," said Leah.

"Love!" said her aunt. "How can you know, Leah? You are far too young to know whether you are in love or not. How can you distinguish, at your age, between love and infatuation?"

"I am almost twenty," said Leah. "I have known him now for more than a year. You would not let him come to the apartment, nor here. You said nothing about not seeing him elsewhere. So I saw him elsewhere. I had to."

"I should be very angry at that," Miss Leckton said. "As it is, I am deeply disappointed in you."

"Why, Aunt Carrel? You said in January that it was all too soon. That I was too young. That I didn't know him, or know about him, or his family. I have grown now to know him. I have found out about him—and his family and home."

"From him, I suppose?" her aunt said. She was unable to keep the sarcasm out of her voice, though she had the sense of its being the wrong note to strike.

"Yes. And from others who know of him," Leah said.

"This is all ridiculous and impossible," said Miss Leckton. "I really feel it no part of my duty toward you to allow him to see you. I do not want him in my house."

"Then I shall see him outside it," Leah said. In spite of the firmness of her words, her voice continued to have the warmth and softness that characterized it.

"See him?" said Miss Leckton. "Why, may I ask?"

"Because he is coming down here to ask me, finally, to marry him."

"Finally?" Miss Leckton picked up the word. "That at least is good. I am glad it is final."

"It is final because he has to go back to England. At once," said Leah.

"Oh?" Miss Leckton said. "So? Why is that? It must be very urgent to make him desert you."

"He is a lieutenant in the naval reserve. He has been called back to active duty."

"*He* is a lieutenant? In the British Navy? A Jew?" said Miss Leckton. Her surprise was so genuine that she spoke without considering her words.

Leah looked again at her aunt and slowly the color began to flood her face until it was (in sharp contrast to her former pallor) suffused with a warm pink on cheeks and forehead.

"You say that to me?" she said softly. "To me, Aunt Carrel?"

Miss Leckton knew then that she had made a tactical blunder, and she felt, obscurely and confusedly, that there was something curious in the fact that it was a blunder, that she should think it so. She could feel no real compunction over what she had said—after all, the girl must come to realize in time the limitations of her ancestry, since they were unalterable. Nevertheless she was troubled by the fact that this was not the thing to have said at that moment, and that she was extraordinarily reluctant to pursue the line of reasoning. It was as though life was repeating itself most uncomfortably; the memory of her talks, her mother's talks, with Dora, their efforts to dissuade her from a marriage with Sam Davids, rose up in her mind. Then there had been in neither of them any reluctance to face and to point out the obvious implications of the act of marrying a Jew. What had happened to her—to the world—that one felt a restraint now in proclaiming what was still equally true, equally obvious? Was this the effect of age on her?

"So he is going back to England," she said, shifting her ground, speaking to bridge the moment of emptiness until new arguments should come to her. "Going back to rejoin the navy. Though why that should be necessary now, I cannot see. A rather alarmist gesture. And therefore he comes here to ask you to marry him. Finally, you say. Well, my dear, now you can finally refuse him, and that will close this most unfortunate episode."

The color had begun to drain away from Leah's face and forehead, and by the time Miss Leckton was done speaking, the girl was pale again.

"Believe me, Leah," she said. "That is the right thing to do."

The girl did not answer at once.

"I don't think so," Leah said at last, very slowly.

"Think what?" Miss Leckton said.

"That I shall refuse."

"Oh," said Miss Leckton. "This is a most surprising development. I had no idea things had gone so far. I had not even thought he had written to you. Or that you had seen him."

"He has written," said Leah. "Often. I have taken the trouble to get the mail as it came."

"Ah," said Miss Leckton. "This too behind my back?"

"I am nineteen," said Leah. "My letters are my letters. I was not sure, Aunt Carrel—you can correct me if I am wrong—that I should have received all of them if you had had them first."

"How dare you say that?" cried Miss Leckton, but she knew it to be a defensive gesture. She saw now that it would have been better had she not taken two of Herbert Golotz's letters and destroyed them. That was in February. She should have arranged for Leah to let her see them, somehow—as a protection, if for no other reason.

It occurred to her then that she had failed, rather obviously, in that very job of protection; that the whole episode could not have happened—at all events, so very unexpectedly —if she had been more up on what Leah had been doing.

66

How, for instance, had she succeeded in getting at the mail so regularly before anyone else? Or had she managed to persuade George Potter, or his son, Desmond, who fetched in the mail from the postbox, to separate her letters? If so, it had been very smartly done, for she had seen many other letters that had come for Leah this summer. That would be something to investigate: it was not a tolerable situation. She would know what to say to George or Desmond. And (her mind reaching further) where had Leah seen Golotz? In New York? That would, of course, be simple. But here? Not easy. Perhaps at Stockbridge? That would mean a gross betrayal by the Woodings, with whom Leah had stayed. Or perhaps not. Perhaps they had not known about Golotz—that she opposed him so strongly? And had not Leah told them? It was all a tissue of deception and subterfuge, very unpleasant.

"I suppose you saw him at Stockbridge?" she asked.

"Yes," said Leah. "He stayed at Lenox, with Charlie Codworth."

"I suppose you told Mrs. Wooding that ... how I feel about Mr. Golotz?"

"No," said Leah. "Look, Aunt Carrel. What use is this? You told me I was a fool to see Herbert. You told Herbert to keep out of your house, very clearly. I disagreed with what you said. I thought I was in love with him, and I had to find out. So I saw him when and where I could. If I had found you to have been right, I'd have come and told you so. Now I know what I feel about him. I know what he feels about me. Don't you think it is a waste of time to discuss how and when and where I got to that point? He arrives here after lunch. He said he would come about two o'clock. He is going to ask me if I will marry him straight away and go back to England with him when he leaves next week. I am going to say—yes. I can say it in this house. Your house. Or I can say it outside the house. That is as you choose. He is coming here so as not to have this happen without your full knowledge."

Leah's words aroused in Miss Leckton a bitterness of anger,

and she forgot what she had been going to say and spoke quickly, making no attempt to keep the bitterness out of her voice.

"So," she said. "You are going to marry him. I realize fully that there is no way to stop a fool from his folly. But I will point out to you that this is a very fine expression of gratitude to the aunt who has harbored you since your ... since you became a charge upon her. Since you were eleven. Eight years of care. Eight years of care—and of expense. You propose to go with what? The things I have supplied to you, yet against my wishes?"

"Oh," said Leah. "Oh. I had not thought about that. I ..."

"You hadn't thought," said Miss Leckton, interrupting her. "You hadn't thought. What assurance have I then that you have thought about the whole proposition? For instance, what will you use for money? Do you not realize that there is nothing coming to you—without my consent—until you are twenty-one? That is almost eighteen months away. Does your Mr. Golotz realize that? Does he know he is getting someone who is penniless now? Does he know that you can't touch a penny of your principal until you are twenty-five? Does he know how small that principal is? Will he be pleased to know you have estranged the aunt who has been as a mother to you? That you can hardly expect her to help you financially now, or remember you—later on? Do you think that is going to please a Britisher—who commonly marries an American girl only for her money? Is he not judging you as a prospect—by *my* houses, *my* establishments? I say a Britisher. I am not mentioning any other of his—characteristics, which might make him be disappointed in a wife with no fortune. Do you feel this will be a good start for a successful marriage?"

"I don't know. I have told him of these things," said Leah, speaking very quietly, very softly. "I told him, too, that you disapproved—he hardly needed to be told—and that perhaps you'd say—what you have just said. He said it made

68

no difference at all. That was in the early spring. He still wants to marry me."

"I am not convinced," Miss Leckton said. "He is just too smart, that's all. He is gambling on the chance I shall change my mind, once you are married. It is an old trick."

"No," said Leah. "He is not like that, Aunt Carrel."

"You're a fool, Leah. Simply a fool. You don't know anything. You are still very young, very ignorant of the world. These international marriages rarely work. Very rarely. Believe me. I have seen them. The British are not like the Americans. He will be a very different man—indeed, a very different husband—when he has you in England. You can be quite sure of that."

"We have talked of that," said Leah. "He has told me of these things. I don't care. I am in love with him. I have been in love with him since I first saw him. He is kind and good. He is very well off. He does not need my money. He needs me."

"You are a fool," said Miss Leckton.

There were a great many things she wanted to say to Leah then, but she was conscious of an oppression that made it difficult to say them: as though to do so, to cover all this ground again, to repeat the arguments that, to her, were so overwhelmingly conclusive—and had such an intolerable echo of Dora—was too great an effort. Perhaps, thought Miss Leckton, it is because of the quality of the day, this sticky, heavy warmth in the air, the early morning awakening. Nevertheless, the effort must be made, however useless. One could not be defeated so swiftly. She must make it clear to Leah that this would create a final breach, that what she had said about the lack of help was meant, was not merely a threat. She was about to say these things when Catherine came into the dining room.

"Excuse me," said the maid. "I thought you had finished."

"No," said Miss Leckton. "We shall be through in a moment. I shall ring to let you know."

"Very good, madam," Catherine said, and she withdrew into the pantry again.

69

"Well," said Miss Leckton. "There is not much I can say, Leah. But I want you to understand, beyond any question, that I meant precisely what I said. That you can expect no aid from me in such a fantastically impossible venture. You understand that, don't you? That this is your sole responsibility?"

"I understand," said Leah.

"Very well," said Miss Leckton. "And understand, too, that what I am doing is for your own good, not mine. Well? What are you going to do about it?"

"I am going to call up the garage at Cottrellton," the girl said, "and ask them to send a car here. I'll meet Herbert at the train and we can have lunch at the Inn."

"And then?" her aunt inquired.

"I'll telephone you," said Leah. "I'll let you know before I leave. I shall take nothing you don't approve."

"Oh," said Miss Leckton.

There seemed to be no question of the girl's determination to do this fool thing. Her mind was closed. Obstinate. Selfish. So self-centered that there was no way to pierce through to her reason by argument. But the man? Might he not be more amenable? More open to reason, to the difficulties of what he was doing?

"How old is Mr. Golotz?" she asked.

"He is twenty-nine," Leah answered. "He will be thirty next month. The tenth of October."

So she already knew his birth date, thought Miss Leckton. Very pretty and touching, indeed.

"No," she said. "I do not think that any of this is right. It is so wrong that it appalls me. But right or wrong, I shall do my duty. He may come here, to the house, as he proposes. At two o'clock, after lunch. I cannot have a publicly advertised elopement. When he comes, I shall expect to talk to him. Is that understood?"

"Yes," said Leah. "He very much wants to talk to you. That is why he has come down."

"Possibly," said Miss Leckton. "At the last moment. Having practically seduced my ward in the meantime, behind

70

my back. It will be better for him to realize how I feel, of my reasons against it. To hear of it from me, without the—shall I say, softening?—of your interpretation."

The girl said nothing.

"Thirty," said Miss Leckton. "Eleven years older than you. Even there, it is bad. Too great a disparity in age. He must see that."

"May I please be excused now?" said Leah.

"From breakfast, yes," said Miss Leckton. She rang the silver bell, and rose, and Leah got up too. "But these formalities seem rather empty, don't you think? They lose all meaning when so much else cannot be excused."

"I'm sorry," said Leah. "I am trying to decide the whole course of my life."

"That is precisely what I have been saying," Miss Leckton replied. "You had better not decide it mistakenly. These matters are not so simple to rectify later."

She stood by her place and watched Leah walk slowly toward the door to the hall. Miss Leckton was folding her napkin automatically.

"As your mother discovered, I make no doubt," she said.

Leah stopped and turned.

"What do you mean?" she said. "What are you trying to say, Aunt Carrel? That Mother was not happy with Father?"

"Oh, I didn't say that," her aunt replied. "But there must have been many moments—in New York—here—at various places where the Lecktons were welcome when . . . well, when she must have wondered. To put it mildly."

"Is this something you know?" said Leah. There was a strange quality to her voice, Miss Leckton noticed, that she had never heard in it before. It was almost like anger. "Is this something you *know,* or that you are just guessing at? Now? For my benefit?"

"It is better not to discuss it," said Miss Leckton, closing her lips in a thin line, assuming the expression of one who is keeping silent against her will, with great self-control. The shot went home, she thought.

Leah stood a moment looking at her, and then turned again and left the room swiftly.

Miss Leckton herself turned back to the table to deposit her napkin. Leah's napkin, she observed, was still crumpled by her plate. Even such little considerations, the girl could never learn. How could you expect her to be considerate—let alone grateful—about the larger ones?

Miss Leckton walked around and picked up Leah's napkin and began to fold it, an act she could neither explain nor resist. As she did so, she saw the slip of paper still there. Without hesitation she picked it up and read it. It was written in Leah's clear, round hand.

"Ordered home for active service as predicted leaving Wednesday September 28. Shall take eight o'clock down and get lunch Cottrellton arriving your house at two. We must decide now darling time grows deadly short. If married at once a few days together before sailing. No faith this German business. Try to persuade your aunt talk to me so all in open now. All my heart."

It was unsigned.

"This will take some doing," thought Miss Leckton.

She went to the window and looked out. The wind was blowing fresh from the northeast, the clouds were getting thinner. It was odd it should be so warm, so oppressive, with the wind in that quarter. "Yes," she said. "This will take a lot of stopping. I hope the girl is not pregnant." But that was a thought so hideously repugnant to Miss Leckton that she immediately put it out of her mind, although she could not prevent the blood from running up hotly into her face and neck.

It was at this point that Mrs. Kluger came into the library, bearing Miss Leckton's supper tray.

72

VI

SOMEWHAT to her surprise, Miss Leckton noticed that this interruption of her recollections (which had been uncommonly vivid) was not at all abrupt, and that she seemed to slide easily from the state of recollection into that of existing in the present. It was almost as though Mrs. Kluger's arrival had been a continuation in time of those things she had been considering and remembering, and so strong was this sense of continuity that Mrs. Kluger had set the tray on a small table beside her and had departed again for the kitchen before it occurred to her employer either to speak to her, or to recall exactly the reason for doing so. She had, she now realized, wished to make a last—and probably quite futile—appeal to the woman not to go home to Chog's Cove. But the confusion of time, this merging of past with present, this odd sense that what was now taking place was not a repetition of a storm but an extension of the former storm, confused her mind until it was too late to speak. And yet, she thought, coming back now to a more detached point of view, a more actual consideration of events, it really made but little sense, because the gale of 1938—let alone the hurricane into which it developed—had not started to blow, to manifest itself at all, until long after her morning conversation with Leah.

Quite automatically she looked at the clock on the desk. It read three minutes past seven. The woman had been

73

prompt, you must say that for her; though perhaps her promptness was not to be admired in this instance, since it could have stemmed from her obvious eagerness to get supper over with and leave the place. Miss Leckton felt a swift constriction of her heart as this thought came to her. Not wishing in the least to examine into the reason for her sensation, she tried to set her mind on something else. Her effort was successful, because she remembered the barometer. She rose from her chair and went over to it. It read 29.60.

Not much of a drop, thought Miss Leckton, but a drop, nonetheless. She reset the index hand and returned to her chair and her supper. Tomato soup, Italian bread and margarine, flounder and potatoes and peas, chocolate custard and cream, cookies. One became tired of fish and fowl, and it was a poor commentary on the state of the country that really fresh fish was almost unprocurable in a seaside community like Cottrellton. Still, there was one thing about having Mrs. Kluger: whatever her religious leanings might be, she was not a Catholic, and did not always have to have fish on Fridays. Miss Leckton began to eat. The smell of the food provoked her appetite, which was a normally hearty one, and she consumed her supper with considerable relish.

It was possible for Miss Leckton to control her thoughts quite well while she was eating. But the moment she was done and had rung the bell for her coffee, she found herself again conscious of the storm. One could not ignore its sound nor its smell. The roar of the wind could be plainly heard now, accentuating the loneliness of the house, the absence of other human beings; the smell of the salt sea was strong in the room. It probably had come in when she had opened the window before supper. It was, she thought, better than the smell of tobacco, at all events. Thinking of tobacco, she thought again of Leah, but her mind leaped past that and settled arbitrarily on the departure of her guests—it seemed to her an ironic term—on the morning after the storm of 1938. Perhaps it was the effort to remove Leah from her mind for the moment, that suggested this removal—singularly involuntary on her part, she thought—of those people.

74

Harry Frosten had left no one knew when. Apparently he had taken nothing with him except the half-emptied bottle of brandy, although it still rather surprised her that he had not, in all that confusion, run off with the silver. Perhaps the fact that she knew who he was by then, knew where he came from, and that he knew that she knew, had deterred him. One would never be able to be sure. Birac had left before breakfast, with Mrs. Barber. He had written the note to her, with his address, and put it on the hall table. Very polite. He had manners, as one would expect of a Frenchman of his class, but there must have been something wrong about him, or else why was he doing the sort of work he was engaged in, here, in Rhode Island? It was hard to tell about foreigners, however intelligent and educated they seemed. Mrs. Barber. She had called the next day, bringing some jam she had salvaged from her house—her miraculous house, there was no other word for it. A common little woman, a bore, but nice enough. There had been a time there when she had been afraid Mrs. Barber might take the whole incident as an excuse to call, to be 'neighborly'—but that had not happened. Perhaps that was because she had told the maid, Catherine, to thank Mrs. Barber and say that Miss Leckton was resting (she had been checking the small objects in the upstairs rooms at the time, to see if anything had been taken), and that had discouraged the old woman.

Mrs. Cleever had left at about eleven o'clock, with her child and the Italian girl, Lucy. Of them all, Mrs. Cleever was the only one she had been sorry to see depart. Sorry. That was not exactly the right word for it. She wanted her to go and she wanted her to stay. More than that, the confusion Maude Cleever's departure had created in her mind was not one that, even now, she liked to think about. No one had ever affected her so before, and she dismissed the memory of it (too readily, she knew) each time it cropped up in her mind, excusing this by her fatigue, the tension of the time. Maude Cleever was a lady, she spoke the same language. That had been a great bond, that was probably the reason anyway. Thinking about it now, rather circumfer-

entially, it seemed to her amazing that Mrs. Cleever had had
sufficient vitality, generosity, to find the strength to take
along the Italian girl with her. That whole incident was
singular—but most fortunate, most fortunate. George had
taken them on foot to the main road, which was about a
mile from the house, and had borrowed a truck from the
Newsomes (from whom Miss Leckton got her milk in those
days), and had driven the lot of them to Providence. She
remembered the letter that Maude Cleever had written to
her, a really charming letter, thanking her profusely not only
for harboring her and the baby, but for being the medium
(quite unwittingly—perhaps unwillingly? thought Miss Leckton) of bringing Lucy into her life. If Mrs. Cleever had only
known, she thought, how relieved she was to get rid of the
Italian girl—not to have to continue to be responsible for a
girl of fifteen who had seemed likely (and had in fact proved
later) to be an orphan! It would have been the sort of irk-
some, unwelcome responsibility that it was difficult to avoid
assuming—at least for a while, until some sort of suitable
place could be found for the girl. It was odd—the disturbance,
the confusion were somehow connected with this—that
Maude Cleever had kept the girl with her. Miss Leckton recalled her own intention, frequently thought of, never put
into execution, to invite Maude Cleever to stay with her.
Each time she had known that she would not, that it would
have been difficult to get her to come without her adopted
Lucy, that she did not want both of them—and that even if
she could have persuaded Maude Cleever to have come alone,
the girl Lucy, the thought of Lucy, would have spoiled the
visit. That was the odd part. It was not pleasant to think
about. It was something one did not wish to examine, that
one put away.

Yes, of them all, only with Maude Cleever had she felt the
smallest reluctance to part—and that reluctance, both vivid
and genuine, was tempered with a huge sense of relief, wholly
disproportionate to the event, as though one had been spared
something; as though—her mind flicked into images—one had
found the switch in one's room, at night, when one woke,

76

wandering in the darkness of the sleep-filled night. The light brought everything into focus. But this was exaggeration, this was nonsense. Basically, Lucy had gone, was off her hands: that was the thing.

This time Miss Leckton saw Mrs. Kluger as she came down the hall with the little silver tray, its coffee pot and sugar bowl, the black lacquer coffee cup. As she saw her, she determined not to speak to her of her leaving. It was an instantaneous decision, and she felt happy to have made it as soon as she realized she had done so. It was awkward and demeaning to plead with people like Mrs. Kluger; and, still under the spell of her clearly recollected sense of relief at the departure of all those people, she found an almost equal relief in the thought that at least she would not have to cope with Mrs. Kluger—for who could tell when a servant might not become hysterical?—during the course of the storm that now she fully accepted as inevitable.

"This is Sanka," said Mrs. Kluger, as she set the coffee tray on the table in the place of the dinner tray she had removed to a chair. "You sure you wouldn't like real coffee tonight? I got some made. Wouldn't take but a minute to change it for you."

"No, thank you," said Miss Leckton. "Sanka will do quite well. I do not sleep well with coffee."

"Uh-huh," said Mrs. Kluger. "Affects some that way. Me, it don't affect any."

She picked up the dinner tray and left with it. So loud now had become the noise of the wind and the water that the tinkle of silver against glass on the tray made a ringing but remote sound, as though it was something heard very clearly at a great distance.

As she drank her Sanka, Miss Leckton reflected on what Mrs. Kluger had suggested. Coffee, indeed! She had never had coffee at night except on those rare occasions in New York when a dinner party at her apartment had seemed unavoidable. No. She was glad to have answered at once and so firmly, for by doing so—particularly by the phrase 'I do not sleep well with coffee'—she had neatly and firmly informed Mrs.

Kluger that she viewed this night as any other night; by implication suggested that Mrs. Kluger's own desertion was the act of one unduly frightened in advance of the possible cause. Sanka at night. Coffee in the morning and also (again in the small cups, as now) at lunch. Coffee was a pleasant ending to lunch.

They had had coffee, she and Leah, on that other day. She did not need any special incident to remember that, for it was habitual, but, as a matter of fact, Leah had spilled her coffee that day, all over the raw-silk doilies that Papa had brought back from the Greek Islands in 1908. It had been (except for the continuance of her pallor) almost the only sign of the nervousness that Leah must have been feeling. Well, thought Miss Leckton, why wouldn't she have been nervous? Sitting opposite me, at my table, eating my food, wearing the clothes I provided, within my house, and facing the ultimate consequence of her practised deception.

It had been while Catherine was mopping up the coffee that the doorbell had rung. That doorbell! So loud, so brazen, so penetrating! It had rung so many times that day, though this was the first time. It had been a bronze bell, like a cowbell, actuated by a wire and a spring, pulled into loud and disagreeable summons by a knob outside the door. Thank goodness, it was disconnected now, and the new electric bell rang only in the kitchen wing. But that time, at the end of lunch, it had given its usual jangle.

Leah had jumped to her feet.

"All right, Catherine," she had said. "You go on with what you are doing. I'll answer the bell." Then she had run out of the room before Miss Leckton could stop her.

Miss Leckton remembered that the whole incident had annoyed her—its totality was aggravating beyond the minor quality of all its component parts. The coffee was bad enough. It was bad enough to have Herbert Golotz coming here on such an errand—or, to be sure, coming here at all. But it was particularly annoying to her, as it always had been, to hear Leah order the servants to do this or that, under her aunt's nose. That was a line she had never been able to define with sufficient clarity to make Leah see it. It was necessary, of course, to bring Leah up as a lady—whatever one thought of her father's position in the world—and to teach her to use and to employ servants, to be at home in the sort of houses to which she—through her mother and her aunt—would have the entrée. But that should not include a complete sense of ownership, if only because the cultivation of such a sense would weaken—as it had, indeed, obviously weakened—the girl's sense of obligation to her aunt and hence, her aunt's authority. I have been too kind, too easy on her, Miss Leckton thought. And Herbert Golotz is the fruit thereof.

Miss Leckton would have liked to have finished her coffee, but she did not feel she could absent herself, leave these two young people alone. She could hear the front door open, and their voices, and then silence; so she rose and, without even folding her napkin, walked out to them. She had had a passing notion to tell Catherine to bring fresh coffee and cups into the living room, but she decided against it. The less social this call, the better.

Herbert Golotz was standing near the door, which was closed. Leah was facing him, her back turned to her aunt.

"How do you do?" said Miss Leckton, walking toward him.

Golotz stepped aside and past Leah, and advanced to meet her.

"How do you do?" he said. "Very good of you to let me come like this. I thought it better to talk to you." He held out his hand and, because she could not think how to avoid it, she gave him a limp and unwelcoming handshake.

There was no doubt about it, the man was very well dressed, in grey flannel trousers with a soft brown tweed jacket, a grey shirt with a small check pattern in it, a tie that went with the shirt but didn't match it too exactly. He wore his clothes easily and, Miss Leckton admitted with reluctance, like a gentleman. He was tall, with wide shoulders, rather heavily built, but certainly not good-looking. He had a straight, rather short nose, very heavy black eyebrows that practically met in the center; thick, slightly wavy black hair, neatly brushed into a parting; a sensitive mouth, rather large, with full lips very clearly cut; and an abnormally heavy chin on which, though it was well shaved, showed the dark, almost blue areas of the heavily bearded. Not good-looking. But not soft, either. Not hard, exactly—what was the word for him? Determined? Obstinate? A little of both perhaps. He looked, she noted, far too sure of himself, but that was a characteristic of the British and not always to be counted on.

"It's blowing better than half a gale out," he said. "You have no boat to worry about, have you?"

"No," Miss Leckton said. "Why do you ask?"

"This wind," Golotz said. "If this were the Bahamas, I'd say you were going to have a hurricane. The wind smells like it, do you see?"

"But this is not the Bahamas," Miss Leckton said. "Fortunately." The conversation seemed to her far too casual. "Suppose we go into the living room," she said. "There we can have our talk."

"Very well," he said. "Will you lead?"

"This way," said Miss Leckton. She started to walk back along the hall toward the living-room door, but she stopped almost at once and turned to Leah. "Leah," she said, "I wish to talk to Mr. Golotz alone."

"Oh," said Leah. "Oh, no! I must be there."

"No," said Miss Leckton, her lips closing firmly after the word. "No. I shall see Mr. Golotz alone or not at all. There are several things I wish to say to him that I prefer to say without your presence. I suggest that you wait in your own room. Or the upstairs sitting room, if you prefer. I will call you before Mr. Golotz goes. No," she said quickly, as Leah opened her mouth to speak. "I do not propose to argue about this, Leah."

"It's all right," said Golotz to Leah. "Better this way, I expect."

Leah drew a deep breath and exhaled it in a sigh. "Very well," she said. "I'll be in my own room."

Miss Leckton stood quite still then and waited. This had its effect on Leah, for the girl finally walked past them to the stairway and went up it, pausing only briefly once to make a small gesture to Golotz, the embryo of a wave, with a little, crooked smile. As soon as she was out of sight, Miss Leckton led the way to the living room and closed the door after them.

She sat in a chair near the south windows, putting Golotz on the sofa next to her. Through the window she could see that the man had been right when he said it was blowing. It was, and very hard indeed. The water was covered with close-running whitecaps, and the wind was blowing the tops off the waves. The long drooping branches of the elms swung in the wind and streamed with its gusts; the leaves were coming off, here and there, though they were still green. The flowers—dahlias, asters, marigolds, calendulas, California poppies—were being flattened by the wind in spite of the clipped yew hedge that lay back of the beds in a long soft arc, protecting them from the east, south, and west. It was the regular equinoctial storm, of course—September 21st. Nothing really out of the ordinary—except the wind had risen very fast. It was not blowing like this when she had gone about her early morning's work, and the sun had even been shining around eleven, with a strong breeze from the eastward. Now it was overcast—an even high sky, with a yellow tinge to it, as though the sun had not yet declared himself beaten. Well—the weather was not important; Golotz was. She looked at the clock. It was a quarter past two. If she were to get a rest, she would have to get rid of him rather expeditiously. So then.

"How did you come over, Mr. Golotz? From the station?"

"I took the local taxi," he said. "I've taken him for the afternoon. He is waiting for me now, outside."

"Oh, yes," she said. "I see. My niece tells me that you must go back to England."

"That's right," he said. "I've been ordered back into service. The Navy. I'm in the Reserve, you see. I expect they've got a bit of wind up with all this Hitler business. I can't say it looks too fine. Do you think?"

She noticed that he spoke easily and directly, with a total absence of nervousness that surprised her, considering what he had come for.

81

"How do you happen to be in the naval reserve?" she asked.

"My mother's people are all Navy," he said. "Have been for a long time. I've an uncle who's an admiral, though I don't think a very good one. I've several cousins in it, too. I was sent to Dartmouth, like the rest of them."

"Oh," she said. "I see."

"Look here, Miss Leckton," he said. "I suppose there's no use in our beating about the bush in the matter, is there? Things have gone rather far for that. I expect you want to know what I mean to do, that sort of thing, and why, and all that. Is that right? Or has Leah told you enough?"

"No," she said. "I had heard nothing. I may as well tell you that the whole thing came to me with a great shock, for the first time, and only this morning. I had thought I had made myself clear last winter. Evidently I did not."

"I see," said Golotz. "I understood you to feel that Leah was too young to know her own mind then—she was only eighteen, to be sure. And also, you didn't know anything at all about me except that I was an engineer, visiting the States for professional reasons. I hope in the meantime that you have made inquiries about me? There's really nothing mysterious about me, you know."

"No," said Miss Leckton. "I did not inquire. I—well—to put it plainly, Mr. Golotz, I had not intended my niece to see any more of you, so there seemed no particular use in making researches."

"May I ask why you felt this way about me?"

It was a disconcerting question. Miss Leckton realized that this interview was not going the way she wanted it, that it had begun to slip out of control. She began to feel angry at this very self-possessed foreigner. She had, moreover, no intention of answering his question.

"I do not see," she said, "what good purpose will be served by any such discussion. Let us keep to the essentials. You are British. My niece is American. She is also extremely young and, in my opinion, immature. You have known each other only a little more than a year. I do not know how often you have seen each other, since I was not aware of the fact that you *were* seeing each other, but it cannot have been often. I do not think these conditions create a proper background for marriage. And beyond this, you are returning to your own country, to go into active service in the navy, and that does not sound to me like a very settled home life."

"No," said Golotz. "It does not. Very well, then. Let's stick to it as you outline it. We have met pretty often. Two or three—sometimes four or five—times a month. Here and there. In other people's houses mostly, and quite openly. We have got to know each other extremely well. I do not think your niece is at all immature, but on the contrary, much more mature than the average American girl of her age, or even older, that I have met. And I have met a great many. As to the question of being married to a sailor, I agree it is hard. In return I will point out that we are not yet at war, that war may be somewhat postponed now, since the Czechs are being—I think the American phrase for it is 'sold down the river'? But most thinking people now feel that Hitler isn't going to rest on his laurels, that sooner or later he'll break out again, somewhere else, for something else. That will mean war. In the face of that, we wish to be married now—so that we may have as much of a life as possible before the balloon goes up. We shall want to be married with your consent, and your blessing. I suppose it is unnecessary to say that, or tell you how much that would mean to Leah. I may as well add that both Leah and I are quite prepared to marry in any event. It would simply be painful and difficult to go against you."

"So you have come, then," said Miss Leckton, "not to ask my consent, but to present me with an ultimatum."

"Miss Leckton," said Golotz, "I am very much in love with your niece. I am not a boy. I have never before found anyone whom I wished to marry, and now I have. If you had troubled to find out about me, you would, I am sure, agree that I am not either wicked or grasping or particularly selfish, and that I do come from a good family."

"A good family," she said. "Well, that is all according to

one's standard of judgment. What one considers as 'good.' "

"I suppose you mean the fact that I have some Jewish blood," he said, with great calmness and detachment.

"I did not say so," said Miss Leckton. She was both surprised and upset by his directness.

"I had noticed how strong the feeling is here about that, in the States," he said. "It surprised me. I had not thought that would be so here."

"I have not said anything about it," Miss Leckton said.

"No, not directly," said Golotz. "I understand from Leah that her father was Jewish."

"Mr. Golotz," Miss Leckton cried angrily, "let us discuss only those things that are necessary and not indulge in unpleasant examinations. May I ask if you realize that Leah is entirely dependent on me financially? That she will have no money of her own until she is twenty-one, that even then she will have but the small income of her inheritance, and that the principal will not come into her control until she is twenty-five?"

"Yes," said Golotz. "She told me all that. Early on."

"You surely cannot expect me to continue to help in a marriage of which I deeply disapprove?"

"No," he said. "I didn't expect you would. It really doesn't signify. I am pretty well-off. I have plenty to do for both of us. Even after the death duties, I shall have another pretty sizable bit of cash when my father dies. I rather incline to the belief that it's not a bad thing for a wife to have a bit of money of her own, though that's not as popular at home as it seems to be here in the States. But there's no rush about it."

"So you propose to marry my niece—my ward—right out from under my nose? Regardless of my approval?"

"It depends entirely on Leah," he said. "She says—has said —she would marry me when I said the word. I have said it now. If she will come with me now, we shall be married. I am extremely sorry if this puts you out. But I cannot see that you have given me—as yet—any reason for deciding against our marriage. If we are to marry, there is obviously no use in further postponement, is there? We shall have, as it is, but a scant week here before we sail for home."

Never in her life before—not even when Dora had, in floods of tears, fled up the stairs crying out that no matter what happened she was going to marry Sam Davids—had Miss Leckton felt angrier or more utterly trapped. There seemed to be nothing she could say or do which would cause this cool individual to swerve from his purpose. Her only hope—a last one and a slim one—was to leave him and go to Leah, and to persuade the girl that she must not marry this man.

Thinking this, she looked out the window, planning how she should approach Leah, what she could say that would prove conclusive, convincing. She was not seeing what went on outside the window: her eyes were turned inward on the scenes of her imaginary interview with Leah.

It was at this moment that the deck chair which had been placed near the sundial by the flower beds suddenly lifted and overturned and, driven by the wind, rolled over and over toward the house, until finally it crashed against it directly below her. Its motion caught her eye and her attention. Its speed was so odd and so abnormal that she found herself wondering what could have made this happen: she was still but half way back to reality, unable to relate the cause to the effect.

Golotz had jumped to his feet, he too looking out the window.

"I say," he said. "This *is* a real blow."

Miss Leckton also rose and came to the window. Together they stood looking out at the storm. The long branches of the elms were waving about in a mad sort of motion, the flowers were bent flat by the gusts. As they looked, they saw George Potter walking toward the sundial. He was finding it difficult to walk against the wind, had to bend forward into it.

It was obvious to Miss Leckton that George had thought of the deck chairs. One lay flat on the ground, collapsed by the sundial, its canvas bellying up and down in the wind, the chair lifting a little from the ground and then settling

85

back. As they watched him, George reached it and picked it up and they could see that he had some difficulty in holding it, for he turned it this way and that to try to arrange it so that it presented the least resistance to the wind. Then he looked around him for the other one, but he failed to spot it, and he started back toward the east side of the house. In a moment, Miss Leckton realized, he would be out of sight.

She unlatched the window with the intention of raising the lower sash to call out to George, tell him to get the other chair.

"I shouldn't open that window if I were you," Golotz said.

Miss Leckton looked at him and she was so surprised that she said nothing.

"It's blowing pretty stiff," he said. "Make quite a do in this room, I expect. And I don't think the man could hear you, you know. Not against that wind."

Reluctantly Miss Leckton took her hands from the window. It irked her to be told what to do or not to do in her own house—particularly by this man—but the truth of what he had said was too apparent to disregard.

"I must speak to him," she said.

"Could I get him for you?" Golotz volunteered.

"No," said Miss Leckton. "No, thank you. If you'll excuse me." She turned away at once toward the hall, and Golotz followed her to the door, opened it for her.

Miss Leckton walked rapidly toward the front door at the north end of the hall. As she did so, there was a peal of the doorbell, as loud, as insistent as always. Confused by it, she stopped, not knowing whether to go on and open it herself or to wait for Catherine to come. She was aware that this was an unusual moment for visitors, could think of no one likely to call; and behind her she felt strongly the disturbing presence not alone of Golotz, but of the entire and unsettled problem his presence raised. Her indecision surprised her and troubled her: she, who was accustomed to decide rapidly for herself and others.

As she waited, still unsure, the bell rang again.

VII

SO strong was the recollection now of that loud sound of the old wire-pulled bell, so vivid the remembrance of her own confusion (coupled with a sense of outrage at the impatience of those who had rung it again at such a short interval) that Miss Leckton rose from her morris chair and stood by the window that she had prevented George from shuttering. Still living in two worlds simultaneously, and liking neither of them, she focused her attention on the darkness outside the window in an attempt to define these two existences, divide them more clearly.

Her mind still attempting to reduce this merger of time, to place the connection simply on the accidental recurrence of a certain weather rather than on the uneasy sense of one circumstance being the cause of the other—or, at least, the forerunner, as well as the premonition, of disaster—she saw lights blinking on and off, on and off, near the tool shed. For a moment she could not decide what this was. Then she realized it was undoubtedly Mrs. Kluger testing the lights of her car, possibly already leaving.

Miss Leckton turned back to the room. That woman, she thought, had not even troubled to take out the coffee tray. The clock on the desk said seven-thirty-five. It was outrageous. She started to go over to the bell-push by the fireplace, to ring for Mrs. Kluger, but stopped as she realized it would do no good, it would ring merely in an empty kitchen. The picture of the kitchen's emptiness expanded suddenly and violently into a realization of the emptiness of the whole house, the wind rattling the shutters of unoccupied rooms, the clocks that ticked against no hearing, the lights that lit for no eye, and she felt weak and sat down again quickly in her chair and poured herself another cup of coffee, her hand shaking just perceptibly.

There seemed no way to escape either from this affliction of the discomfort of indecision or from the sense of events continuous beyond any rational basis. This was how she had felt, she thought, when that old bell had rung before—no, not quite the same—then she was angrier, less aware of the storm, but equally confused.

Then, too, she had not known what to do. She could not and would not return to Golotz in the living room. She could not—it would be like running away—retire to the library, from both Golotz and these importunate, these untimely visitors. She could not just stand there and wait for Catherine to come and open the door. If she did, how could Catherine say she was not at home; or to which room could she withdraw to await Catherine's report? Nevertheless, so powerful was the urge not to let this person, these people, ring that bell a third time that she strode to the door herself to open it. As she put her hand on the knob, she was conscious that Catherine had emerged from the dining room into the hall behind her.

The door was a heavy one and it usually required a considerable effort to open it; but this time, as she released the catch, it opened itself and the wind blew against her, lifting her skirt embarrassingly, disarranging her hair. Behind her she heard the sound of paper crackling and, looking back, saw the newspaper on the hall table blow off and scatter in angular confusion on the floor and Catherine bend to retrieve it.

"Take the door, Catherine," she said, but she had to repeat it, raising her voice. "Take the door," she cried.

Catherine picked up as much of the paper as she could encompass with one sweep of her hands, put it on the chair

88

by the hall table, and stepped quickly to the door. The paper at once blew off the chair and sailed in the disorder of its parts down the hall. Miss Leckton, one hand to her hair, the other to her skirt, stepped out on the stone landing, and Catherine closed the door almost shut behind her.

Standing on the top step, within reach of the bell-pull, was a man of medium height, heavily built, wearing a lightweight green overcoat. He had no hat, and his thick red hair, rather long and untidy, blew in the wind. Below him, at the foot of the steps, was a small woman, dark-haired, in a dark blue dress and coat, a small, ugly blue hat on her head, a sallow face, foreign looking. Behind them, drawn up just short of the steps, was a limousine, its black paint worn to a muddy bronze color, and behind its wheel she recognized Walter Carey, the taxi driver from the railroad station. He was there for Golotz, she remembered, not for these people, who had evidently walked in.

"Yes?" said Miss Leckton.

"How d'ya do?" said the red-headed man. "I'm real sorry to disturb you any. You the owner?" He had a strong Rhode Island accent.

"Yes, I'm Miss Leckton. I'm the owner," she said. "What is it, please?"

"How d'ya do?" the man repeated. "It's my wife. She don't feel too good. I'm Mr. Grover La Perche. This is Mrs. La Perche. We was wondering some if she could jest rest up here a while, while I go git some gas."

"Gas?" said Miss Leckton. She had to shout to be heard and so did he.

"Why, yes," said La Perche, running his hand over the wind-blown exuberance of his red hair. "Never did have it happen to me before. No. Not in twenty years of driving. Car's right out of gas. It's there." He turned and pointed.

Miss Leckton looked in the direction of his finger, and saw a small car parked on the turnout of the road, just beyond the bridge over Ten Acre Creek.

"May I ask," she said, "what you are doing there? This is

89

a private road. There is a sign at the entrance to it, at the main road. Did you not see it?"

"Well, yes," said La Perche. "I seen the sign, but I didn't think it would bother any if we jest come down the road a piece. We come down from Lonsdale, we wanted to see the storm, the breakers. Hadn't seen a good spot to see the breakers from till we got here. And then the car run out of gas. First off, I thought she was jest choked up some, maybe the feed line was stoppered up some, and I coasted her down to where she is. But I looked then, and she's dry. Not a drop. And then my wife says she don't feel too good, feels sort of dizzy. So I thought I'd ask could she set in here for a spell, while I walk up the road and git some gas. I seen a station not above a couple miles back."

This is intolerable, thought Miss Leckton. The shouting fatigued her, the wind kept pulling at her hair, her skirt, and its discomfort added to her exacerbation with these people who trespassed so lightly and then asked favors.

"The sign at the gate was put there," she cried, "to prevent people from doing what you have done. It was quite clear, quite explicit. It said 'Private Road.' It said 'Absolutely No Trespassing,' in large letters. You would have done better to let your wife sit in the car, not make her walk up to the house. I am sorry she is not well, but it is all quite impossible. Too many . . . it is quite impossible. She can sit in your car."

"Well," said La Perche, "it's this storm. It don't feel normal. It frightens her. She didn't like for to set alone there, feared I'd be too long. It sure blows real hard, don't it? There's talk on the radio of a hurricane, maybe."

"No," said Miss Leckton, "I am sorry. It is quite out of the question. No. Not here." The wind blew in a gust just then that lifted her skirt indecently in spite of her hand on it, and she let go of her hair to hold the skirt down, and her hair blew loose from its pins. It enraged her, made her feel trapped by the wind, by these people, by Golotz. "Not here," she said again, shouting over the wind. "You'll find quite a good safe spot in Cottrellton, it is but six miles from here. I am sure Mr. Carey here will drive you and your wife back to your car, and you to the gasoline station. But I cannot accommodate you here. I am sorry."

She looked at the woman then. It was evident that she was not well, her color unhealthy under the sallow skin; it was equally evident that she had not heard what had been said, for she was smiling a small, forced, and timid smile. The man said nothing, merely looked puzzled and rather hurt, and ran his big pink hand over his hair again. Miss Leckton turned at once to the door. There was no use in prolonging this. As she turned, Catherine let the door blow open, and Miss Leckton entered the house, and together she and Catherine, using their combined strengths, pushed the door closed.

The newspaper settled to stillness on the floor, its pages scattered about. Standing with his feet apart, his hands clasped behind his back, just within the frame of the living-room door, was Mr. Golotz.

"Oh," said Miss Leckton, and her hands went up to her disordered hair. "Do pick up that paper, Catherine."

The maid began at once to collect and fold the scattered sheets into order again.

"You will have to excuse me a moment," Miss Leckton said to Golotz. "I must ask you to wait a moment. Do sit down in the living room or something, will you?" She wanted to add, 'and don't just stand there looking at me,' but she controlled herself. "I shall be with you in a moment."

Golotz bowed slightly, without speaking, and disappeared into the living room.

"What impertinence!" said Miss Leckton. "They had run out of gasoline, and wished to wait here. After having trespassed to get here. Saw the sign and paid it no attention. Such people are impossible. Give the paper to that gentleman, Catherine, and then that will be all for now."

"Yes, madam," said Catherine. Her face, as usual, betrayed nothing of what she was thinking. Miss Leckton, as she went upstairs to her room, found herself wondering about it, speculating on how much Catherine could have heard through the crack of the door, and was impatient with herself for wanting to know. What difference did it make?

On the landing she paused long enough to look out. She could see Grover La Perche putting his wife into the back of Carey's taxi and following her in. Well, she thought, that was good. They had taken her suggestion. Carey would not be gone long; not long enough to delay Golotz's departure. She went to her own room and tidied her hair in front of her mirror. How savage the wind was! One could scarcely think properly in a wind like that, it made things complex that should be simple. She had been too polite, too thoughtful of those people. She should have sent them off with a flea in their ear. And downstairs was still Golotz. Leah was in her room. Too many things to tackle at once. Taking a deep breath, patting the last strands of her hair again into neatness, she decided to speak now to Leah. It would be of no use to speak to that man any more. His mind was closed.

As she walked toward Leah's room, it occurred to her (as it had occurred before) that it had been a ridiculous performance of Dora and Sam Davids to leave Leah's money as they had. If they expected her to take over the control of the child in the event of their death (as they obviously had, or why else had they left Leah's money in trust with her?), why had they not left her full control of the funds indefinitely? Only so did one retain control; only so would she now have been able to break up this unfortunate affair with Golotz. One was landed with the social and moral responsibility for the care and upbringing of a girl, but was not provided with the final weapons to make compelling an authority necessary to that task. As she thought of this, she thought at the same time, as though her thoughts could carry an overtone to their main course, of how much of a sacrifice it had been for her—not financial exactly, for Leah's trust fund provided almost enough for the child's care, but in all other ways—to be saddled with a child one had not wanted, had not begotten (thank God!), and whose very existence one had opposed—if one could consider opposition to Dora's marriage in that light. The whole tenor of her thoughts now, coupled with the nervous exasperation of Golotz's presence, the scene with the La Perche man in the discomfort of the high wind, enraged her, and she felt her temper slipping away from control. She made a distinct effort to master it, and knocked on Leah's door.

There was no answer and Miss Leckton entered the room. Leah was not there, not in the bathroom, whose door stood open. The bedroom was somewhat disordered, a towel on the end of the bed, one drawer of the bureau half opened, the runner on top of the dressing table askew, the toilet articles shoved together at one side of it, as though they had been moved to make a clear space. The silver brush and comb, the hand mirror, the whole matching set, with Dora's monogrammed initials on them, were there complete. Glancing around, Miss Leckton saw the cupboard door open, the hanging rod still supporting many dresses. It was only when she turned on the light in the cupboard, looked more closely, that she saw a few empty silk-covered hangers. In the bathroom, into which she peered, all the pretty bottles and flasks she had provided were on their glass shelf. The toothbrushes were gone, there were no salves or cold creams. The room looked untidy, indeed, but as though a guest had just moved out of it.

She has packed up, thought Miss Leckton; and her anger grew within her. There was nothing to be done here, she must go downstairs to find Leah. The girl must have gone down while she was fixing her hair. It made her job more difficult. Everything seemed to be made difficult for her today. No one seemed to consider her or her comfort or convenience or feelings—only their own needs. People were so damnably selfish!

Miss Leckton went down the stairs. As she did so, she became aware of the Piranesi engravings on its wall—why, she could not imagine; they were as they had always been, since long before her governorship of the house; they were not things she often looked at, thought of. Now, their familiarity was changed: they were, suddenly, the symbols of her existence, the possessions of her parents and grandparents, and

93

they spelled out both the order and the quality of her existence, the direction in which she, and all the Lecktons, had
gone, the direction which Leah should have followed, had she
not been diverted by this regrettable intrusion of an alien
force into her life. What would become of the engravings?
What was their end to be, when she should die? The threatened and imminent defection of Leah seemed now to Miss
Leckton to make her feel both old and insecure—she who
was not old, had never been insecure—as though there were
now no point in the orderliness of these engravings, spelling
out a tradition more than a decoration. These thoughts
made her feel curiously weak inside herself; but the weakness
did not persist. She heard voices below her, very faintly—the
wind was making a good deal of noise even within the house,
she noticed—and, identifying them as Leah's and Golotz's
voices, she felt immediately a resurgence of anger that swept
the weakness away, and a violent desire to exercise the
power that she felt to be her inborn as well as her acquired
right. It was in this mood that she swept into the living room,
past two of Leah's suitcases that stood outside the door.

Golotz and Leah were standing by the window, their backs
turned to her. Golotz held the folded newspaper in his hand.

"Well," said Miss Leckton with an acid smile, "you seem
to have wasted no time, Leah."

As they turned to her, she examined their faces. Leah
looked as though she had been crying, her eyes were rather
red and her lids swollen. Golotz faced her with an expression
of polite impassivity, and she was struck again by his well-
developed control of himself, though she was not at all sure
what sort of thoughts and plans that impassive expression
might cover.

"I see," she went on, "that you did not wait for our decision, but decided for yourself."

"I waited and waited, Aunt Carrel," Leah said, her voice
controlled but full of an inner nervousness. "I packed my
things, so as to have something to do. I knew what Herbert
would say."

"Oh?" she said. "Then his coming here was not to find an

94

answer to a question, was it? It was to complete a decision. It was a mere formality, his talk with me?"

"I came," said Golotz, "to tell you that I was going to marry Leah if she still wanted to do that. I didn't like the idea of not telling you, myself. I thought I had made that clear."

"Oh, quite clear, crystal clear," Miss Leckton said. She could feel her self-control slipping away. "It was so good of you to think to do this. It was so good of you to come here to take away from me, on an hour's notice, the niece I have raised and cared for, for whom I have spent the best years of my life—not that anyone asked *me* to take care of her. Oh, no. I'm not consulted. The child is dropped in your lap, as it were, and they say, 'Now look after her, you're her aunt. Feed her and clothe her and educate her. Give her a good background, do, so that someday some man—it doesn't matter who, some stranger from God quite knows where—can come along on an hour's notice and take her away from you.' That's what they say. That's why I'm so happy at this event. This event about which I was not consulted."

"I might point out to you," said Golotz, his voice still very calm and unhurried, his accent a little more clipped, more pronouncedly British, "that you hardly have made it a simple matter to consult you, Miss Leckton."

Ignoring this, Miss Leckton turned to Leah.

"Well, Leah," she said. "What are you going to do?"

"I am going to leave now, with Herbert," Leah said.

"And where are you going? If it is permitted me to know?"

"To New York," said Golotz. "Leah will stay with Mrs. Fox, a friend of ours. We shall be married Friday. We hope you will be there."

"And this Mrs. Fox," said Miss Leckton. "Who is she? Is she also British? Is she by any chance a Christian?"

"She is American," said Golotz. "Mrs. Anthony Fox. She lives on East Sixty-third Street. Her husband is a vice-president in the Madison Trust Company. I expect you can find out about them quite easily. They are friends of the Woodings, whom you know."

95

"What little confidence I had in the Woodings has fairly well evaporated," said Miss Leckton. "After their performance at Stockbridge—which I heard about only this morning."

"Will you be coming to New York?" said Golotz. "Or, would you prefer that we remain here, get married from here? That would, of course, be preferable and far nicer for Leah."

"Since my preference has not been consulted about the main issue, I cannot see why you should consult me as to minor ones," she said. "I shall have no hand in this marriage. I do not wish it misunderstood now that I would forbid it if I could—that I heartily disapprove it. That I shall expect Leah to realize that this is so, and that she must suffer fully the consequences of her own wilful act. Do you understand that, Leah?"

"Yes," said Leah.

"Very well," said Golotz. "Seems to me a poor sort of business, this. Sorry it had to go this way. I expect we had better leave now, Leah. We're not getting any forrader here. Miss Leckton seems to have made up her mind and we've made up ours. Come along." To Miss Leckton he said, "Thanks for letting me come here. I shouldn't have liked not to have talked to you."

"You shouldn't have liked," repeated Miss Leckton. "This whole thing revolves entirely around what you and Leah like. No one seems to consider for a moment what *I* like, what *I* feel."

"Good-bye," said Golotz. "Are you coming now, Leah?" He bowed slightly to Miss Leckton and walked to the door.

"Yes," said Leah. "Good-bye, Aunt Carrel. I am sorry you feel like this. Life isn't normal now. I must seize my happiness while it is there to seize. Good-bye. I have taken only my own few things, some underclothes. I've left the others, as you wanted. I'll be at the Foxs's if you want to reach me."

Miss Leckton stood very straight in the center of the room and did not speak. Within her, her rage was mounting so fast that it choked her. The curious thing about it was that she no longer cared at all whether Leah married this man or not, but only (and deeply) that she had lost the power to prevent it, that a public defeat stared her in the face.

Leah, looking white and frightened and very young, and saying, "Excuse me, please," like a small child leaving the table, slid sidewise past her aunt and followed Golotz into the hall. Miss Leckton simply stood where she was, unmoving except for the fingers of her hands, which she laced together and unlaced, the knuckles white with her tension.

She could hear them in the hall, and she could hear the wind, too. It was high and loud, and it came in gusts now that slightly shook the house. The clock on the mantel said ten minutes past three. Miss Leckton was waiting to hear them go, to hear the sound of the door, and she was torn by the desire to stay here, in silence, letting her disapproval show in that fashion, and by a violent urge to rush out into the hallway and hurl her anger at Leah, in words at least, though blows would be more satisfying.

She was totally unprepared, then, to see Leah reappear in the doorway, her raincoat on, wearing her little brown felt country hat with the pheasant feather, her handbag clutched in both hands in front of her.

"Good-bye," said Leah. "Good-bye, Aunt Carrel. Thank you for all that you have done for me. I shan't forget it. Good-bye." The girl was not really weeping, for her voice was clear and warm, but the tears were coming out of her eyes and running down her face. She stood an appreciable moment so, looking at her aunt, and then turned swiftly and as though with a real physical effort that showed in the swing of her shoulders, and was gone again into the hall. Miss Leckton heard the front door open, heard the wind, heard the newspaper blow off the table, saw a piece of it come sailing untidily past the living-room door.

Whatever it was that had held her immobile now released her. She ran into the hall and was just in time to see the front door close in her face. She ran to it, opened it—it swung in on her with great force, hitting her in the forehead. She avoided the door and it swung fully open, and she ran out onto the steps. She could see Golotz's back as he climbed into the car after Leah.

"Go, then! Go!" she cried out. "Go, and never come back! You may never come to me again. Do you understand? Never come back! Never!"

The wind whipped the words from her mouth and blew them away to the stormy west. The car door shut, the car moved slowly, moved faster, was going away.

"Stop that car!" she cried. "Mr. Carey! Stop that car!"

But the car moved on, gained speed, turned north, went down the slope to the bridge, crossed it. Beyond the bridge she noted that that other car had gone too. Soon Carey's taxi was out of sight as it swung east into the oak woods on the rise. They were gone.

Miss Leckton went back into the house. The newspaper was scattered all over the hall, the cover had blown off the hall table, the rug was turned back. With great difficulty she shut the door, and suddenly felt her hair fall in disorder around her face. The hall seemed empty. The house itself seemed empty.

VIII

THE fingers of Miss Leckton's left hand ached. Looking at them, she was surprised to see that they were still tightly gripping the tiny handle of the lacquer coffee cup, which was half full. She drank the rest of the coffee, finding it cool, and set down the cup. Automatically she looked at the clock again. It said seven-fifty. She must, she realized, have been clutching the cup for at least fifteen minutes. It seemed to her that she had been a great distance in that time, and that the pursuit of the past had tired her.

She rose, in an attempt to shake off this feeling, and took the coffee tray. It would be as well to carry it to the pantry, wash the cup, put it away. There was no one else to do so now, and it would occupy her.

She was just turning into the dining room when Mrs. Kluger came through the pantry door toward her. The woman had on a transparent white raincoat, the hood thrown back. She was wiping her face with a very small handkerchief edged with coarse lace.

"I was jest coming to git it," said Mrs. Kluger.

Miss Leckton stood where she was and let Mrs. Kluger come to her and take the tray.

"You have been out?" Miss Leckton asked.

"Yes," said Mrs. Kluger. "A bad night. It's hard to tell whether it's rain or spray. That wind, it's certainly blowing real hard. But my car is fine. Started right up."

Rather stiffly, Miss Leckton made a final attempt to prevent the departure that now seemed so imminent.

"I hope you think it is safe to drive a car on a night like this," she said. "I should think it very foolhardy."

"Well, it's risky," said Mrs. Kluger. "No denying. But gracious, there's risk everywhere, ain't there? Risk your neck every time you cross the street in Providence, these days. I'd say there was risk to stay here, if it comes to that. You're real near the water. But still and all, you got through the last hurricane, so I guess you needn't to worry. I'll just wash up this, and I'll be going. Good night, Miss Leckton. I'll be back tomorrow, God willing." She walked toward the pantry door, the little tray held lightly and easily in one hand, the other still busily mopping at her face with the little handkerchief.

There was nothing Miss Leckton could think of to say to her, nothing. She stood until the woman had gone through the door to the pantry, stood until the door had ceased its swinging back and forth and had settled again into immobility. Then she moved. She walked into the office, switched on the light, glanced at the arrangements there, switched off the light, and left again. She walked through to the living room, turned on a lamp by the sofa there, surveyed the room. It was in order. It was in as good order as she could manage now. She was about to switch off the light when she decided not to do so. It was better to leave a light on, it was more sensible. It was a little more cheerful—though the situation hardly lent itself to any cheer.

She avoided the library, went upstairs, visited each room. In each she turned on and off the lights, leaving only one lamp burning in her bedroom, leaving the lights on in the upstairs hall. It occurred to her as she went downstairs again that it was foresighted to do this: one could move more swiftly in a moment of emergency. But as this thought came to her, it brought with it a sense of panic, the fear of just such emergencies, and as the feeling spread within her—a definite sensation of chill that moved outward from her stomach to her extremities—she thought, "Perhaps the lights will go out."

So strongly and unpleasantly did this affect her that she almost decided to run out to the kitchen, plead with Mrs. Kluger to stay. She knew that it was fear that suggested any such move, and she made a terrific effort to overcome it, and stood still on the stairs. It was impossible, Mrs. Kluger would throw the Potters in her face, unaware that they too had, in a way, already deserted their mistress; nor could she explain that desertion to this woman. No. Nor could she beg. After all, Mrs. Kluger herself had said that the house had ridden out one hurricane—why should it not be equally safe for another? There was little comfort in the thought; there was no certainty.

Very slowly she completed her passage down the stairs, walked to the library. She went to the barometer. It read 29.45. A low glass, very low. The clock on the desk said eight. She reset the index hand from the former reading of 29.60. It was a big drop, very fast for one hour. It did not make the future seem secure. There was more security in the past.

She stood by the unshuttered window, looking out at the darkness, at the light from the tenement dormers, the lilacs thrashing below the sills. She was trying to recapture the sense of relief she had felt earlier when she had realized that this time there would be no one to bother about, no one to cope with, that she would know now how to deal with visitors, invaders of her privacy, problems within her house. No Leah now, no Herbert Golotz. "I have," she said, "only myself to consider." But this had lost its power to support her now.

Standing there, she saw the lights (that she had identified before as those of Mrs. Kluger's car) blink on, brighten. As she watched, wholly fascinated, the lights came around the tool shed and flashed straight into her eyes, momentarily blinding her, making her duck her head sidewise. Then they swung away, and in a moment, she could pick out the red of the tail-light. The little red spot diminished, faded rapidly, then abruptly disappeared. Miss Leckton knew that the car was below the rise of land, going down to the bridge over Ten Acre Creek, and she watched to see the light again as it should climb the opposite bank. But she could not see it. This abrupt invisibility of what should have been clearly visible bothered her. Was the car stalled? Its lights out? Would the woman return on foot? Defeated? Or was it that the night was so thick it had swallowed up the car and its bright lights?

She stood for she knew not how long peering in the direction of the bridge, but she could see nothing there. Well, she thought, if the woman's car is stalled, she will have to come back to the house on foot, with her tail between her legs. It occurred to Miss Leckton that she could lock the kitchen door, make Mrs. Kluger ring the front doorbell. There would be considerable satisfaction in that. "Well, Mrs. Kluger!" she would say. "So you decided to come back after all!" It would be only just to have it happen so: it would put Mrs. Kluger in the same relation to the storm as herself, instead of leaving Miss Leckton the only one to be the victim of the elements. There had been something vastly annoying in the attitudes adopted by Mrs. Kluger and the Potters, that they were quite free to move, to come or to go, without regard to herself, her wishes, her judgment. It had begun when, she having decided the hurricane was going to arrive, they had succeeded in making her feel that they had snatched the decision from her or, at least, had shared in it.

Miss Leckton turned away from the window and went out to the kitchen. It was quite dark, and she put on the light over the sink. Then she went to the door and locked it. She was about to turn off the light, but she changed her mind. Mrs. Kluger would see it.

She went back to the library and sat down to await the sound of the bell. She waited for five minutes, ten minutes, a quarter of an hour. If Mrs. Kluger were coming back, she should be here by now. Why had she not come? Had the water risen again, as in 1938? Was the woman drowned? If the water had risen, had it come again to the house, here?

She ran out to the hall, took a torch, went to the living

room, turned off the lamp, shone the torch through the window. It was hard to see with any clarity, there was so much moisture on the window, but after a little she could make out, through a broken slat in the shutters, the edge of the juniper bushes that made her foundation planting, the grass at the edge of them. The water had not risen, or not so high; not yet.

She switched off the torch, put on the lamp, returned to the library. She was conscious now that she returned there because she felt more safe within that room, more removed from the furious sound of the storm. As she sat down again, she was sweating freely, all her clothes stuck to her, her girdle was most uncomfortable. With her handkerchief, she mopped her forehead. The smell of lavender in the handkerchief was so accustomed, so pleasant, that it restored her a little, made things seem, for a moment, usual. One's handkerchief always smelled of lavender.

Perhaps Mrs. Kluger had tried the kitchen door, and finding it locked, had gone to the Potters' tenement? Why had she not thought of that before? She picked up the telephone and called 72-J. George answered.

"Hello?" he said.

"George," she said. "Is Mrs. Kluger with you?"

"Why, no," he said, his voice sounding surprised. "Why, no, Miss Leckton. She ain't here. She left in her car. Must be some time ago she left now."

"I know," Miss Leckton said. "I saw the car go. But I could not see the lights on the far side of the bridge. I thought the car might have broken down, she might have come back."

"No," said George. "I think she made it all right. I been out and around."

"Oh, you have?" Miss Leckton said. "There is no water risen yet, is there?"

"No, Miss Leckton. Tide was low this time. The water's sort of high in the creek, but ain't over the bridge. I took a turn down that way with a torch. Thought we'd better know. I'll go again pretty soon. You want me at the house for anything?"

Miss Leckton could find no way to say that she did want him, that it was outrageous that he and Ella were not with her, that it was wrong to leave her alone.

"No," she said."No. I am quite all right."

"Well, I'll be over soon now," said George. "I'll come in and look at things when I go out again, in about a half an hour. You got the kitchen door locked, Miss Leckton."

"Yes," she said. "Since I am alone here." Then, in a sudden access of a most enjoyable, a reconstituting indignation, she added, "I don't want another invasion of the house this time. I don't want any more Frostens here or those people. Once was quite enough."

"Yes, Miss Leckton," said George. "You want me to ring the front door when I come? I dunno you'd hear the bell, would you?"

"Ring the front door," she said. "I'll let you in." Then she hung up. She felt a great deal better.

"Indeed," she said aloud, "this is better than 1938."

IX

BETTER than 1938. Why? Well, perhaps because she had been so fully occupied, mentally and physically, that she had been unaware of the advent of the real peak of the storm until it had hit the house and thus caught her unprepared, off guard.

It must have been, she thought, about a quarter past three in the afternoon when Leah and her Golotz had left. She remembered now that she had rung for Catherine Lovatt, had told her to pick up the front hall, remove the newspaper, that she would want her in Miss Leah's room in fifteen minutes. Then she had gone upstairs to tidy her hair again. This time, she had decided, she would take her hat down with her, so that she could protect her hair if she went out of doors again. She would have to find George Potter or pick up that deck chair herself. It would do no good to the juniper bushes by the house, flapping against them like that. In the meantime, there was Leah's room to attend to. That was the only satisfaction that remained, the one gesture she could make now, this minute.

She got to Leah's room before Catherine did. At once she began the job of emptying all the drawers, putting their contents in neat piles on one of the beds. The bureau was emptied by the time Catherine arrived.

"Get some dress boxes," Miss Leckton said. "And we'll

pack these things in them. Some string too, please, and some paper."

"Are you going to post them, madam?" Catherine asked.

"No," said Miss Leckton. "Why do you ask?"

"I'd bring stouter paper, if they're for the post," said Catherine.

"No," Miss Leckton said. "Any sort of paper. I am giving them to the Salvation Army."

"Very good, madam," said Catherine.

She turned and left the room so quickly that Miss Leckton could not make out her expression. It would have been difficult, in any event, the woman's face was so withholding. Miss Leckton was sorry now that she had given herself the satisfaction of revealing her intention to Catherine. It was hard to know how people of that sort would respond to what was certainly an act of retributive justice, but possibly of a harsh appearance to those who had not the whole key to it. Well, harsh or not, that was what she was going to do. She began taking the dresses from the cupboard, laying them one on the other in piles on the other bed. The cupboard was emptied of all but its shoes—of which, she noticed, there were not many: Leah must have taken most of them.

As soon as Catherine returned with the boxes, paper, and string, Miss Leckton set her to packing up the things on the bed.

"You needn't be too careful about the folding," she said. "It's not important. Get as much as you can in each parcel."

She helped Catherine to make a start, then left her to go on with the job. Miss Leckton now began a thorough search of the bedroom and the bath. She emptied the medicine cabinet of all that was in any way personal to Leah, leaving only the standard contents, iodine, adhesive tape, a bottle of aspirin, a can of bicarbonate of soda. She scoured the rooms, putting all that she found—bottles, note paper, old letters, hairpins, odds and ends of childish things thoughtlessly kept in the small bureau drawers—into a scrap basket, until it was full. The silver frames that had held the photographs of herself, Sam Davids, Dora, a family group, all stood empty, she

106

saw. Leah had not taken the frames. That was right. They did not belong to her. Only one photograph remained in its frame: the rather poor (because it was too flattering) picture of Dora in the oval frame with the repoussé work. She put all the frames together on the bureau, took some black tissue paper that Catherine had brought her, wrapped them into a tidy bundle, and put them in the back of one of the drawers in the dressing table. Surveying her work, she was pleased. It was complete, the room was restored to her, taken from Leah. She recalled the verse in the Bible that said, "And whosoever shall not receive you, nor hear you, when you depart thence, shake off the dust under your feet for a testimony against them." It seemed a little wrong-side-to, but essentially it was right. She was shaking Leah's dust off the room, the house. A testimony against her.

"I have put the things together, madam," said Catherine, "and marked it here on the boxes. This is underclothes and night things and like that, and these are the dresses, and this the shoes. Where will I put them?"

"Just leave them all on the bed by the wall," Miss Leckton said. "That's good, Catherine, very neat."

"Thank you," said Catherine. She piled the boxes on the bed. "Anything more now?"

"No," said Miss Leckton. "That's all for the moment, Catherine."

The maid straightened up from her work, stood facing Miss Leckton. All of a sudden a most curious expression came on her face: it was both attentive and puzzled, her mouth a little open, her forehead wrinkled, her eyes slightly narrowed.

"My God," she said in a low voice. "What's that?"

"What's what?" Miss Leckton asked.

"The house," said Catherine. "It's shaking."

It was true, Miss Leckton could feel it now. The house shook slightly, was still, shook again. Standing still and silent to try to place the cause, she could hear very clearly the uproar of the wind, a deep note neither quite whistle nor quite moan, unpleasant. The shaking of the house was periodic but without rhythm; it was noticeable only when one stood so, attentive to it. She had no idea how long it had been happening.

"It's the wind," Miss Leckton said. "That's all. Just the wind. It's blowing hard outside, a September storm. We usually have them this time of year, as you know."

"I never felt the house shake before," said Catherine. Without another word she left the room.

It was the first time, Miss Leckton thought, that she had heard Catherine say anything that did not directly have to do with her work. Well, it was quite a storm. She went to the south window to look at the weather.

It was not too easy to see. The rain—or was it spray from the ocean?—hit hard against the panes; then the gust that had blown the water would subside and the water would run down in blurred rivulets; then the wet gusts would strike again. Nevertheless, by peering intently she could catch occasional glimpses, not too obscured or distorted, of the salt water; she could see that the whitecaps were almost continuous, that they were being formed by the tops blowing off the waves rather than by the breaking forward of the waves. It made the sea look very odd and flat, almost as though it were being stirred from beneath into white patches. The tide was very high. The big rocks, The Ewe and The Lamb, were wholly submerged, the waves were breaking against the sea wall that contained the earth of her sloping lawn, not in recurrent combers, but in a steady, almost incessant succession of white foam, as though one wave was doing it all, was sufficiently solid to be flung over and over again, at intervals of a second or so, against the stone of the shore. If the water on the windows was spray, not rain, it must come from there, she thought.

She noticed now that occasionally the water was forced up from under the meeting rail of the double-hung window, making little bubbles that grew and exploded rapidly. She touched the bubbles with a finger, put it in her mouth. It tasted of salt. A bad storm, she thought. It took a very high wind to force water through these tight, well-constructed windows. However, it was doing no harm. She turned around, looked once more at the room, now so neat (except for those boxes on the bed), so impersonal. A guest room now, no longer "Leah's room." Not Leah's room ever again, not if she knew it!

It was then that the thought had first crossed her mind about the will. If she did nothing about it, the place would go to Leah—*and* Golotz. It was an appalling thought. She would have to make a trip to Boston later on and see cousin Ellett Pursey and get him to change her will. Then she could let Leah know that she had done so—though there was really no need to wait, she could write to Leah and tell her that this was her intention. The sooner the consequences of her selfish, her wholly self-centered, act were brought home to the girl, the better. Indeed, it was a pity she had not thought to say this more explicitly to Leah, in front of that man. Thinking about this, she realized, however, with a recurrence of anger mixed with frustration, that it would probably have done no good. The girl was quite out of her head; one cannot touch someone in that condition with the rational, however important.

The clock on the mantel in Leah's room said four o'clock, but she knew it to be a quarter of an hour fast at least. She should go and get hold of George Potter about that deck chair. It was getting late, though. If she did this, it would be so late she would have no rest before tea, and she felt very tired. Well, it wasn't important about the chair, it couldn't do much harm. She left Leah's room, walked to her own. There she took off her shoes, lay down on her bed.

Usually she pulled the light coverlet over her when she lay down, but today seemed incredibly warm and oppressive, and she threw the coverlet back over the foot of the bed. Then she closed her eyes, breathed deeply once or twice, tried to relax. It was not easy. She found herself reliving the scene with Leah and Golotz, their departure. A great many things occurred to her that she could have said: remarks that would have been most telling. Little by little they became blurred, more general in application, were directed to a group of people, to Dora, and it was then (as she was on the verge of sleep) that the knock came on the door.

Rousing herself enough to prop up on one elbow, Miss Leckton called, "Come in!"

The door opened and Catherine appeared.

"I'm sorry to disturb you, madam," Catherine said. "But the electric power has gone off."

"Oh," said Miss Leckton. "Did you call up and report it?"

"We tried," Catherine said. "But the telephone is out, I think. It don't answer."

"Very well," said Miss Leckton. "I'll come down."

"Yes, madam," said Catherine, and she withdrew, shutting the door with her usual soft care.

What a bother! thought Miss Leckton. Sometimes when the electricity went off it took the power company several hours to make the repair. She looked at the clock. It was five minutes past four. Perhaps they'd get it fixed by six, which would hardly delay dinner. It must have been the storm that did something to the wires. Maybe the garage telephone was in order.

She got up. This was not her day to get any rest. Well, she could go to bed early. Perhaps she'd go to bed really early, have supper on a tray, and read. There was no one to consider now save herself, thank God!

She put on a felt hat, secured it firmly with two pins, an elastic band under the coil of her back hair. She put on next a pair of heavy brown oxfords with crêpe soles, good, serviceable, waterproof shoes. Then she went downstairs, got into her raincoat, buttoned it up, fastened the belt, went out to the kitchen. Catherine and Anna Mulvey were there.

"Now," said Miss Leckton, "let's see the range."

She walked to the range, turned the switches on, all of them, and waited. Nothing happened, no heat came in the coils. She switched all the coils off. It was true. The power was off, but it was always best to make sure for yourself. She pulled the switch cord on the light over the sink: there was no light.

"You can make my tea on the silver kettle," she said. "We have alcohol?"

"Yes, ma'am," said Anna.

"I'll see about the range," said Miss Leckton.

"It's this storm," said Anna. "A terrible storm."

"A real September blow," Miss Leckton said. She looked out the west window of the kitchen. The waves were piling up on Cato's Beach in a continuous froth of water, no breakers at all, far up the beach, the foam at the foot of the beautiful high dunes. She had never before seen it so high, nor like that in the manner of its breaking. The house shook now more often, more violently, than when she and Catherine had been in Leah's—no, the guest room. She must think of it now as the guest room. Shake off the dust.

She left the kitchen and went to the library. There she also tried the lights. They were off. She lifted the telephone, jiggled the hook. It was immediately apparent that the instrument was dead: there was not even the slightest humming sound. A bother. She would have to send George to report this.

She went out to the hall, opened the door. This time there was no immediate inrush of air. The north side of the house seemed to be in the lee now, the wind must have shifted to the southward; it had been almost due east earlier in the afternoon. She closed the door and started to walk across to the garage. As soon as she was well out on the driveway, the wind struck at her, and she nearly lost her balance and fell. A savage wind. She looked at the elms on the lawn. Those she could see were waving their branches crazily. There would be damage, boughs broken, if this wind did not soon abate. Well, she thought, it can't keep up like this long. The wind, for all its power, was uncommonly warm, and it blew a warm salt spray onto her face.

She climbed the wooden steps on the east side of the garage up to the second-floor entrance. It was necessary to hang on tight to the railing to prevent oneself from being blown off the steps. When she reached the platform at the top she tried to turn the handle and enter, but the door was locked. She pushed the doorbell, again and again, with one hand, all the while holding tight to the railing with the other. She could hear no ringing within, but that did not surprise her, so furious was the noise of the wind. After a while, she gave up pushing the bell and pounded on the door with all her force. She must have been at this for three or four minutes before she got any response. Then the door opened suddenly and she almost fell into the little hallway, the wind coming in with her and making a terrifying uproar in that small, confined space.

She turned around to see Ella putting her whole weight into the effort to close the door. After several tries, it was closed, and Ella turned the key in the lock. One could hear again.

"My!" Ella said. "That's surely a wind!"

"Yes," Miss Leckton said. "Your bell is out of order."

"The electricity has gone off, Miss Leckton," Ella said. "It went off about fifteen minutes back."

"Is your telephone working, Ella?"

"No, ma'am," said Ella. "It's off too."

"Where's George?"

"He's gone up the road a piece to meet Desmond. He's late from school. We was worried, this storm and all."

"How long since he went?" Miss Leckton asked.

"Just before the lights went," Ella said. "Desmond usually gits here about half past three. We was worried."

"Yes," said Miss Leckton. "Yes. I know. But I wanted George. I wanted him to report that the power had gone, the telephone was off. When do you expect him back?"

"I'm hoping he'll be here any minute now," Ella said. "Any minute."

"Did he take the car?"

"No, ma'am. He walked up toward the postbox."

"Well, send him over to the house when he gets back, please," she said. "I would like to get the power back on before it's time to cook dinner."

"Yes, ma'am," said Ella. "I'll tell him."

"I really don't know why I ever expected to find him,"

Miss Leckton said. "Everything has gone wrong today. Every-thing."

As she said this, there was a horrid tearing noise that coin-cided with a deep vibration through the tenement hallway. It was followed by the sound of a loud report, like a gun going off near by, and the tenement shook again and there were more noises (mixed with the sound of the wind) like wood being rent apart with metallic overtones.

"Oh my Lord Jesus!" cried Ella.

She turned away from Miss Leckton and flew to the inner door, opened it, disclosing the living room-kitchen of the place. As she opened the door, a little dark-brown-and-black puppy leapt out into the hall, barking loudly, followed by two cats. Ella entered the kitchen, disappeared from view.

The puppy came and put its paws up on Miss Leckton's skirt, barking frantically.

"Down," she said. "Down, down! Do you hear me? Down!" She pushed it away, and it circled around her, barking with-out cessation. The two cats leapt up on a chair and sat there, their backs humped, their tails erect, looking fixedly at the puppy.

In a moment Ella returned.

"It's not up here," she said.

"Please put these animals away," Miss Leckton cried.

Ella stooped down and grabbed the puppy, threw him gently into the kitchen, picked up the two cats, and set them also inside the room, closed the door. The puppy continued to bark, there was the sound of furious scratching on the door. Ella banged her fist on it.

"Be quiet, Dobie," she said. The scratching and the bark-ing stopped. To Miss Leckton, Ella said, "That noise, it came from outside."

"Yes," said Miss Leckton. "I must go and see what has happened."

"I'll come with you," Ella said. "I'll get my coat on."

"No," Miss Leckton said. "I must go at once. Open the door, please."

Ella went past her to the door, opened it. The wind entered, the sound and the rain entered; Miss Leckton, her head down, leaning forward, moved into the force of the wind, groped for the handrail, began to descend the steps. She did not hear the door shut behind her, nor did she look back. It was all she could do to go down the steps; the raincoat flapped up, her skirt billowed, the wind pushed against her in sharp gusts. It was easier to move—though still difficult —when she got to the bottom. At once she saw what had happened.

One leaf of the garage door had blown off its hinges, lay flat in the driveway. The other, by whatever freak of wind pressure, had also torn loose, split, and had crashed back into the car, smashing the headlights, the whole front of the radiator. As she looked, horrified by this damage, suddenly the wind blew again with extreme violence, pushing her against the wall of the garage, and it picked up the other leaf of the door, stood it on its edge, and the door sailed off, clear of the ground, to crash into and through the privet hedge that lay to the west of the garage. The hedge was sheared as though by a sharp knife. The door faltered there, touched the ground, turned over, rose again on its edge, and went, tumbling over and over like the top of a cardboard box, out of sight down the slope toward the rocks and the turmoil of the sea.

Flattened against the garage wall, Miss Leckton had watched this flight of the door with the utmost surprise. The door was heavy, it was seven feet high, about four feet wide. She had never imagined that wind could do such a thing as lift a door of that weight. How had the two leaves blown open? The wind was against them, they opened outwards, against the wind. What mad trick of suction had pulled them loose? They must have flapped violently, slammed, broken. And the car. Smashed.

Suddenly she felt that this was no place for her to stand. If the wind could do that to the doors, what could it not do to her? She was not frightened, but she was abruptly aware of her own weakness, her helplessness in the face of this storm. With an effort she moved away from the solid wall of the garage. As she did so, she saw George and Desmond coming toward her.

George had the boy next to him, linked to him by his arm around the boy's waist. They were walking in a queer, uneven, staggering sort of way, leaning back against the gusts of the wind, then straightening suddenly as it abated for seconds, their feet going down like the feet of someone who feels his way in the darkness over familiar ground.

There was no use to try to speak to them, she realized, so she waved her arm, moved heavily toward them a step or so, then waited for them, her feet apart, her body braced. They saw her and came to her. She could see that the bottoms of George's trousers were soaking wet, his boots oozed water with each step. When they came up to her, she pointed to the car.

Together George and Desmond moved past her, went to the open doorway, looked at the car. She saw George disengage his arm from Desmond, pull at the section of door that had rammed into the radiator. It gave, lifted, then suddenly blew back with a violence so great that the noise of wood against metal could be heard over the wind. George turned and came toward her. He tried to say something to her, but she couldn't hear him.

Forming the words carefully with her lips, she said, without trying to shout, "Come over here," and she pointed to the house. Then she turned and made her way toward the front door. As soon as she was near it, the wind let up; she could straighten and she walked, with an astonishing sense of lightness and ease, up onto the stone platform. As she stood, she took a deep breath, realizing then that she had not breathed properly since she had left Ella, that the wind made breathing difficult.

When George came up the steps with Desmond, she spoke to him. One had to speak rather loudly, but it was possible to communicate without actually shouting.

"Well, George," she said. "It was not very clever of you to leave the garage doors unfastened."

"Oh, no, Miss Leckton," he said. "They was fastened tight shut."

"They could not have been," she said. "They blew open. Against the wind."

"I did them myself, last thing before I left for the boy," George said. "Bolted them shut. Yes, indeed."

"Well, I suppose the car's gone, anyway," she said.

"Looks like it," said George. "Water running right out of the radiator. I'm certainly sorry."

"No use to be sorry now," she said. "Too late. And I wanted you to take the car and report that the telephone is off, and the electric light. Mine and yours."

"It don't surprise me," George said. "This storm. Branches breaking off the oaks up yonder." He waved toward the far hill. "I don't believe we could of got the car out now, Miss Leckton, anyhow."

"Why is that?"

"Water," he said. "Water's over the bridge now, almost eighteen inches about. I had to wade. I carried the boy. Tide's awful high. Never did see it so high. I'd hate to drive the car through that ugly water, this wind."

"Over the bridge?" she said.

"Yes, clear over it," said George.

"How shall we report the telephone?" Miss Leckton asked. "And the electricity?"

"I dunno, I'm sure," George said. "The telephone and the light too is off up to Newsome's and at the garage. I tried to call the school to see where at was the bus. Couldn't do it. But it finally came. Nearest telephone after that is to Mr. Pollock's, that's three miles. May be off too."

"It may not be," said Miss Leckton.

"No, that's so," said George. "But I'd sort of hate to leave here right now, Miss Leckton, I surely would. Let this blow over a little. You going to need me, maybe, if this wind rises any more."

"Rises?" she said. "It can't blow worse than this. I never saw it blow so hard before."

"That's so," said George. "But Chet Gould, at the garage,

he's got a radio in his car. It's predicting this is going to be a hurricane, blow worse than now."

"Nonsense," said Miss Leckton. "I have no faith in that sort of report."

Nevertheless she knew that George was right about one thing, although she was not going to admit it to him. The Pollocks' telephone might well be out, it was on the same general line with her own. It was a long way. If the wind did rise, she would need George here. The electric people might fix the power anyway. They usually did.

"All right," she said. "Let it go now, George. You'd better take that child indoors. He's wet. His mother is worried about him. Unnecessarily worried."

"Yes," said George. "You want me for anything here?"

"No," she said. "Not now. I'll let you know."

She rang the doorbell. Even over the storm she could hear that infernal clangor within.

George nodded and took Desmond with him. She watched them for a moment, fascinated by the effect on them of the wind as they came out of the lee of the house. Then she turned about. When Catherine opened the door, she entered swiftly, and the maid closed the door instantly.

As Miss Leckton wiped the moisture from her face with her handkerchief, it occurred to her that she had forgotten to tell George about that deck chair. Stupid!

"We have had to put towels and dishrags on the windows of the dining room, madam," said Catherine.

"Why?" said Miss Leckton.

"The water was blowing in," said Catherine. "The cloths seem to stop it. In the middle of the windows."

Remembering the bubbles of salt water in Leah's room, Miss Leckton said, "Oh, yes. Quite right." She patted her hair, her hat. "I'll have tea in the library whenever it's ready," she said.

"Yes, madam," said Catherine.

Miss Leckton went into the library. The noise, even here inside the house, more or less on the lee side, was appalling, and the air was chokingly close, damp, and warm. This is an unusual storm, she thought, and she walked over to the barometer. It shocked her to see what it read: 29.00.

"That is terribly low, the lowest I ever remember to have seen it," she said aloud.

Turning, she looked at the clock. It said twenty-five minutes to five. Miss Leckton set the index hand on the barometer, and sat down in her chair.

At that precise moment the hurricane had struck.

X

MISS LECKTON found herself bracing against the fierce intensity of that memory, ready (again) to spring to her feet in order to meet the demands of the storm.

She could feel now, and to her surprise, the slight tremors that shook the house as the gusts of wind, pouring out of the darkness, struck against the walls: they should have been heavier; the surprise lay only in the slightness of the sensation conveyed. Within herself she was feeling the house shake as it had shaken before, like a doll's house moved by a malign and adult hand.

That violent first tremor of the earlier storm had been accompanied by a simultaneous change in the sound of the wind. The noise, which before had been a roar, not quite incessant but with brief intervals between prolonged gusts, then had risen to an unpleasantly high-pitched note that was altogether different in tone, having the qualities of hysteria and of malice. Mixed with this had been another noise that sounded, through the open door to the living room, like heavy hail striking dangerously on the glass of the windows.

The tremor of the house was not single, it came again and again, and added to this increase and change in the sound of the storm it brought Miss Leckton to her feet. Quickly she walked through to the living room, to the south windows. It was not possible to see clearly through them, that was the first thing she noticed. Then she saw that the water was running down the insides of the panes, was bubbling in a pulsing flow through the meeting rails, up from under the sills, and that the sound of hail was caused not alone by the water that struck furiously on the glass but by a mix of coarse sand, some of which was finding its way through the meeting rails and was making dirty brownish streaks on the panes, the white woodwork.

A swift examination showed that the water was forced through only the two south windows of the room, that the window on the east side was merely wet, not leaking. It was obvious that the copper screening of the porch outside it was protecting it here. Through this window she could look: to see that the porch furniture lay now in a jumbled heap against the heavy wooden railing at the north end of the porch; and that the Cape Cod hammock had lifted off its southern hook and was flapping with terrific force against the pile of furniture, smashing wicker chairs and tables as it swung from its solitary remaining support. Then she turned her eyes to the eastward; although it was impossible to be sure, so dense was the flying water, it looked to her as though the sea had risen, beyond all reason, and was breaking around the ends of the flower beds in thick, nearly continuous short waves. Horrible!

Miss Leckton turned away then, and ran toward the dining room. As she got to the hall she paused to look at the south door. There was no water coming through its sides or its sill, and this surprised her until she remembered that the screen door was still up outside and was undoubtedly acting as a major protection. It was a terrible pity, she thought, that she had had the screens taken off the outside of the windows so early.

In the dining room she found the same conditions at the windows, except that the cloths the servants had placed there seemed to be absorbing most of the water. Swiftly she went to the pantry and through it to the kitchen. Anna and Catherine were standing near the west window, looking out.

"Catherine!" cried Miss Leckton. "Anna! Please!"

She realized as she spoke that she had unconsciously pitched her voice to override the fierce high sound of the storm in the other rooms, and that here there was noticeably less noise.

The cook turned toward her at once; so, but more slowly, almost reluctantly, did Catherine.

"My God," said Anna. "The water!"

"I shall need help," said Miss Leckton. "The south windows are leaking in the living room. I have not got upstairs yet. I'm going now. Please collect more cloths, dishtowels, anything of that sort, and put them on the rails and sills of the windows, to stop the water blowing through. Do it as you did in the dining room. I'll do the upstairs. At once, please, the water is ruining the wallpaper below the sills, the carpet."

"Yes, ma'am," said Anna. "Did you see the water?"

"What water?" Miss Leckton asked with annoyance.

"The ocean," said Anna, and she pointed out the window. "My God, it's terrible!"

Impatiently (the quality of impatience that seizes the adult in dealing to allay the ridiculous and unbased fears of the child) Miss Leckton took three swift steps to the window and looked out. But once there, she forgot her impatience, stood looking at the scene.

The ocean was a dirty yellow, quite flat, with light patches of a most disagreeable ochre color. The tide had risen now until the salt water wholly covered the beach, reaching up to the sand dunes, over the rocks and shore ledges below her house, and it flowed over a point of marsh into Ten Acre Pond. The low area of lawn to the westward was half covered with the water that broke and surged and eddied: it was over the sea wall, which showed but briefly between waves. The whole scene was dim, because between her and the familiar dunes there was an incessant horizontal veil of driven spray, so thick that she could not see the near side of Ten Acre Pond. It was so ugly, so angry a spectacle, that she finally turned away from it less because she meant to get about the business of the windows than because she did not wish to look any longer: there was terror in the weather, one must not let it seize one.

She made an effort and said, "Yes, a very bad storm indeed. And now we'll do the windows, please."

"Yes, ma'am," said Anna. "Will that water get any higher, d'you think?"

"No," said Miss Leckton. "It's quite abnormally high now. Have you got cloths?"

"Yes," said Anna. "We'll fix them windows, Miss Leckton. We'll find plenty to use. I hope to God you're right about the water."

"Of course I'm right. I'll go upstairs now," Miss Leckton said, and she left them.

She went quickly up the stairs, got bath towels from the linen cupboard in the hall, moved to the sitting room. The water was leaking here. She tucked the rolled towels across the meeting rails, across the sills. The east window in her room, the window in the hall, the two south windows in Leah's room: all were leaking water steadily. The wallpaper, the paint below the windows, were already soaked. There were small puddles on the floors.

It all took but a couple of minutes. She was hurrying, consciously, so as to get downstairs again and oversee the work there. The brittle sound of gravel flung against the panes of glass sharpened her sense of hurry; it made her feel she should be everywhere at once, as though, by being so, she could avert the cracking of the glass.

Then it occurred to her that the thing to do was to close the shutters, that they would (for all that they were slatted) protect the glass, break the force of the water. She had on her raincoat and her hat, she would not get too wet. It was only as she unlatched a sitting-room window, put her fingers on the metal handles of the sash, that she recalled what Golotz had said. Perhaps he was right, perhaps one shouldn't open the window to the wind. Yet unless the window were opened, she could not close the shutters, and the glass might give to the wind. She stood for a moment in indecision, then decided to go ahead, to have a try: she was not going to allow the memory of what that man had said to control her actions. She closed the door to the hall, the door to her room: that would stop the draught. Then she returned to the window, seized the handles, and heaved it open.

At once the storm entered the room; she was almost blown away from the window. The salt rain, the sandy rain lashed at her face as she bent down, got on her knees, thrust her head out, reached out, blindly and gasping for breath, to unhook the leaf of the shutter. It was not hard to release the catch, but she found it next to impossible to move the leaf—the wind was holding it flat against the house wall. With a tremendous effort she pulled it forward, hung on, pulled again, and it slammed shut and latched, barely missing the fingers of one hand. Once more, alarmed now, she reached out for the other leaf. Again she released the catch, tugged, heaved at the leaf. Perhaps she pulled too hard, or the wind affected it, she did not know; but in a second the leaf came off its little iron hinges, slammed violently against the house below the window, lifted and turned (she had let go of it by now) as though of its own volition, slammed back against the house, cracked and broke into two uneven halves, and rapidly blew away, scraping along the house to fall out of her sight. And there was no noise that she could hear, except the overwhelming sound of the storm itself.

Conscious of immense fatigue, of defeat, she withdrew into the room, closed the window with difficulty, latched it. Her coat, her face, the upper part of her dress, were drenched. She could taste the salt, feel the sand, on her lips. The room was in a mess. The table covers, photographs, had blown off the tables; the pictures hung askew on the walls; there was a large wet area on the floor by the window. There was no use to try to close more of the shutters—it was too late for that. The alarming thought came to her of what might have happened to that shutter in its falling progress across the house, and she ran out of the room, down the stairs, and into the living room. As she arrived, the deck chair crashed through the window below which it had lain, breaking the lower half of the sash into jagged fragments. It lodged there, halfway

123

through, sawing up and down against the remains of the mullions, and the storm entered the room.

The effect of the wind was so violent that Miss Leckton found herself for a moment unable to do more than fight for her balance and for control of herself. The rug blew into a billowing thing and upset a chair, a small table fell over, its vase crashing to the floor, the cushions from the sofa moved about on the floor in a crazy circular motion. The noise was appalling; it made it hard to think of anything at all except its volume, its menace.

Then the door to the library blew shut. Even in all this uproar she could hear that slam, and could find it possible to marvel that the door was intact and closed.

Immediately the objects in the room slowed down their motion or ceased to move. The pillows stopped rolling and tumbling around, the rug billowed less violently, a round table that had been sliding across the floor, stopped. Miss Leckton realized what she must do. She started for the door to the hall, to close it. As she reached it she saw Catherine standing in the hall, her black skirt blowing in the wind, her mouth open, her eyes staring.

"Come here!" Miss Leckton called loudly. "Quickly! Come!" She beckoned the woman toward the living room. Catherine responded quickly, and as she entered, Miss Leckton closed the door. It required effort to get it half-closed, but as she overcame the wind, the door was torn from her hands and slammed shut like its fellow.

The diminution of the gale within the room was instantaneous. It was not that it had stopped blowing, but that the wind seemed now to have less force to move the objects. The noise was as great as ever.

Together (and almost as though they had previously rehearsed what they were to do) the two women began to arrange the contents of the room. They put the tables, the chairs, the pictures, in the corner by the fireplace, as much as they could crowd in there. They rolled back the rug till it lay in front of the hearth. They lifted down the pictures, stacked them against a section of wall, covered them with cushions,

124

with a table cover. They put the ornaments in the ashes of the fireplace, and Catherine closed the damper of it, for water was coming down the chimney in a slow stream and the ashes had begun to blow into the room. There was nothing left to move except the sofa between the two south windows: it was being drenched with the blown water. Together they heaved it, lifting and pulling, working it toward the north of the room.

It must have been while they were doing this that the great wave struck, because so much had happened by the time Miss Leckton next looked out the shattered window. She had gone across the room to it, with Catherine, in the hope of removing the sawing deck chair. Looking out she could see that the water had risen and was foaming and breaking over the garden, that there were no elms at all within her view, no yew hedge to be seen.

What shocked her was not that the elms had broken or had been blown down, but that they were not there at all, there was nothing to see, nothing but the dirty, yellow, angry water swirling, breaking, clutching at the lawn, digging at the ground. She stood quite still, the drenching wind blowing in her face, one hand clutching the weaving motion of the deck chair, and looked. The elms were gone. She tried to remember, as though it were now of the utmost importance, how many there had been that one could see from this window. Five? Six? She couldn't remember. She had the crazy notion, so strong that it was like a physical sensation, that she could restore them, could undo this disappearance, if only she could recollect their number. Then the deck chair gave a sharp and living twist, and flicked out of her grasp, fell downward and clear of the window, and as suddenly swept upward in a curving arc to disappear from her vision.

Miss Leckton, still looking to see the chair return to earth, felt her sleeve pulled hard from behind, and turned. Catherine was pointing to the east window. Miss Leckton looked there.

The big posts of the porch were leaning against the sash, a tangled mass of copper screening around them. One could not see more, for beyond the posts was a thick clutter of boughs and leaves. As she watched, the whole mass slowly moved, the window buckled in, the glass panes cracked and fell inward, and the posts fell forward into the room. There was no increase in the sound, no change in the amount of wind that entered: the tangle of wire, branches, leaves, posts, filled the window thickly.

"Come!" said Miss Leckton, and she took Catherine by the arm and walked swiftly to the door to the library. She tried to open it, but could not: it had jammed shut. As they went to the other door, Miss Leckton was aware of a growing sense of panic that she knew she must suppress and overcome. She tried to keep her mind from putting into words the thought that this door too might not open, that they would be closed into this room and its desolation, its horrid uproar. But the door opened (with their joint efforts), they left the room, and the door slammed shut behind them. The hall was unbelievably quiet.

It was so quiet, so usual, that Miss Leckton felt her legs give under her, and she wanted badly to sit down. Perhaps it was the contrast, or perhaps the exertion and the tension she had just undergone. If Catherine had not been with her, she would have collapsed onto the chair near the door. Instead, she reached out her hand to the wall to steady herself.

"We had better look in the library," she said. She was surprised to hear how normal her voice sounded.

Without replying, Catherine walked away from her to the dining room and looked in.

"Had I better close this door?" she said.

"The windows?" Miss Leckton said.

"They're all right," said Catherine.

"No trees there," said Miss Leckton. "Yes, close the door. We'll close all the doors."

Catherine closed the door and rejoined her, and together they went into the library.

The first thing Miss Leckton noticed was the amount of light in the room. It was so unusual that she thought the room was broken open until she realized its quietness, that

126

the storm (however loud) was outside it. Then she saw the reason for the light.

The porch was gone, completely, and one could see the sky through the east window. It was not, in itself, a reassuring spectacle. But the window was intact. Miss Leckton went over and peered through it, through the water and the sand that blew against it.

She could see but dimly, yet enough to count the effects of the storm. There were the stumps, twisted and shattered, of three elm trees in sight. The porch lay broken under the weight of one huge bough of the elm that had stood at the southeast corner—that same elm which smashed the window in the living room. The great bough lay so that it broke somewhat the force of the wind against the window; but it alarmed her, for she wondered what supported it, whether it had pierced the wall of the house.

"Let us go upstairs now," she said.

Again as she went up the stairs (this time less easily, more slowly, with greater effort) she noticed how very hot she was: the sweat was literally running off her face and forehead, her clothes felt wet through. Well, she thought, I still have on my raincoat. It would be comfortable to take it off, but would it be wise? Things were happening so fast, such awful, such unpredictable things.

It was while she was debating the question of whether or not to take off her raincoat—almost as though this were a question of high importance, a point that might decide, in itself, great issues—that she noticed the extraordinary bad taste in her mouth. It was not one she recollected as ever having tasted before. Her mouth was dry, her throat felt constricted, and this taste, at once strong and bitter and a little sickening, seemed inescapably connected with the dryness, the constriction. It made her want to swallow at rapid intervals, and yet there was so little to swallow, and each effort to do so produced the bitterness as an aftertaste. It was a taste she was to remember later, and although she was never willing to give a name to it, within herself, unphrased, she knew it as the taste of fear.

Her own room, when she and Catherine reached it, presented a curious sight. To begin with, it was much lighter, as had been the library, and she recognized this as from the same cause: the downfall of the elms. But one branch of the big elm that had crushed the porch had broken cleanly and been split into a sharp white blade of wood, and it had pierced precisely the center of one of the lower panes of the east window, knocking the smashed fragments of the pane onto the floor. The water was running off the end of the branch, and a large pool had already formed on the carpet. Not a great deal of wind came through, so nearly did the broken branch fill the hole it had created; but the sound of the storm had risen high here.

Miss Leckton simply stood and stared at the window. It seemed to her that the room had been violated, and that there was nothing she could do about it. It was with some surprise, then, that she saw Catherine come past her, holding a large bath towel and a small one. The maid at once and neatly stuffed the smaller towel around the branch and against the unbroken mullions of the pane, blocking the hole up quickly and efficiently. Then she mopped up the pool and the glass on the floor. Miss Leckton merely continued to watch her, for she felt an inertia that seemed momentarily impossible to overcome, as though she could fully satisfy her need—the well-realized need—for action, by this vicarious means.

The maid took the towels into Miss Leckton's bathroom and reappeared without them.

"I'll close all the other doors, madam," she said.

So usual was her voice, her manner, so accustomed was the lack of expression on her face, that it stirred Miss Leckton out of her immobility.

"Very well," she said. "Do that. And I shall take off this coat. I am very hot in it."

It appeared to her then that this was a perfectly even balance of work: Catherine would do the doors, see to the other rooms; she would divest herself of this coat, rid herself of the horrible sense of sweaty heat, and thereby become herself again. She had already undone the belt and begun to unbutton the coat when Catherine left the room.

But no sooner had the door closed on Catherine than the spell was broken. It was impossible to remain here, in this room, the end of the elm branch gleaming whitely at her, the storm and spray pelting, rasping at the window. What was happening elsewhere? What other windows were broken? Into what rooms had this tempest entered, to unleash what fury against her possessions, against her security?

Forgetting about the coat, she ran out of the room, omitted to close the door, remembered, closed it hastily, ran down the hall, looked into the closed sitting room. Except for the frightening sound of sand on glass, the steady drip of water from sills to floor, all was well. She left, ran toward Leah's room. At the door she met Catherine. The woman had newspapers in her hands.

"Nothing there, madam," Catherine said. "I have put paper on the floor below the windows. Will I do this in the sitting room? The water."

Pulling herself together with a great effort, patting her hair, Miss Leckton said, "Yes. Yes. A good idea."

This maid was astonishingly collected. She didn't even look hot.

The loud and brazen front doorbell rang.

XI

HEARING now (within her mind) that bell whose sound was intolerable even over the calamitous voice of the hurricane, Miss Leckton lifted her head and looked toward the door to the hallway. She found that she was staring at the lamp-lit wall that made the side of the stairs, with an intensity calculated to augment her hearing. Had she heard the bell—any bell—or was this merely the powerful echo of her recollection? And why should she be trying to hear a bell now?

With a sense of relief she remembered that she was expecting George Potter. Perhaps it was he, perhaps he had rung the front doorbell. She felt a wave of pleasure run through her: a warm tide of feeling, physically perceptible. But as she listened again, hearing now the violence of the storm that raged in the night outside her house, she remembered that the electric front doorbell rang now only in the kitchen, that it would be extremely difficult for her to hear it over the storm, even if all the doors were open. As she thought of this, she thought too of the fact that all but the swinging doors in the pantry were open, and that that was as bad now as it had been before. If the windows gave again— even though there were now no elms, no deck chairs to blow against them, even though the shutters were closed—it would create havoc once more. The storm, an entity as real and as evil-intentioned as a personal devil, would enter the room, enter the house. And she was alone to repel it.

For the first time Miss Leckton seriously imagined the idea of abandonment of her house. It was not that she meant to leave it now, but that she had a picture of herself, quite clear and distinct, within one of the ample and comfortable rooms of the inn at Cottrellton or in her own living room in New York. It was as though, transported magically to either of these safe havens, she would still be conscious within them of the storm that beat against this house, would be filled with an uncertainty as to its fate, but one so removed, in a physical sense, as to make of that very uncertainty an almost comfortable emotion.

Shaking her head briskly, she tried to dismiss the image, but as its shadow persisted, she rose again. The stronger motion dismissed it. She looked at the clock. It was five minutes to nine. It was five minutes too early to read the barometer, she thought, feeling that it was a necessary discipline to withhold from that action until the exact hour should arrive. Nevertheless she could not resist a glance at it across the room and even from that distance she could see that the black hand of the reading had slipped perceptibly below the brass hand of the index. In five minutes she would take the exact reading. Not until then. But the glass had fallen again.

"What did you expect?" she said aloud.

Expected or unexpected, it was an unpleasant fact, and it was while she was absorbing it (and at the same time attempting to rid herself of it) that she found she had the bitter and recollected taste in her mouth. If it was indeed the taste of fear—a word she did not use—it was surprising, because she did not feel any emotion at the moment except one urgent to activity, to be doing something, to create a situation better than that in which she now found herself. The thing to do, then, was to go to the kitchen—where she could hear the bell when George rang it—and get a glass of water, perhaps with lemon in it, something, anything, to take this taste from her mouth. Of course, it was possible that George would use the heavy brass knocker on the front door, though unlikely, and it was probable she could hear that quite well in the library. But that would mean she would have to remain here, both in inactivity and with a continuance of the taste in her mouth, and perhaps to experience a recurrence—no, surely to experience a recurrence—of the recollections with which she had so often been assailed. By going to the kitchen she could do something about the doors. She shut the door between living room and library.

She went out to the hall, closing the door behind her. She closed the door of the living room, went into the dining room and through the pantry to the kitchen. There was nothing one could do about the pair of swing doors there; they would either, in the event of calamity, operate to help by their weight and inertia, or they would not. She was seized with a clear recollection of the force of a hurricane wind, of its overwhelming, its terrifying power, and again the sharp taste, the acrid taste, increased in her mouth, and she felt her throat to be as dry and scratchy as a throat at the advent of a bad cold.

There was something remarkably quiet and equally discomforting about the kitchen, its single white light burning over the sink. It was a room that was waiting for something to happen; it waited on events to be filled. The sound of the storm outside it, clear and unmistakable, was the envelope that contained (and isolated) this room and herself. Miss Leckton felt, suddenly and with great precariousness, that she—the owner, the rightful heritor of its silence and its use —could not fill it unaided, could not shake it from this passive waiting on the event.

She had rarely talked aloud to herself but she found herself doing it now, in the hope, perhaps, that the sound of her own voice could dispel this atmosphere she did not like.

"One must do something," she said. "One must not give in to silly, schoolgirl feelings." She seized (from what region of her memory she could never determine) on the British phrase: "One must put up a good show."

As she heard the words, they offended her because she

placed them as British. They made her think of Golotz: Golotz the Britisher, the Jew. The Jew who had been superficially, in his manner, a gentleman. The man who had momentarily dominated her, who had imposed his will on hers. It was intolerable to think about, it made her angry to remember. It was against every canon of her belief, her creed.

"No," she said aloud. "No. I won't think of it."

But the thought was not easy to get rid of. She could see the image of Golotz standing in the hall, near the doorway, his hands behind his back, looking at her, his face abnormally, cruelly, rudely expressionless, as it had been when she had come in from dismissing those people, the La Perche people. By a reasonable transference, she could hear what she had just said coming now from his mouth, saying (as he had not said in fact), "One must put up a good show."

With an angry movement of her shoulders, Miss Leckton went to the kitchen cupboard and got out a tumbler. Then she went to the icebox and looked in. Milk was there. That would stop this horrid taste. It would be good, it would nourish her, too. She poured the tumbler full, shut the icebox. As she did so she gave a jerky start, spilling a little of the milk. A bell was ringing over the door to the pantry.

"That's George," she said. "I must let him in."

As she walked to the front door, she was conscious of the excellence of the picture she presented: the usualness, the commonplaceness of the lady carrying a glass of milk; not hurrying, because she might spill the stuff; a little hungry; drinking milk, not sherry—not brandy, as last time.

She was so seized with this conception of herself, so greatly restored to composure, that she carried the play through to the end, holding the milk carefully in her left hand, opening the door (with some extra effort and care) with her right. It did not occur to her then that the presence, imagined or real, of George Potter waiting outside the door to enter, could have anything to do with this return of self-confidence.

George Potter was indeed outside the door. As soon as he saw her, he took off his hat and entered the house, his face shining darkly with moisture, his raincoat wet, his rubber boots making damp marks on the waxed boards of the floor. He took the door from Miss Leckton and closed it.

"Well, George," said Miss Leckton. "I had almost given you up."

She took a sip of the milk. It seemed very good to her, the bitter taste had disappeared from her mouth.

"I come over a while back," said George. "I rang the bell, but I guess you didn't hear it, Miss Leckton. It's a long way to that kitchen from your library."

"Yes," said Miss Leckton. "I was going to telephone over. Oh. Is the telephone still working, do you know?"

"Yes," he said. "We used it. Only about ten minutes back."

"Excuse me a moment," Miss Leckton said. She was still under the spell of relief, still playing out her part of composure. "I want to read the barometer. I have read it each hour. It's so interesting."

She went into the library, leaving the door open behind her, and to the barometer. It read 29.20. The time was five minutes past nine. She reset the index hand. Then she returned to the hall and to George.

"What is happening outside, George?" she inquired. As she said this she realized, with a slight sense of shock, that she had asked less because she was interested than because, having got George here, she needed to detain him as long as possible. The odd thing was, she thought, that there was almost nothing that she could suggest for George to do.

"It's blowing up all the time," George said. "Yes, indeed. It blows harder and harder. Mighty like last time. That wind, it's warm. The water, though, it ain't high this time. It's up, but nothing like before. It's still under the bridge, it hasn't come over the sea wall any. I been down there. You can't see much, the spray is pretty thick and all, but I took a torch, I could see there wasn't no water."

"I see," she said. She drank again from the glass. "Well, that's good, George. Perhaps this will be better. We've taken better precautions. I'm so glad we got those shutters closed. I am going to close all the doors on all the rooms, upstairs and down."

"Yes," said George. "That's a good idea. You want me to do that?"

"No," said Miss Leckton. "I'll do it. I have really nothing to do here now." She was sorry the moment she had said this.

"I put paper, those bundles of newspapers, some in each room," said George. "For window leaks."

"Perhaps they won't leak," Miss Leckton said. "Perhaps with the shutters shut, it won't come through again." She was conscious now of the need to keep talking, of her desire to invent something to detain George. Standing in the hall, his hat in his hand, his wet raincoat and boots shining, he had the impermanent air of someone about to depart.

"They maybe won't," said George. "We can hope so. There's nothing outside loose can blow against the house this time. I cleared all that sort of truck off, put it in the garage or the tool shed. I nailed up them garage doors."

"Good," she said.

"Well, unless you want me, I'll be going. I'm going to look around once more before I go in. You let me know if you want me."

"How?" said Miss Leckton.

"You can telephone," said George. "Ain't that the quickest?"

"Unless the telephone goes off."

"Oh," he said. "Yes. Well, I'll come around again about an hour. What you want me to do, Miss Leckton? Ring that bell only sound in the kitchen?"

"Well, ring the bell," she said. "And if that doesn't work, use the knocker. I can scarcely leave the doors unlocked. Not after last time. Now being alone here."

"You want to shift over to the garage," said George, "and you'll be welcome, we'll make you comfortable. We ain't much for company these days, but we're someone."

"Thank you," said Miss Leckton stiffly. "I shall stay here. Someone has got to be responsible for this house. I wouldn't think of imposing myself on Ella. Not *dream* of it. In the midst of her grief. I shouldn't think of adding *my* worries to her own. I shall expect you here about ten."

"Yes," he said. "Ten or before, if it looks like it's necessary."

He turned away and opened the door. The sound of the storm was very ominous outside in the blackness. George went out and shut the door behind him.

Miss Leckton finished her milk and set down the empty glass on the hall table. Then she closed all the doors in all the rooms; undid the bundles of newspapers; laid thick wads of them under the windows on the floor; rolled other wads to jam across at sills and meeting rails; pulled down the shades, and drew the curtains; left a light burning in each room. The last room she did was the guest room.

As she went downstairs again to retrieve the glass in the hall, it occurred to her that the lights might go off at any moment. It was a really appalling thought. Before, that had meant mostly that the electric range was off, there had been daylight to cope with the worst of the storm, its southeasterly phase. Now there would be darkness. If the lights went off, should she leave candles burning about the house? No, one couldn't do that. The wind might force its entrance to any room, at any time, and while it might merely blow out the candle, one couldn't count on that. It might roll it, fling it, blow it, still lighted, against curtains, under a bed. Then there would be a fire. That was too terrible even to contemplate briefly. The choice lay between fire and darkness. Darkness, darkness, however bleak, however depressing, was preferable. She must keep an electric torch with her always.

By the time Miss Leckton had reached the foot of the stairs and turned toward the table in the hall, the bitter taste was back in her mouth.

Taking the glass in her hand, she found herself reluctant to go to the kitchen with it. The emptiness of the kitchen seemed greater and more unpleasant now than that of any other part of the house. That was simply something she knew now. She remembered her relief when she had last been there and the bell had rung: the bell had meant George at the front door. Here. Behind the door she was now looking at, had been someone she wanted to see. And now she had seen him; she had had the moment of security, the moment of self-possession, the fortifying opportunity to repulse his invitation to the garage-tenement; and he was gone again. He would not be back until ten o'clock—a long time off when you were alone, at night, with the wind around you. It was all very disturbing, very new, too many novel sensations. The bitterness increased in her mouth. Yesterday, at this same hour, she could have said she would be incapable of feeling the emotions that now possessed her at the arrival (indeed, at the departure, however temporary) of George Potter. Yesterday she would have reflected, rather, the feeling she had had when that damnable old bell rang, announcing the further inconvenience, the turmoil, the outrage of her privacy, that those who had rung it betokened.

She put the glass down again on the hall table and went into the library. She shut the door after her, but immediately opened it again. Shut, the room was too unpleasant, too cooped up. Or perhaps, she thought, in avoidance of the truth, it was because she could better hear the bell, the brass knocker? More than likely. She sat down in her chair. How different, she thought, was this solitude from the arrival of Birac and Mrs. Barber!

Miss Leckton had followed Catherine Lovatt down the stairs, and had stood at the foot of them while the maid opened the door. Without any word at all—without so much as a by-your-leave—there had entered an ill-assorted couple, a man and a woman. As usual, the sound of the hurricane, that high-pitched and tearing sound, had entered with them, and it was quite possible that, had they spoken, Miss Leckton would not have heard them. Catherine closed the door as soon as they had entered.

The man was of medium weight, very solidly built, with no hat or overcoat, a thin blue cotton shirt, grey flannel trousers. He had fair hair, long and fine, that hung lankly over his forehead, was plastered wetly to his rather elongated skull. His face was heavy and very red. He was dripping wet. He stood firmly in his wet and dirty white sneakers, his arm around the waist of the little, stout woman he supported.

The woman wore a dark red topcoat with a mangy fur collar, a battered little dark red hat, from under which her grey hair fell in wet and untidy strands. Her head hung down weakly and her face was hidden by her hat brim. Like the man, she was soaked through, and both of them were dripping water in an already considerable puddle on the floor.

Miss Leckton walked toward them.

The man lifted his head (he had had his eyes fixed on the woman he supported) and looked at Miss Leckton. She was immediately struck both by the directness of his gaze and by the brilliant blue of his eyes.

"How do you do?" said the man. "I am sorry we are making such a formidable mess on your floor. Where shall we go?"

Miss Leckton didn't know at all what to say. She knew that she wished they would go away, that she didn't want them here at all; but there was something so forthright and yet so polite in the man's voice—although he spoke with a distinct foreign accent—that she could think at the moment of no way in which to dispose of them. Not yet, at all events.

The man looked down at the floor.

"If you could give me a help," he said, "we can get this woman somewhere, some place where she will change her clothes. She is very wet. She is also quite weak now. Perhaps a little brandy for her, if this troubles you not too much?"

"Where will I take her, madam?" said Catherine in her cool, detached manner.

Miss Leckton found her voice.

"I really don't know what you are doing here at all," she said. "I really don't know why you have come here. I was not expecting anyone."

The man gave her a sharp look, and then smiled, showing a lot of rather large, irregular teeth as he did so.

"Of course," he said. "It is all very unexpected. I do not know much more than you do. I will be very glad to explain to you. The storm, you see. I think this woman is very weak now, and that it will be best that she be dry first. We make a very awful mess here, we are so wet. Is there, perhaps, a bathroom? The salt water will not be good for your floor."

"To your room, madam?" Catherine asked. "Or to Miss Leah's?"

"Take her to Miss Leah's. No. Take her to my room. This man will have to use Miss Leah's bath." Miss Leckton said this because she felt she could not say anything else.

The little stout woman now raised her head. She did so with obvious effort.

"Well, I am grateful," she said weakly. "I am truly grateful. I'm about done in. My! Awful!" She hung her head again.

Without waiting for more, Catherine went to her and took her free arm.

"Right this way," she said. "We'll go up now and get you dry and warm. Just lean on me, madam. We'll have you all right in a minute." To the man she said, "We've got to get her upstairs. Can she do it, sir?"

"Yes," said the man. "I will carry her, if it needs."

"Straight ahead," said Catherine. "Then up the stairs."

"Right," said the man.

Miss Leckton watched them go, standing aside to let them pass her. Everything that happened today seemed to be just beyond her power to control. Except the La Perche people.

She realized, as she watched the slow but perfectly steady progress of these people up her stairs, that there were things she should be doing—so many things! The storm was something in itself one should be looking out for; one should be, as it were, on patrol against it. Then there were these two strangers. There would be dry clothes needed. It offended her to have to supply them, but it was obviously better to do so than to have them—the woman particularly—become really ill here. As she had feared with the La Perche woman. There would have to be something given to her, tea, brandy. Medicine? Well, no medicine yet.

"You can open the package of clothes," she called up to Catherine. "There is that jersey dress. If it is too small, you can take my dark blue wool for her. I'll order tea. I'll get something for the other one from the garret." She didn't say 'for the man' because she could not make up her mind what

139

he was, and it seemed ridiculous, considering his appearance, to call him a gentleman.

"Yes, madam," said Catherine. "I'll attend to it."

They were at the head of the stairs now, so Miss Leckton went swiftly to the kitchen. Anna was standing there, looking out the west window.

"Tea!" said Miss Leckton rapidly and loudly. "We shall have to have tea at once. Toast, too. Right away!"

"All right," said Anna, turning suddenly, her face showing a mixture of alarm and anger. "All right, ma'am. There's no need at all to shout at me. I'm not deaf, ma'am. I'll get the tea. No need to shout at all."

Miss Leckton had not been aware that she had shouted until Anna spoke, and it shocked her both to realize that she had done so and that the cook should address her in this manner. But this was no time to argue or reprimand.

"Very well," she said. "It is these people. Two people, strangers, just arrived, from the storm. They are wet through."

"Aah," said Anna. "The poor creatures!"

"Get the tea as soon as you can," said Miss Leckton.

"And what will I make the toast with?" Anna asked.

It seemed intolerable to Miss Leckton that she should have to arrange for details of this sort when there was so much to do that needed her attention.

"I don't know," she said. "Use your ingenuity. Make toast somehow. Something hot to eat. Light the fire in the dining room, if you wish. But get it done. Use the spirit-lamp for the tea. Put the tea on the dining-room table."

"I'll try," said Anna. "The poor creatures! Were they hurt?"

"No," said Miss Leckton. She controlled the annoyance that Anna raised in her. Everyone was always concerned with the comfort and health of someone else, but never of her. "No, just wet through. I must go now. I must get clothes."

"Aah, God be praised!"

Miss Leckton fled out of the kitchen. She did not want to hear Anna say 'the poor creatures!' again.

She went up to the garret, to get at the cedar chest wherein were stored some of her father's clothes, a few suits of Sam Davids'. Sam was about the size of this man, this intruder. When she got there, she was appalled by what she found.

The roof was leaking in five places. They were not small leaks, they were steady rivulets, thin but persistent. Some of them were falling directly on the trunks and chests stored there.

She did not know what to do; hesitated, wondering whether to move the things now, get help, get something to catch the water. Anna was at the job of tea. Catherine was coping with that woman. Better not disturb them. She tugged the chests into different positions, moved a trunk. She found a commode, a bed-pan, two old-fashioned ewers and a basin (with blue flowers on a light cream ground), and these she set under the leaks. It seemed no time at all before she could hear the sound of water change from the sharp note of drops falling against metal and china to the splash of water falling into water. They would soon have to be emptied.

She opened a cedar chest, pulled out the first things she laid hands on: a pair of bright blue flannel trousers (so like Sam Davids to wear such things!), a red flannel blazer, a couple of white shirts with sports collars (like something one used to see at Long Beach, she thought, wondering if it were the Jew or the southerner in him that had selected them), a pair of brown and white rubber-soled tennis shoes, a pair of red leather carpet slippers (in case the shoes didn't fit). She could find no socks at all, only a pair of wool golf stockings of a shocking black and white plaid pattern, with large tassels at the garter strings. There were no underdrawers to be found. Her mind avoided the unpleasant thought of what this man would do without underdrawers, she dismissed it swiftly from her consciousness. She rolled the clothes into a loose bundle, shut the closet, and left the garret. She went down to the door to ... to the guest room. Standing outside it she wondered uncomfortably whether to knock or not. The man might be naked. She wanted to call for Catherine, but realized that that would not do. Taking a slight breath, she knocked and waited.

In a moment the door opened a crack and through it she could see the head of her unwelcome guest. His hair was now combed neatly and brushed back straight from his forehead without a parting. Seeing his face so, she realized for the first time what a long nose he had, what a high forehead.

"Yes?" said the stranger. "You wish?"

"I have brought you clothes," Miss Leckton said. "I trust they will fit. They were all I could find."

"You are too good," the man said. "This is really marvelous luck. Your husband's?"

"I am not married," Miss Leckton said stiffly.

"So?" said the man. "That is hard to believe of such a lady as you." He smiled at her, opened the door a little further (he was evidently hiding his body behind it), reached out one bare arm and grasped the bundle Miss Leckton held out to him. Miss Leckton averted her eyes. She heard the door close, and his voice saying, "Thank you a thousand times."

"There will be hot tea downstairs in a few minutes," she called through the door.

"That will be marvelous," he said. "O.K. I am so grateful."

Miss Leckton went to her own room. The door was closed, and she had to knock again. It outraged her to have to do so.

Catherine came to the door and opened it.

"She's in the bathroom, madam," Catherine said. "I've got her dry and half dressed. She's too stout for Miss Leah's clothes, so I've had to take some of yours. They are too long for her, but I will do what I can."

"Yes," said Miss Leckton. "Very well." She knew that she sounded grudging. "Bring her to the dining room when you have her dressed. There'll be tea."

"Yes, madam," said Catherine, and she closed the door again. Miss Leckton felt as though she were being barred from her own room.

On her way down she debated whether or not she'd get out the brandy. Well, perhaps she'd better. She went to the office and unlocked the cupboard there, took out an unopened bottle of brandy, locked the cupboard again. She opened the bottle in the pantry, got some glasses, put these and the bottle on the dining-room table. Then she got teacups, saucers, spoons, plates, and set the table with three places. She chose the pottery cups and dishes that were the remnants of the set her mother had used for picnics. No need to use good china for this.

When she had done all she could think of, she stood uncertainly in the dining room, wondering what to do next. She had an urgent desire to go to the living room, see what had happened there, but she dared not open the door. How awful it would be if the door were opened, the storm leaped again into the hall! Thinking this, she went rapidly into the library, got paper, printed on it in bold letters, 'DO NOT OPEN THIS DOOR!!', got a thumbtack, and pinned the paper to the living-room door. Then she went to the side-lights of the south door and looked out.

Dimly and occasionally through the sandy water that was striking against the small leaded panes she could see the storm and its effects. She could see the white and yellow water up on her lawn, over the garden beds, no sign of the yew hedge; and there was the hideous absence of trees. It struck her then that she did not at all understand how these two people had got to her house, for since the crazy water had risen so high here, it must have completely covered the bridge over Ten Acre Creek. Had they swum? Was that why they were so wet, the woman so exhausted? Yet she had not looked as one would expect someone to look who had been totally immersed.

Miss Leckton found herself growing angry again at the fate that had pursued her this day. First Leah and then Golotz. Those awful La Perche people. Then the storm, the car, the garage. The light and telephone gone. Now these people, strangers. Now! Of all times!

The front doorbell rang again.

XII

WITHOUT a moment's hesitation, Miss Leckton hastened toward the front door. This time she herself would see to it that none entered. There would be no welcoming in by Catherine of more of these intrusive strangers. This was too much.

She had gone but four steps on her way when the whole house shook violently, a tremor that she could clearly feel in the boards under her feet; and simultaneously, there was a horrible rending sound from the living room, loud enough, within the house, to be heard over the tormenting high scream of the hurricane.

Miss Leckton stopped dead: a prey, once again, to that hideous indecision that had so frequently beset her this day. What should she do? Answer the door, drive off these people? Or go to the living room, look in, see what had happened? Yet if she delayed, even briefly, someone else would come to answer the door; and if she opened the living-room door, the tempest would seize her hall again, it might not be possible to close the door once she had opened it—now it stood firm, at least. Later, she was to learn that the noise and the tremor had been caused by the further collapse of tree and porch posts through the frame of the broken east window; now she could imagine only some far more serious disaster.

The situation, intolerable enough as it was, grew only to become more intolerable. She was filled with emotions composed of fear, anger, and confusion, in almost equal parts. Where were her servants? Why had she to be left alone at the moment of crisis, her household occupied with tasks dictated by the comfort and convenience of strangers greatly unwanted? What had happened to her house? What would happen if she did not herself repel this new invasion?

With a great effort, she seized control of herself, decided what to do. She walked to the library door, looked in. The door to the living room was still shut; there was no change she could discern, no wind here, no water. Then she turned away and, her anger mounting now to the ascendancy as her confusion was banished, her fear momentarily allayed, she flung the front door open, stood forbiddingly in the open doorway.

"No!" she cried out. "No! This house is full. There is no place here. Do you hear? There is no place here!"

She had been shouting—nearly screaming, so intent was she, so loud the storm—at the woman who stood there, but she had not observed her. She was hardly aware, indeed, whether it was a man or a woman; it was, to her, simply another person come to trespass on her life, her privacy, her comfort, her convenience.

Getting no reply, she looked at the woman, saw her now more fully for the first time. The result of observation and perception went through to her mind and emotions with shocking force.

There stood before her one of the most beautiful young women Miss Leckton had ever seen. Not even her disarray, the obvious fact that she was soaked in water from head to foot, could detract from her beauty: indeed, in a way that Miss Leckton did not even attempt to define, her state enhanced her beauty. She was fairly tall, of a strong and wonderfully developed figure: large, firm breasts clearly and cleanly outlined beneath the wet silk of her dress; full, finely rounded hips; long, straight legs without shoes or stockings. She wore no hat, and her dark hair, cut short, hung wetly about the oval of her face. The features were perfect: big, dark brown eyes, widely set, a straight nose, a full mouth, its lips large and finely cut, a strong but softly rounded chin. It was a face that Miss Leckton was never to forget: even on this first view (this startled and almost unwilling observation) she was made aware deep within herself that here was all that was desirable in woman and that her desirability was frightening. In the woman's bare arms was held an infant, wrapped in a blue blanket that dripped from its saturation of water in a steady stream onto the stone of the steps.

The woman was simply looking at her, her lips slightly parted, her eyes wide and soft and yet somehow searching. She neither stirred nor uttered.

Miss Leckton opened her mouth to speak, but no words came. Moved by an impulse too strong to be contested, she stood aside, and the woman with her baby walked past her into the house. Miss Leckton followed her in and closed the door. She could hear, in this new comparative quiet, the woman heave a deep sigh.

The idea of attempting to keep the woman out or, even now, to get rid of her, was replaced in Miss Leckton by an urge to explain, to make clear her first shouted denial; and although such explanation was something quite alien to her own character as she had always conceived it, yet she could not stop from trying it.

"I did not realize," she said. "It is the wind and all these people. So many people, all in one day and the storm. Everything happens at once..."

The woman interrupted her.

"Could I go somewhere to dry the child? A dry blanket, or clothes, or something? A blanket, perhaps. Have you a bathroom? We are very wet. He has been wet so long."

Her voice, Miss Leckton noted, was that of a lady. It was also warm and rich: it moved the listener, she felt, beyond the content of the words.

"I'll see," Miss Leckton said. "There are no proper clothes, I fear, but a blanket, surely." As she spoke she realized rather abruptly that she was enormously tired, that it was going to be a great effort to take care of this woman and her child— and that that was both what she must do and wanted to do.

She wanted to do it beyond reasonableness—the want came deeply from within. "Come this way," she said. "I am Miss Leckton. Miss Carrel Leckton. We'll see if those people are out of the rooms upstairs."

"Thank you," said the woman. "I am Mrs. John Cleever."

"Oh, yes," said Miss Leckton. She led the way to the stairs, began to mount them. "You're Providence, aren't you?"

"Yes," said Mrs. Cleever.

They were halfway up the stairs when the door to Miss Leckton's room opened and Catherine came out, followed by the little woman, now dressed in the fantastically misfit clothes that had been provided. But seen now, her grey hair neat, if still damp, in a bun at the back of her head, her soggy hat removed, she presented a far more lively appearance. Catherine, holding the wet clothes bundled into a soggy towel, stood aside to let the woman go past her and to the head of the stairs.

"Well," said the little woman, "I certainly do thank you, Miss Leckton. I certainly do. And you too," she said to the maid. "I surely feel better. I was pretty near to done in if it hadn't been for that kind gentleman that helped me and for you. My! is someone else in trouble? This your family, now?"

"No," said Miss Leckton. "Is the room free now, Catherine? We shall want a blanket for the baby, right away. Are there more towels?"

"Yes, madam," said Catherine. She put the bundle down on the floor and went to the linen cupboard.

"Oh, a baby!" said the little woman. "My goodness, is he all right?"

"I think so," said Mrs. Cleever. "I hope so."

"Give him to me," said the woman. "I used to be a trained nurse, before I got too old for it. I've worked with babies all my life. A boy?"

"Yes," said Mrs. Cleever.

"How old?"

"Eighteen months."

"Give him to me. We'll fix him up. We'll see he's all right."

The little woman almost pushed past Miss Leckton in her eagerness to get to Mrs. Cleever.

A little to Miss Leckton's surprise, Mrs. Cleever surrendered the baby immediately to the arms of the other woman.

"Now," said the little woman. "We'll get you both dry. We can use your room again, Miss Leckton? Is that right? You been so kind, you have. Real kind. Maybe you'll let me have Miss Lovatt, here, to help me."

It was all happening so fast that Miss Leckton felt somewhat bemused by it and yet relieved.

"Yes," she said; and to Catherine, "I suppose you can find something for Mrs. Cleever to wear?"

"Now you come right along with me, Mrs. Cleever," said the little woman, heading for Miss Leckton's room. "My! A lovely boy! My, he's handsome. He'll be all right. Just a little wet, won't hurt him any. I'm Mrs. Tessie Barber, Miss Leckton, a neighbor, sort of, I've a house below Olneys Ridge yonder. Or I had one there. What a terrible storm! Come along." She entered the room, Mrs. Cleever following her. In a moment Catherine, carrying towels and a white blanket, joined them and closed the door.

As soon as the door had shut, Miss Leckton turned and began to descend the stairs again. She was conscious now of her own fatigue, of the weight of her raincoat flapping as she walked, of the oppression of the hot air, of the sweat that covered her body. She felt confused again, too many things to do and to understand, too much to sort out. All these people, unwanted, or, like Mrs. Cleever, neither wanted nor unwanted, but powerfully imposed on you almost as a need: they had, in a manner, taken possession of her house, they had invaded her, the situation was not at all under control. And always the storm forced itself on your attention, shaking the house, making its high and terrible dissonance around you and above you, the sea and the wind making concert against you.

Wearily she took off the raincoat, dropped it on a chair in the hall. She felt no cooler without it, but it was good to be rid of it. Then she went into the dining room, sat down

148

heavily at the head of her table. There was something she should do. What was it? Too much to do. Too tired now.

She reached out and took the bottle of brandy and poured a little into a glass, swallowed the liquor. It felt fiery as it went down her throat, into her stomach. Almost immediately, it began to have its effect on her: she felt stronger. This was obviously what she had needed.

The room was very hot. She had grown accustomed to the oppressive warmth of the air, but now it had become almost unbearable. Then she noticed that Anna had lit the fire, a small but brightly-burning blaze. She rose and went to the west window. Perhaps it would be safe to open that for the moment; it was the lee side of the house. With considerable caution she edged the window up a few inches. As there was no effect beyond the heightening of the noise of the storm, she raised the bottom sash a foot. The cotton net glass curtains behaved curiously: they would suddenly billow out, drop, then bulge out the opening, then drop—each motion was abrupt and brief. Very little air came into the room and what did enter was moist and warm, and smelled strongly of seaweed.

What else was there to do? Oh, yes, two more teacups. She got them from the pantry, got spoons. Food for the baby. What did one give an infant that age? Milk, probably.

She went to the kitchen.

"Anna," she said, keeping her voice level this time, "how much milk have we? A lady with a baby has just come in from the storm."

"You don't say!" said Anna. "Well, imagine that! A little small baby, ma'am?"

"Eighteen months," Miss Leckton said.

"A boy? A gyurl?" Anna asked.

"A boy," said Miss Leckton.

"Aah, the sweet little thing," said Anna. "Yes, ma'am, we got milk. We got about two quarts of it with a bit in another bottle. And we got lots of cereals, farina, and oatmeal, and all like that, like Miss Leah liked. They'll be fine for the little feller. Only I don't see how ever I'll cook them, outside I cook them on the fire."

"Yes," said Miss Leckton. "Have you made the toast?"

"Yes, ma'am," said Anna. "You'll see it in the covered plate like, by the side of the fire, just back of the screen. Will I get it for you? The tea's on the table. The kettle should be on the bile now."

"No, thank you," Miss Leckton said. "That'll be all right, Anna. They're not down yet."

"And how many have come already?"

"Four," Miss Leckton answered. "Four. A woman, says she used to be a trained nurse, an older woman. A man. A young lady, Mrs. Cleever, from Providence, I knew her people slightly, with the baby." It surprised her to hear herself talking like this with Anna, and to find it agreeable and relieving. "I do hope no more come. Six people have come in all. That should be enough. After all, I am not running a hotel."

"No, ma'am," said Anna. "It's the storm."

"The storm," said Miss Leckton. "Yes. But I don't see that the storm excuses people from barging in on a house they have never been to, simply ringing the bell and walking in. It's not as though things were simple here, as it is. I never had such a day. Never!"

"Aah," said Anna. "And you all sad at Miss Leah's leaving, too. She'll be the one to miss."

That remark brought Miss Leckton up short. It was her own fault, she thought. This was the result of such talk with Anna. How could one expect the woman to understand that situation? And it was one that certainly would not be explained to her. Although it was really an impertinence of Anna to mention it at all, it would be best to overlook it now, everything so upset; take it for granted it was kindly meant, however stupid and ignorant.

"I must see to the tea," she said abruptly, and she returned to the dining room, to find she was no longer alone there.

The man was standing uncertainly in the doorway. He had put on Sam Davids' clothes and presented a grotesque appearance in them, as one would expect, although they fitted him

150

well enough. He had on the red carpet slippers. His appearance gave her a curious satisfaction, almost as though she had thus had a sweet, though wholly private, revenge on him for this intrusion into her life. Looking at him, she had another thought, scarcely expressed, a swift, shadowy conception that flitted through her mind and left at once: it was that Mrs. Cleever would hardly pay any attention to him, dressed in such appalling fashion; he looked infinitely less attractive, more vulgar, more impossible, than he had in his wet shirt, wet flannel trousers. And yet, his face was not at all commonplace.

"Is this where you wish me to be?" he asked.

"Yes," said Miss Leckton. "Come in. Since you are all here, I thought you would need something hot."

"That is most kind of you," the man said. "I am so much obliged. One got rather chilled by the water, although it is not cold in this storm."

"Will you have tea?" Miss Leckton asked. "Or some brandy?"

"If I could have a little brandy," he said. "To stop me from shaking inside myself. Then perhaps you will be good enough to give me tea."

"Yes," Miss Leckton said. She poured a liqueur glass full of brandy and handed it to him.

"Thank you," he said. He drank the brandy in two quick gulps. "Ah," he said. "That is good. That is wonderfully good brandy, a good cognac. It is a shame to drink it so."

"It was some my father bought, many years ago," Miss Leckton said. She busied herself making the tea.

"Your father had excellent taste," the man said. "I think I should present myself, I have arrived so very suddenly. My name is ... my name is now Francis Birac, since I am an American citizen."

"You have become one recently?"

"Since six months," he said. "You see, I make my living here, I live here. I shall not go back to France. That is all done. So I have made my name American."

151

"You were French, then? What was your name in those days?"

"I am, I was the Vicomte François de Birac. We come from Angoulême. You know this part of France?"

"Yes," Miss Leckton said. "Oh, yes. I have been to Angoulême."

This, it seemed, was altogether different: he was a foreigner, but a gentleman. It explained his looks, his assurance.

"Tea?" she asked.

"Please," he said. "Two lumps and cream, if convenient. I suppose you did not expect two strangers."

"No," she said. "But there is enough in the house. There has come another woman, with a little baby, since you came. She also was very wet. Do you know the other woman, the nurse, that Mrs. Barber?"

"Mrs. Barber?" he said. "She comes with the baby?"

"No," Miss Leckton said. "With you."

"She is a nurse? I did not know this. No. I do not know her. Mrs. Barber? I did not know the name. I found her in the fields to the west of Ten Acre Pond. Together we tried to reach the road, through the more or less open country, but the brambles, the briers, they are impassable. Then we tried the little road, but it is full of trees that have been blown down by this wind, it did not seem a safe venture. So we have come across on the bridge, seeing your house. This woman, she was very exhausted, she was not able to walk around very much longer. There was a great deal of water over your bridge, but some large trees, elms I think, have been jammed against it and over it, and I got this woman, this Mrs. Barber, over on the trees. I did not know she would have the strength to do it, but she did. We were very wetted on the other side, the water is waist deep, and it is a strong current. But we succeeded. It is so that we have come. She was very exhausted, as I am telling you. This is why I have brought her to the house. With rest and dryness, she will soon recover, I think."

"Let us hope so," Miss Leckton said. "It's bad enough as it is, let alone having anyone fall sick."

"The baby," said Birac. "The baby is O.K.?"

"I hope so," she said. "I believe he is just wet. He is upstairs now being dried off, put in a blanket. Mrs. Barber seemed—for all that she was so 'exhausted,' as you say, when she arrived—to have recovered very rapidly and insisted on taking charge. As she is a trained nurse—if she is—she might as well make her talents useful."

"Yes," said Birac. He drank his tea and looked at the windows. "I hope your windows will hold against that storm," he said.

"Yes," said Miss Leckton with a slight shudder. "I pray God that they will. The windows in my living room—across the hall there—have crashed open. Things blew against them. You must not open the door there."

"No, of course," he said. "You do not have the shutters?"

"There are shutters," she said. "But one cannot close them from the inside. The storm enters the room so terribly. One blew right out of my hands."

"One could close them from the outside," he said. "There is no man here?"

"My chauffeur," she said. "He lives over the garage. I have not had time to get him." It annoyed her very much to be questioned like this. Who did this man think he was, anyway? What did he know of what had gone on here? Wasn't his own presence one of the reasons she had not yet got George to help her? And if it had not occurred to her to tell George to pick up the deck chair, how should one be expected to anticipate what this wind could do, and what difference would it have made, since the elm had done far more damage? "I have done all that I could," she said with precision and coldly, "in the very much interrupted time at my disposal."

"Of course," Birac said. "You have been invaded by all of us castaways. You have been most kind and considerate. If you could lend me a raincoat, I could get your man and together we could close the shutters from the outside. Those on this room, the ground floor, at least. You would like this, perhaps?"

There was no denying that that was a good suggestion, Miss Leckton thought. Certainly it was only just that these people who trespassed so lightly, should be useful to her—like Mrs. Barber.

"Yes," she said. "That is a good idea. I can lend you my raincoat. The chauffeur, George Potter, lives over the garage, up the outside stairs. Directly across from the front door."

"I will go now," he said, putting down his cup.

"Finish your tea," Miss Leckton said. The part of her which suggested this was purely automatic. "Finish your tea. And tell me how you came here."

"I think it will be good to do the shutters now," he said. "I have had the tea. It has done me a lot of good. As for how I came, it is merely odd, not interesting. I was examining the dredge of Ten Acre Pond—the one that builds the causeway. I am the engineer for this project. The storm struck, the water came, a tidal wave, I think, and it picked up this dredge and it flung it high up on the land, sucked it back and out over where the dunes once were, returned it to high land once more. I was not at all hurt, merely terrified. I jumped out and walked through bushes to dry land. There I found Mrs. Barber. The rest I have told you. It is fantastic, is it not? I should have been drowned very quickly. I do not know why I was not. I shall be frightened more later. I have not yet had time to be so."

"Goodness!" said Miss Leckton.

"The raincoat?" he said. "I do not think I have the pleasure to know your name."

"Leckton," she said. "Miss Carrel Leckton."

"Thank you. The raincoat, Miss Leckton?"

"There's toast here," she said.

"May I save it to later?" he said.

"Yes." She got up and went to the hall and he followed her. She gave him her coat to put on. It was a little small for him, but not very much so.

"Out here," she said. She opened the front door and pointed to the garage. "You will have to knock, loudly too, on their door. The bell is not working."

154

"Thank you," he said. "I will be right back."

In the hall he took off his slippers and his stockings.

"Excuse me," he said. "I would not get these wet."

He rolled his trousers up above his knees and, barefooted, left the house.

Miss Leckton watched him till he was on his way up the steps to George's tenement, and then closed the door. The sound of the hurricane, the spectacle of the horizontal rain and spray driven in a thick grey veiling before her eyes, the sight of the huge rocks and the debris of God alone knew what docks and dwellings that lay scattered over the devastated lawn, the swirl and crash of water over once dry, once safe land, were too appalling to be contemplated.

As she got to the foot of the stairs, on her way back to the dining room, she saw Mrs. Cleever coming down alone.

The young woman was dressed now in a powder-blue silk dress of Leah's. It was tight for her, and it accented her figure in much the same way as had her own wet clothes. Her dark hair, still damp, was more neatly done; one could see its wave, and the straight beauty of neck, the width and whiteness of forehead. Watching her descend, Miss Leckton felt her heart constrict once and perceptibly. One did not often see such a sight, after all. Even the dress, which she had thought unsuitably mature for Leah, looked beautiful now in spite of wrinkles and ill-fitting lines.

"Oh," said Mrs. Cleever, "how good of you to take us in like this—from this terrible storm!"

"Not at all," said Miss Leckton.

"Indeed, it is kind," said Mrs. Cleever. "And what a miracle to find that Mrs. Barber here! She and your wonderful maid have taken over the care of my Winlock. It is nothing short of a miracle. I, who am so ignorant, so incompetent—and having just lost my Phyllis." She was at the bottom step now, and Miss Leckton could see that there were big tears running down her cheeks.

"Your Phyllis?" she said, not understanding at all.

Mrs. Cleever nodded, her lips trembling. She swallowed, tried to speak, could not.

155

"You had better come with me now," said Miss Leckton. "There is tea ready. I think you need it. A glass of brandy, too."

Mrs. Cleever nodded again.

"Does the child need anything now?" Miss Leckton asked. It took a tremendous effort to say the simple sentence, full of the implications of more work, more worry, on top of her present confusion and fatigue.

"No," said Mrs. Cleever. "But I'm not sure. I'd like to ask Mrs. Barber. I know so little. I am so exhausted."

"Come along," said Miss Leckton.

She led the way to the dining room and poured a glass of brandy and gave it to Mrs. Cleever, who drank it quickly.

"Sit down," said Miss Leckton. "I'll make you some tea. Sugar? Cream?"

"One lump, nothing else, thank you."

While Miss Leckton poured the tea, Mrs. Cleever sat inert in her chair, her hands and forearms resting heavily on the table. Miss Leckton gave her the cup, fetched the plate of toast from the fireplace, put it beside her.

"There," she said. "I believe that will help. Now I must go up and see how they are getting on upstairs."

"Oh," said Mrs. Cleever. "Must you go? I don't want to be alone."

It seemed a curious remark to Miss Leckton; but the fact of the matter was that she found herself pleased by it even as she disapproved it.

"I keep thinking of Phyllis," Mrs. Cleever said, stirring her tea round and round very slowly and regularly. "It's all so terrible."

Yielding both to curiosity and to the obvious pleasure of postponing the trip upstairs, Miss Leckton sat down again at her place at the head of the table.

"Who is Phyllis?" she asked. It surprised her to hear the softness and tenderness of her own voice—to this woman, this stranger.

"She was so young, such a lovely person," said Mrs. Cleever, speaking only just loudly enough to be heard over the

156

incessant noise of the storm. "She had been with me six months. Looking after my baby. Winlock. She was so wonderful with him." Then, dropping her voice so that Miss Leckton had to strain forward to hear, she said, "So wonderful."

Miss Leckton said nothing, but waited.

"We were going down for a few days to my cabin at Matunuck," Mrs. Cleever said. "We had planned it long ago. It would have been a holiday, my—my husband was to remain in Providence." Her voice rose a little. "He was not to come at all. Not at all. It was going to be just the baby and me. And Phyllis, of course. To do our own cooking. To rest. To be alone. And then we stopped the car on the road to Wonontaug Beach, and we got out to see the storm. She had Winlock in her arms and the wave came. She fell and was dragged under but she—she raised herself, somehow. She held the baby up and I took it from her. I could not stand in that water, we were washed to the land. The car was gone. Phyllis was gone. She was gone. In the water. Then I walked here, seeing your house. I came over those trees across the water. It was all my fault. It was my fault."

"What was your fault?" said Miss Leckton. There was a quality to the story that both excited her and disturbed her, an undertone to it that she could not grasp but wanted to grasp.

"Phyllis," said Mrs. Cleever. "It was my plan. It was all mine. I was the one who wanted to stop the car. She was only twenty. Now you know. Everything is gone. I took her to her death. Do you see?"

"How terrible for you!" Miss Leckton said.

"Yes," said Mrs. Cleever. "May I have some more of your brandy, please?"

"Certainly," said Miss Leckton.

She poured the little glass full again and watched Mrs. Cleever while she sipped it. The color was coming back into the young woman's cheeks, making her more beautiful than before.

"It is terrifying to see life wasted," Mrs. Cleever said, her voice a little thick, a trifle blurred. She was speaking with an effort now, as though what she was saying was being forced from her. "It is awful to feel you are responsible for the waste—however involuntary your part. It takes time to create any relationship, even the least of them. You are not married, are you? Perhaps you will understand because you are a woman, have had to employ people, make a relationship with people. There are not many you can work with and work in happiness and understanding, are there? Life as we live it —you and I, and all our kind—is hard, usual, cruel, selfish. It is full of children and their animalism. Of men. Of men and women pulling at each other. You try to set up a refuge, a sort of island of protection, don't you? But with how many do you succeed? But I can't make it clear. I am too shaken. This has all happened too suddenly. You see, the girl wanted to come, liked the country, looked forward to it—but still, it was my idea, my conception. Oh, God! You can't talk about things like this. I'm so tired!"

Miss Leckton, listening to her in astonishment, realized how little she understood of what was being said, its obscurity. In a way, she wished it had not been told her, knew that it had a quality almost of confession. Mrs. Cleever might well repent later what she had said now, though Miss Leckton could not say why she thought so. It was nothing that had been said: it was the tone of it. She felt embarrassed, awkward, wishing to stay, to go, both at the same time. This woman had a quality that disturbed her, almost frightened her, while it attracted so strongly. It would have been better, Miss Leckton felt, if Mrs. Cleever had never come. But then it would have been better if none of these people had ever come.

Her train of thought provided her with a decision, and she rose to see to those who were upstairs.

"Help yourself to more tea," she said. "I'll go up now and see about your son."

"Yes," said Mrs. Cleever listlessly. "Thank you."

As she turned toward the window, Miss Leckton saw the figures of George and Mr. Birac outside it. They were closing the shutters, their bodies but dimly perceived in the failing light and through the wet and muddied panes. It occurred to her that now she would have to provide some sort of light. Candles, she said to herself.

"I'll light some candles," she said. "When they get those shutters closed, it will be dark here. The electricity is off."

She fetched the two silver candelabra from the sideboard, placed them on the table, and began to light them.

Mrs. Cleever looked up at the south windows.

"Oh," she said. "Who is closing the shutters?"

"My chauffeur," said Miss Leckton. "And another man, he came just before you, a Frenchman. There. That's better."

The candles made a warm and becoming light.

"Oh?" Mrs. Cleever said. "A Frenchman?"

"He's an American now. His name is Birac. He was the Vicomte François de Birac before. He's a complete stranger to me. I don't know any more about him than what he has told me—if that is true."

"I see," said Mrs. Cleever. "That is true of all of us, isn't it?"

Her remark drew Miss Leckton's eyes to her. Mrs. Cleever's hands were engaged busily with her hair, arranging it, primping at it, and they dropped from her hair to her dress, fussed with it, straightening the wrinkles, pulling it neat. It was immediately and completely obvious to Miss Leckton why Mrs. Cleever was doing this, that it had taken merely the mention of Birac to produce these actions, and she was aware of an emotion within herself that was hard to define, but which included, more clearly than any other component, a dislike of the Frenchman and a violent recurrence of the wish that he had never intruded his presence in her house.

Without another word, Miss Leckton left the room, determined to get done with her unpleasant duties upstairs as quickly as possible. If she were quick, she could be back before Birac re-entered. There crossed her mind again—not with pleasure, but with something approaching satisfaction— the recollection of the clothes she had lent to him. Then she started up the stairs. . . .

.... The lights in the library faded to dimness, came up again to a sudden and high brightness, then went out. The shock of the darkness (with which increased the apparent intensity of the storm's voice) jolted Miss Leckton to her feet. She could see absolutely nothing. Looking in the direction of the window she had been at such pains to leave unshuttered, she could see only darkness, so thick, so full of the terror of high wind.

XIII

THE paralysis of her power to act which assailed Miss Leckton at this moment, was caused by a division within her mind. She was thinking, as nearly simultaneously as is possible, of two separate things at once. With one part of her mind she was attempting to recall what it was she had planned to do in this exact event of the failure of the lights; and it was notable that she did not for a single moment attempt to create a new plan, but devoted so much of her mind as was not otherwise and involuntarily occupied, to trying to reconstruct what had previously been decided by her.

Overlaid on this was a new and fresh train of thought about Maude Cleever: for now, for the first time, Miss Leckton was assessing the remarkable speeches that Mrs. Cleever had made to her at the tea table six years ago; and it occurred to her as almost unexplainable that the loss of the girl called Phyllis could have so affected Mrs. Cleever if Phyllis were regarded merely as a nursemaid. Surely, even in those days of shortages of good and competent servants, even allowing for an abnormal devotion to the welfare of the baby Winlock (a devotion which had not been particularly manifest), it was all out of proportion; and although it was possible to attribute much to the simple cause of shock and fatigue, both of them natural and great in the circumstances, Mrs. Cleever's rapidity in recovery denied the simple explanation and complicated her curious testimony.

It is possible that Miss Leckton might have arrived at the beginning, at least, of a conclusion in this analysis of Maude Cleever (in spite of that dichotomy of mind that fumbled in a panicky fashion toward remembering what she had meant to do if the lights went out), had not she seen a slowly increasing glimmer of actual light appear in the dormer window of the garage-tenement.

The lights, she thought, have come on again over there.

As she thought this, she recollected the telephone. Had it gone off? Was it still working? One should find out.

At once her mind cleared. She felt for the electric torch she had put on her desk, found it and lit it. With its white light, she found matches, lit one of the two candles on the mantelpiece, transferred it to the desk. Then she sat down, switched off the torch, and picked up the telephone.

It was working. She called the garage and got George.

"Are your lights on again?" she asked.

"No, Miss Leckton," George said. "No. They're off now. We got the oil lamp lit now. You got your candles all right?"

"Yes," she said. "I suppose it is no use to report this failure, is it? After last time?"

"No," he said, "but I already done that, Miss Leckton. They're swamped up there to the Electric Company. They don't know nothing except that all the lights is going off everywhere. You want me to come over now?"

"Yes," Miss Leckton said. "Yes."

"Right away," he said. "Which door now?"

"The kitchen," she said.

"I be there," George said. "You need anything I can fetch?"

"No," she said, and she hung up.

There was a definite and real sense of comfort in the thought that George was coming over. There was something to do once more, something to interrupt this process of sitting and waiting for God knew quite what, alone. She did not allow her mind to go ahead, to speculate on what would happen when George left again. One could meet that when it had happened.

She rose and took the torch. She remembered now clearly what she had decided to do about the lights. She was not to touch the switches, lest she leave the current turned off. She was not to light candles in the rooms—the unoccupied rooms—the empty rooms: it might prove dangerous. She was to survey the house, with her torch, see to its state, see to leaks. She could begin with the kitchen, since George would come there. Together they would go over the house.

Standing for a moment in the hall, the beam of the torch directed on the waxed floor in front of her, she felt the house shaking. This was what had happened before; so it had begun: the house had shaken, heavily, in recurrent quivers at brief intervals. The wind was louder now, higher in tone, almost as high as it had been in 1938. It was at this juncture then that those people had begun to come: there was a difference now—there was no one here. There would be no one, this time. She wondered why she knew this so absolutely. Was it because that was the way it would happen, or because that was the way she had determined it? Would she, after all, repulse invaders this time? Send them off her peninsula—if it had become a storm-girt island? There flashed through her mind the phrase "For unto every one that hath shall be given, but from him that hath not shall be taken away even that which he hath." What made her think of that? Well, this was no time for texts and parables, she must go out to the kitchen.

Entering the kitchen in the dark was, to her surprise, a comforting thing to do. Suddenly it had been restored to her, it had lost that unfriendly quality, the sense of strangeness and loneliness that had filled it when she had come before to find the solitary electric bulb burning over the sink. Now, in the dark, it was empty: her kitchen at night, deserted as it always was when the light was put out. Even the ray of the torch seemed friendly now against the sound of the hurricane that had come, she knew, at last.

Miss Leckton's acceptance of the hurricane was an involuntary act. And although the thought was simple and simply accepted, it nevertheless frightened her. Now she knew that

163

she must wait it out: that there was little or nothing she could do; that action would be restricted to minimizing the effects of possible calamity. Now too, and for the first time fully, she was conscious of her singleness. The feeling she had known before, even in 1938, of needing to be in all parts of the house at once, was made almost unbearably acute and disagreeable by the fact that she did not want to be in any part of it: wherever she went, she would be single, the absence of other humanity would be palpable. Alone—and, she thought, cruelly deserted—her preparations against the storm were feeble, would prove wholly useless. The bitter taste returned to her mouth, she felt her stomach grow weak, she was slightly nauseated. However pleasantly relieving it would be to drink something now in order to mitigate that taste, she could think of nothing she could be sure of retaining. Then she remembered the sherry. However hot it was, however much trouble, she would get that out of the cupboard; but after George had left, after George had left. It would not do to let him see her resort to the sherry: it implied an apparent weakness, however well justified the drink might be for purely restorative reasons.

She heard a sound—a rattling noise, very faint over the uproar of the wind. Locating it, she turned her torch on the door to the porch. Through the glass she could see George Potter. At once she unlocked the door, let him in.

"We got it now," George said. He shook his head as he took off his wet hat. "We got it for sure now."

"Yes," said Miss Leckton. "And the water, George? Has it risen?"

"Yes," he said. "But it ain't at all like last time. She's lapping at the bridge, just over the floor boards, that's all. The waves is just breaking over the sea wall, just a little, I think. I dassen't go too close—you can't see well, the spray is so awful heavy, just with a torch. I don't believe we going to git much harm from the water this time."

"I hope not," she said. "It's bad enough as it is."

"What would you like me to do now?" George asked.

It was unnecessary for Miss Leckton to think what to say:

she knew what she wanted and (uncomfortably well) why she wanted it.

"We'll go over the house, room by room," she said. "Check the windows. That sort of thing. The garret too."

"That's good," said George. "Maybe there'd be some leaks, wind up like this. I hate to think how hard it blows now."

"Come along," said Miss Leckton.

Together they examined each room of the house, using their torches. The garret proved to have but two very small leaks, both easily trapped in basins. Most of the south windows in the house were leaking water, but somewhat less than at the same stage in the hurricane of 1938. It was, Miss Leckton decided, because they had got the shutters closed. Together they made stoppers of the newspapers and laid more papers below the windows on the floors.

The worst leak was in the guest room. Looking through the window, with the beam of the torch, she could see that the slats had blown out of the lower half of one of the shutters; that explained the leak. It annoyed Miss Leckton, because it meant she would probably have to repaper the wall below the window, and she was fairly sure she didn't have enough of the present paper left to do so. She turned her torch around the room, looking at the wallpaper. It was bright and unfaded, the simple, geometric design of red and salmon clear and concise. Well, the room had not been used, she had kept the shades pulled down with great care. It was ready for the guests who might occupy it, but had never done so. At all events, it was not recognizable as the room that Leah had occupied, one would not easily, again, miscall it by her name.

Since this was the last room on the top floor that they had examined, they left to go downstairs, and Miss Leckton realized how little more there was left to do with George, how soon he would be gone again. As she thought this, she thought too that the emptiness of the guest room had an unpleasant quality, as though it symbolized rather too exactly the emptiness of the house, the state in which she now found herself attempting to delay the departure of as insignificant

165

a person (in all her previous life) as George Potter. It seemed to her unfair that this should be so: a queer, distorted, malicious plot, hatched by an unknown, an unnamed mind, to certify her discomfort, to force this bitter taste to persist in her mouth even while Potter was there, to augment the great fatigue she felt growing upon her. How uncomfortable was the combination! How incompatible was the utter weariness she now felt, with the nervous need to action, the necessity to patrol, to be everywhere at once! Whence came the fatigue? There had been far less to do, far less of activity, no damage to run and repair, be shocked by. And—more baffling—whence the nervous craving for action? Was she not alone? Was she not—this time—fully relieved of the unpleasant responsibilities for others that had been so roughly thrust upon her before?

She dismissed this thought at once, though with an effort, knowing as she did so that her very dismissal of it was in itself somewhat of an answer to her own question: what she did not want—and yet paradoxically craved—was the inaction of impotent waiting, full of the thoughts and memories that physical stillness bred so clearly.

When they had been through all the rooms, she sent George down to the cellar to make certain it had not flooded. While he was gone, she went to the library and read the barometer. It showed 28.95 and the time was ten minutes past ten. Curiously enough, the reading cheered her a little, for she thought that it would be very unlikely the glass should fall further than this, and therefore she could look soon for a shift in the wind to the westward. When that had happened, the worst of the storm would be over, for the high land of Olneys Ridge would break the force of the wind. Had not Leah said the storm would start about ten?

Turning toward the hall door, she saw George there.

"Well, George?" she said.

"Dry," he said. "Nice and dry. Not a bit of leak this time. I don't guess she's going to get water into it this time, Miss Leckton, that tide's too low."

"I hope not," she said.

166

"Yes, indeed," George said. "You want me for anything more now?"

Miss Leckton stood silent while she cast about in her mind for further tasks for George; but she could think of none.

"No," she said. "I can think of nothing more. At the moment."

"You like me to stay here a while longer?" said George. "Everything's fine over to our place."

Miss Leckton opened her mouth to say yes, that he could sit in the kitchen for a while, but she closed her lips again without speaking those words. If he were here, it would make it impossible for her (as she felt then) to get the sherry she wanted, and she was so tired now that the idea of the sherry was become of extreme importance to her. Further than that, to have George remain, on such terms, would be a confession of defeat, of weakness; and since it would be but a temporary matter, it merely postponed the moment when she should be alone again. Perhaps then it would seem worse to her.

"No," she said, as firmly as she might, although she could not keep the bitterness out of her voice. "Oh, no. You can return to Ella now."

"I'll be back if I'm needed," said George. "The telephone, it's still working. You want me any time, and the telephone goes off, you just put the candles in this here window, I'll see 'em. I'll keep an eye out. You want to leave the kitchen door unlocked, the way I can get in quick?"

"No," said Miss Leckton. She could not change now. It was, somehow, too late for that. "I wish it locked. As I said before."

"I misdoubt there'll be folks coming," George said. "It's night now, and they've got a lot of people took away from them shore houses on account of this storm. It was daytime before, people come to look at the storm. Won't be no one this time."

"One can never tell," said Miss Leckton. "I should hardly like to have that Frosten man walk in in the middle of the night."

"Wasn't no harm in him," said George. "No real harm.

167

Just shiftless. I doubt he'd come. I heard he was drafted into the army."

"Army or no army, I propose to keep the doors locked," she said. "Perhaps you have not considered that I am now alone here, George."

"If I see it needs a hurry," said George, "I'll knock on the knocker. That be O.K.?"

"That will be all right," she said.

As soon as she judged that the man had departed, she went out for the bottle of sherry. But she was not satisfied to take George's absence for granted, and she took a look in the kitchen before she went to the office. She would have liked to explain to herself why she did this; why, in fact, it seemed so important that George should not see her drinking sherry. She had had wine and sherry all her life, and it had never occurred to her to consider what her servants would think of that. Now, for some reason—perhaps because of the sense of well-being that had been generated in her by the exhibition of herself drinking a glass of milk on George's previous visit?—it was shaming to contemplate, almost as though it signified publicly a weakness she was extraordinarily anxious to conceal. There was nothing shameful, she thought confusedly, about being upset by a hurricane. The taste in her mouth (very bitter and strong now), the dryness of her throat, the queer, almost sick lassitude of her body and in particular of her legs, these were involuntary symptoms, quite beyond control. Was she not in full control of all her other forces?

There returned to her the image, and the physical sensations, of her moment at the window when she had tried to prevent George from closing those last shutters. There was something so wrong, so abnormal, so patently uncontrolled about that incident, that it became larger than life-size in her mind, standing suddenly and precariously for everything she had felt (and indeed suffered) within herself since that hour, now so long, long ago, when she had turned off the radio after its warning of danger to come; when she had decided, against her will almost, that there would be a hurricane. Everything, she thought, was wrong, horribly wrong! What was there about these storms—the very recurrence of which was a shocking and abnormal phenomenon—that created the sense of wrongness in her? Invaded, or alone, it made no difference. Well, there was this about it at least: it was not her fault, it was not of her doing.

Uncomfortably though dimly aware that this might not be altogether true, she turned to the job of moving the stacked pictures away from the cupboard wherein was the sherry. The effort made her very hot, the sweat poured off her body. She found, to her intense annoyance, she had forgotten the keys, and she had to go back to the library and fetch them; the effort so expended seemed tremendous.

Finally she opened the cupboard, got out the sherry bottle—it was three-quarters full—and locked up the cupboard again. Then she got a glass from the pantry and went back to the library. It seemed to her, when she finally sat down in her morris chair, that she could not have gone a step further. Her hand shaking slightly—from fatigue, she thought—she poured herself a glass of sherry. Before she drank from it, she recorked the bottle, put it, not on the table by her side, but on the floor under the table, in the dark. It was an involuntary act. Then she sipped her drink.

Its taste was wonderfully good. It was a good, sound wine, she thought, neither too heavy nor too dry. It cut the abominable taste in her mouth, her throat relaxed, she could feel the warmth of the stuff as it went down to her stomach. This was better than brandy, it was softer, it shocked one less, it comforted as much.

It came to her as she finished her glass and refilled it, that this was the second time in her life she had taken alcoholic drink for a purpose other than purely social or for the sensible increase of appetite. Well, after all, this was the second time she had been subjected to a hurricane. But the difference in the two storms was great, wasn't it? They, which had merged in her mind before so frighteningly, were separate now; she was living in this one only, she was looking back, almost detachedly, on the other. How odd that other had been! How odd those people were!

Thinking about them now in a new security, it occurred to her, suddenly and for the first time, how little she had known or, indeed, knew now, about those people. She knew more about Maude Cleever now than she had known five hours ago. How odd that was! With a strong effort, she removed what she knew from her mind: she was not going to think about that. Not at all! But the others. Mrs. Barber was no harm—a good, common little woman, of no account. But Birac was an adventurer, a ne'er-do-weel. Lucy Lagonegro was a—well, a common, vulgar, ill-educated little Italian girl, however pretty she was. How *could* Maude Cleever have taken her into her household? Again Miss Leckton shied off the thought of Mrs. Cleever. And as for that Frosten! A shiftless, dirty, dishonest, alcoholic native. How had he got here? How had he found Lucy? What would he have done, if he had not been interrupted? It was revolting to think of.

Why should one harbor people like that? It wasn't as though they were—what was the word?—valuable sorts of people. No. Even if (this was a new thought to Miss Leckton) she should have welcomed them more than she had done—which was a debatable point—how could one be expected to welcome any and all riffraff that a storm deposited at one's doorstep? Well, she didn't have to decide that now, thank God! There was no one here now.

There was so little comfort in that last thought, that Miss Leckton stirred a little in her chair, finished her second glass of sherry. The taste in her mouth was gone now. There must be things she should be doing. What things? Must she do anything now? There was no alteration in the high, shrieking sound of the night's storm; the house shook with great regularity and force. What good would she accomplish by moving around the house now? Was she not tired? Was she not better off here, resting? Even if she was alone?

Her head dropped, her eyes closed. She made an effort to raise her head, open her eyes; gave it up as a waste of effort. It crossed her mind again that she had still an unsolved problem in those invaders of her house in the other storm: that she should know more about them; that if she did, it would answer something, something she had just been thinking about, something about their value, her duty toward them. That she knew too much here, too little there. Maude Cleever. No. No. Lucy and Frosten, the unshaved man, the naked girl. The people who came at you, from nowhere, and you had no key to them, no *reason* for having to harbor them, feed them, protect them.

If one knew ... knew ... something unpleasant, now, would be solved ... would open up ... more unpleasantly ... less?

Miss Leckton had fallen into an uneasy sleep.

XIV

LITTLE RIMMON is a fishing village that lies three miles across water southeast of Olneys Point; though by following the curving arc of the low, watery land, the road traverses almost seven miles. The village is built on the sea rim of marsh and sandy dunes that enclose Anamasset Pond, a big body of partly navigable salt water fed by tides that flood swiftly in and out through Anamasset Reach. The village has the sad picturesqueness of a poverty that seems natural and inevitable to its inhabitants.

When the 1938 hurricane struck Little Rimmon, the hungry water of the sea drove over the dunes and devoured most of that village. Except for Lucy Lagonegro, who was fifteen years old and had learnt to swim well, the entire Lagonegro family was destroyed.

It happened with great swiftness. Luca Lagonegro had just come into this four-room one-storey shack. He had on his oilskins; he had just set another pair of mooring lines, of new rope, to his boat. Caterina, his wife, was cooking at the kerosene stove and saying prayers in Italian in an audible monotone, though without panic. The baby, Roberto, was playing on the floor with Amelia, who was seven, and John, who was ten. Maria, eight years old, was looking at a picture book that had doll cutouts in it, seated at the table by the west window. Stefano, fourteen, who had a right leg slightly crippled from infantile paralysis, was cleaning a mess of scup at the sink. All of them, then, except for Lucy, were gathered in the kitchen.

Lucy was tidying up the room she shared with Amelia and Maria, pulling the coverlet straight on the big double bed they slept in together. It was only because she was in that room that she had not perished with the others. It had been built by Luca as an ell to the house, and it was, essentially, a separate twelve-foot-square structure, on its own piling foundations, and the only real connection it had with the house proper was the door he had cut through the west wall. The big bed lay close against the old exterior wall, its weathered shingles still in place as the now interior wall-covering.

When the great wave (the wall of water that was driven by the hurricane over the two high tides the winds had held from ebbing) struck Little Rimmon, it sheared off the dunes, tore through the short length of Anamasset Reach, rushed with inevitable force and uproar over the flooded and turgid waters of Anamasset Pond, struck at the docks, the boats, the houses grouped on the thin strip of land that made the northeast side of the pond itself, and flooded its low, sandy area to a depth of six feet of mad and yellow water. Since the strip of land was less than a quarter of a mile wide, most of the debris that the wave and its parent wind picked up, was flung into the ocean and there was rendered swiftly to its component parts. Its effect on the Lagonegro house was typical of all those destroyed.

Suddenly and with no warning at all the water burst through the door and the windows. Within seconds it had flooded the room, and such was its pressure that the south wall collapsed without noticeable sound in that fury of sound, and the roof fell in and was torn sidewise and ripped off, but not before it had stunned Luca and his wife (in the midst of her prayers) ; killed Roberto outright by breaking his neck; broken Amelia's left leg and hip and partially stunned her; cut Maria virtually in half and so swiftly that she felt nothing before she died. John, untouched, was caught under the west wall when it collapsed; he was pinned there and drowned. Stefano was flung clear by a freak of water pressure, but the knife that he had automatically clung to, cut the artery in his left wrist and, swimming for a little while, half on top of, half under, that swift torrent, he weakened soon from loss of blood and was drowned like the rest of them.

With Lucy it was different. The little addition was torn loose both from the house and from its own piling, and upset onto its side. One moment the girl had stood bending over the iron bed; the next, she was flung forward on it, the pillows at its end breaking her fall. The bed, standing on its head for a brief moment, fell further until the high foot-board jammed against the now vertical ceiling. The force of the water and the wind rolled the whole structure over once more, and then the room broke into parts, the walls splitting outward like the developed drawing of a cube. Protected by the bed and its mattress that lay on top of her, Lucy was not touched by the collapsing floor above her. When the water seized her, she was impelled out from under the jammed bed, gasping and clutching at the buoyant mattress.

For a few, interminable minutes that was all she knew. She could only, and with good instinct, hold her breath. She could see nothing because her eyes were tight shut. She could hear only the sound of water about her ears, that dulled and bubbling sound of underwater foam. The mattress was rolled and tossed, it had a life of its own, it heaved and rippled and its ends slapped forward and back. But Lucy's grip was on its edge, her body lay over the center of it, and she did not loose her frantic hold until she was well clear of the shore.

When she opened her eyes, Lucy could see nothing but the water around her, and that but for a short distance. As the mattress floated in its jerky, undulant progress, it revolved, and Lucy, peering to see where she was, could not tell even in which direction she was going. Near at hand, and behaving in a peculiar and most frightening manner, was a huge piece of piling, and the mattress was going toward it.

From time to time the piling would upend its dark and

creosoted ends, to which were still bolted the heavy and jagged fragments of cross-bracing. Then, after it had seemed to hang suspended in this position for a long time, it would slide swiftly down, in a scything, deadly motion, and float almost submerged.

The idea of the mattress becoming entangled with this menacing thing terrified Lucy, and she began to kick with her feet in an effort to move the mattress further away from the piling. It was then that she became aware of her sneakers, high ones, that she had had for basketball this winter at Cottrellton High School. They seemed very clumsy and heavy, full of water. They impeded her kicking. Very carefully she let go with one hand and tried to reach the laces of her right sneaker. She got the knot undone, was loosening the laces when the mattress struck against the piling, lifted over it. Lucy clutched again with both hands at the mattress' edge.

Then the piling, impelled by the vortex of water in which it drifted, upended again, mattress and all, and Lucy was flung free of the mattress in a neat somersault and plunged into the water without support. She sank a little, rose, was knocked dizzy by the crest of a wave that smote her emerging head, swallowed some salt water. She was really frightened now, and she felt sick at the same time. Before, everything had been happening so fast that she had not had time for fear or for any distinct emotion.

In the grip of this fear, Lucy tried to swim. She neither knew nor cared in what direction she went; she was simply and powerfully moved to be away from the place she found herself in, no matter where; somewhere else would be safe; here was terror and danger. Her cotton dress dragged in the water, her water-filled sneakers pulled her feet down. The waves were not high, but the incessant whips of the spray, the tops that were flung entire from the smallest eminence of water, made swimming virtually impossible. In her terror, her panic, she did not understand that. It is probable that a little more of this frantic attempt to swim would have exhausted her so much that she would have drowned.

175

As her head emerged from the hard buffet of a wave-top, Lucy opened her eyes. Directly in front of her was a small tin washboiler, its top gone, floating at a sharp angle. Out of the washboiler projected the head and shoulders of a doll, its blond hair thick and curly in spite of the wet, its bright pink dress (the color intensified by the wetness) showing cheerfully on the shoulders. One arm of the doll was raised stiffly, as though to wave at someone, and the doll's face was pink and smiling. Its odd craft bobbed and dipped, whirled around from time to time, and drifted past Lucy.

So astonishing was this miniature spectacle, so cheerful and imperturbable was the expression of the doll, that Lucy found her eyes following its progress in the washboiler. To look, she had ceased her swimming and was treading water; and as the doll moved past her down wind, going further and further away, Lucy watched it. It was thus that she gradually realized that she was now facing away from the wind, was merely keeping herself afloat, and that it was not too difficult. From time to time the water flung itself at the back of her head; sometimes she was wholly covered by it; but this was not too hard to cope with, she was swallowing no more water. It seemed to her then that the thing to do was to follow the doll, to drift with it, and that thus she would come to safety. If only, she thought, I could get off these sneakers!

Very carefully, holding her breath, keeping her mouth tightly closed, she began to work again on the sneaker she had already loosened. She could do it only in short inter-rupted movements, for each time she bent her knee to draw her foot upward within reach of her hands, she submerged her head; but by careful persistence she got the right sneaker off her foot.

As the sneaker came off she brought it to the surface in her hand. What should she do with it? Let it go? If she could hang on to it until she got the other off, she could tie the laces together, hang the sneakers around her neck. Carefully she tried to hold the sneaker under one arm, reach the other sneaker with her hands. It was impossible. The waves were breaking too roughly, the storm was too violent, too terrifying for any movement so methodical. She needed both her hands, unimpeded. It would be necessary to let the sneaker go.

As Lucy realized this, it occurred to her how awful that was. Sneakers cost so much money! It had taken so much persuasion, such careful argument, to cajole her mother into letting her buy them. She remembered the shifts she had used—how she had even talked to her about it in Italian, a language she hated to use, but that was so much easier for her mother to understand. And thinking of this, Lucy became aware of her mother, her father, her sisters and brothers, and that she did not know where they were, or what had happened to them. Were they alive? It was not possible to conceive of them as anything but alive. But where? What had that awful wave of water done to them? Would she ever see them again?

Now for the first time she knew herself to be alone, and her heart beat faster within her, in increasing anguish and fright. I am alone, she said to herself. I'm all alone. There ain't nobody but me. There ain't nobody to help me. I got to help myself. God helps them that helps theirself.

Still clutching the sneaker, treading water, her head above the surface only about half the time, Lucy tried to pray. She thought: I must say the Our Father and the Hail Mary. I must say them now.

She tried to pray but she could not remember the words in English. They kept getting mixed up with Italian words— the Italian she hated so much, that symbolized everything you tried to get away from, by being American. The Our Father confused with her love for her father and mother and her contempt of them because they were not really Americans, had not been born here. They spoke two languages, and only one well, the words mixed. She gave up the Our Father and tried the Hail Mary, and that went better, she was halfway through, she had said, "blessed is the fruit of thy womb, Jesus," when the water hit her again and submerged her deeply. It drove the prayers from her head, it drove her down and down. It seemed forever before she got to the top again, could suck in a breath of air, could hear again the terrible sound of the wind. The thing to do was to get off that other sneaker, let this one go, it was a waste, it was probably sinful. She must be sinful, or she could say her prayers. When she had got rid of the other sneaker, she'd float better, she'd try again, she'd pray, say the Acts of Contrition. God is punishing me, she thought, and maybe He is going to let me drown—I'll pray St. Christopher too. Perhaps the sneaker would float, and floating, stay near enough to be grabbed again when she got the other off, using both hands so as to be quick. She put the sneaker on the surface near her, having emptied it of water. It floated a second, submerged, still floated just below the surface.

Taking a deep breath she drew up her left foot, fumbled with the laces. They had got into a knot. She tore at them, pulled, yanked. She could feel the laces, pulled taut, bite into her ankle. Then she had to let go, breathe. As she breathed, a wave-top struck her; she went under. When she came up, the floating sneaker had disappeared. In a curious way it was a relief. It was gone. You didn't have to think about that any more.

Reaching down again, she caught the laces, tugged. They broke. In a moment she had the sneaker off. She just let it go, it was no use. What use was one sneaker? She reached down again, pulled off her cotton socks. She felt lighter, easier, it was far simpler now to keep up in the water. But she realized she was feeling tired, that her arms felt numb, her legs were heavy. How long could people keep afloat? In a storm. In a terrible storm.

After the next wave broke over her, she saw a huge thing like a raft near her, only it wasn't a raft, it was a funny shape, with angles and bumps. It was floating. It was something she could float on, it was very large. She swam toward it, it was only a few yards off. She reached out her hand to touch it, was flung against it. As her body struck it, she realized it was completely studded with the dull-sharp points of nails. They hurt her hands, her shoulders. She tried to push clear, but found her dress caught on the nails. Terrified lest another

178

wave drive her against those many points, she pushed frantically, cutting the palm of her hand in several places. The dress tore and ripped, but she was free. She turned as fast as she could, and swam away. Then, judging herself clear, she once more began to tread water, her back to the wind and the waves. The raft—the thing with nails—was gone as though it had never existed. She felt tired and her very tiredness frightened her.

Her ripped dress now floated up around her, hampering the motion of her arms. It would be good to get it off, she thought, but difficult. It would have to come off over her head. Once she had it off, there would be nothing to bother her, it was all she wore. Could she rip it? It frightened her to think of getting it over her head, having it stick there, the wet cloth over her face. She could try to rip it.

She felt for the rip, found it, followed it up with her fingers, seized firm hold, tugged. The material tore easily until it came to the hems at her neck and arms. Now the whole dress floated around her, only the top of it attached it to her, it was over her arms, it was making it difficult to move. She tore the two buttons loose in the back and, treading water violently, gathered the dress till she had all of it within her two hands, got one arm free and then the other, lifted the dress over her head. It did not catch, it came loose. She was free of it. In her relief, she threw it from her, and it floated near her.

The relief that Lucy felt, while great, was only momentary. For a short while it seemed to her that it was infinitely easier to maneuver her body around in the water, stay afloat, drift with the storm; then she began to feel tired again, her legs in particular grew heavy, and she felt cold. The water had seemed warm, unusually warm, when she had first gone into it, but now it became chilling, and she felt her stomach began to tremble a little with the cold. She tried to swim fast. It was difficult and she tired at once, and the warmth that the action generated didn't last. She began to be frightened again. It seemed to her that this fatigue was growing on her, and that with the chills that struck through her now and again, she was going to perish here, alone, at sea, in a storm. Death was not a thing she had ever before contemplated; it was altogether beyond her to imagine such a thing could happen to her, and yet there existed within her a terror of death, of destruction, that was as powerful as it was undefined.

So strong was the effect on her of this emotion of fear that she struck out again, swimming rapidly, using the crawl with the naturalness of the child who has been taught to swim when young, until she was so tired she could no longer lift her arms forward for her strokes. Treading water again, afraid to float on her back for fear of the heavy blows of solid water that would descend on her face, she saw the dress she had discarded, floating near her, its green-and-white pattern undulating on the surface. It shocked her, because she had thought she had left it far behind. How did it come here? Had she been swimming in a circle?

It was while she was watching the dress in the water that she saw the telephone pole. It was floating along quite near her, very steadily. Unlike the piling it did not upend itself. It did not even roll.

Without hesitation she swam toward it, but this time she approached it cautiously, fearful of more nails. When she was alongside, she reached out her hand to it, felt it. It was of rough texture, but she could feel nothing on it to hurt her. With immense relief, tempered with a sharp dread of what this pole might do, she rested her arms over its large diameter. The pole seemed not to change its position in any way, it submerged only a little more for her weight. It was blissful to hang to it, her feet dragging out behind and below her, no effort needed to stay afloat. She was on the windward side of it, the blows of driven water hit her from behind or from the side. If she kept her mouth closed, breathed cautiously through her nose, she would be all right. The only thing that bothered her now was the thought that this pole might revolve. She could not understand why it did not.

Looking around her carefully, she discovered the reason. The four wooden crosspieces of the pole were still attached firmly to the top of the pole. They acted to keep it steady and, at the same time, to make it float in the one direction, its butt end (which she could not see) pointed away from the wind.

For a little while Lucy was content merely to rest so. She could feel her strength returning to her, and this gave her confidence. Somehow, too, the excitement of discovering the pole, of exploring its surface, had warmed her; the chills had stopped. But now another trouble came: she was conscious that the rough surface of the wood was chafing her chest, the soft skin of her upper arms. If she went on like this, hanging to the pole as it heaved and moved about in the turmoil of the water, she'd soon be rubbed raw.

She was sorry now that she had taken off her dress. Thin as it was, it would have protected her while it no longer hampered her. Why had she taken it off? It was hard to remember, it seemed a long time ago.

Everything seemed a long time ago. The images of her recent past came clearly into her mind now, pictures of her house, her parents, her brothers and sisters, herself making the bed in the ell; they were removed in time, part of another world; they made her feel sad, deserted, lonely; but they were distant. All that counted now was the present, this business of hanging on, of keeping afloat, of protecting her skin from the rough wood.

There was such an incessant curtain of spray that she could not see more than a few yards in any direction; so it surprised her when she saw the dress, still afloat, a large bubble of air caught under its fabric, not above six feet off from her pole. The thing to do was to get it, it would protect her; but the act she must perform to reach it terrified her even to plan. She would have to let go, swim to the dress, bring it back. The pole might disappear (as the big nail-studded raft-thing had disappeared) the moment she left it, turned her back on it. If the skin of her chest and arms had not felt so sore, she would not have attempted it.

She took a deep breath, flexed her arms to push herself off from the pole—then could not. It was as if her arms would not obey her, rebelled against her decision. Once more she breathed in deeply, counted to herself—one, two, three!—and pushed; then turned swiftly, full of terror, swam to the dress, seized it, and began (hampered frighteningly by the act of clutching the wet fabric in her left hand) to swim back. She could see the pole: it seemed far away, the few feet were miles.

But now she was at the pole, her hand reached out—with the same tentative gesture she had first used, as though it might suddenly have developed spikes and nails since she had left it—touched it, clung to it. She put the dress over the pole, leant on it, clutched now with both arms again. The dress felt wonderfully soft and smooth; the pole seemed then to her as though it were home, as though she had returned to all that meant safety and security.

This feeling of safety persisted strongly, and she was impelled again to think of her family. Thinking of them, wondering what had become of them, she remembered that she had not prayed, that she had never finished the Hail Mary, the Our Father, nor had she asked St. Christopher to help her—and yet she had been helped. It was a terrible thing to be ungrateful. Almighty God and the Blessed Virgin and St. Christopher—and St. Anthony, too, who had floated the dress near her—had miraculously looked after her, had seen her in the midst of the waves, had reached out their hands to save her. Her gratitude to them welled up in her like a sense of warmth from a fire, and without difficulty she prayed to St. Anthony to thank him for her dress returned to her. Then she prayed to St. Christopher and she said the Our Father clearly, all the way through, her lips moving a little, and no Italian phrases bothered her; and without pausing and because she had been helped although she had not prayed, she said the Acts of Contrition then and the Act of Love.

In a moment, she thought, she would close her eyes and say the Hail Mary. She would close her eyes because you closed your eyes to pray, and because thus she could see the Virgin in her mind, all the beauty and the goodness of the world contained in her beauty and her smile; seeing her, you would be with her. Although this would be wonderful (it would be full of comfort, it would breed strength in her, warmth in her), yet she put it off. There was terror, too, in closed eyes—you could not see the waves, you could not see what might come at you, nor what was going to happen.

She began to feel cold again, and with the cold came the little chills, growing stronger, shaking her each time a little more. Fear began again to run through her: fear and cold were the same. There was no one to help you, except God and His saints and the Mother of Jesus. Yet you could not come to her, the spray and the waves were barriers between you and her comfort, and it was too terrifying now to close your eyes. Would you ever open them again? And if you did—when you did—what would you see?

All her emotions were simple and direct, they followed one on the other as the forces of fear and loneliness and youth and innocence worked on her in the face of the storm. Thinking back on this in later years, when she had become wholly mature and wholly corrupt and when her battle for her personal redemption was still ahead of her, it seemed to her that this was the highest point of happiness in her life; that all the emotions that flooded her then were as clear and as clean as the storm that bred them; that the terror of the storm was only a power to arouse her, to show forth her own innocence and the simple beauty of trying to live—to live, but to do so within the orbit of the God she had later lost and might never find again—or, finding, discover as a different being, His manifold face no longer full of the sweetness of loving compassion.

Now she gripped tight to the pole, tighter than before, feeling its length heave and sway steadily under her body, the coldness of the water around her legs. The chills shook her now less often, but she felt herself becoming numb. It was hard to move; it was a great effort to have legs at all, they dragged so at your body. It would be best to pray now, for if she did not pray, she would be lost, she would not be able to hold on, the water would take her.

She closed her eyes—it was, as she did so, a sweet sensation, giving rest, no longer a fearful act—and she began to say, not the Hail Mary, but the lovely prayer that begins "Immaculate Heart of Mary, pray for me," and she said it over and over, and as she did so, she could see the Holy Mother of God before her, her powder-blue gown falling over her knees, her face alight with love and beauty and kindliness.

The prayers trailed off in her mind . . . the Virgin became part of the sound of the storm . . . and she did not know anything more for a long time.

XV

HARRY FROSTEN had no sooner closed the slanting cellar doors (it wasn't possible to lock them from the outside) and got the privy and the hydrangea on the rise of land between him and the house, than he remembered that he hadn't shaved.

"God damn it to hell!" he said, and he rubbed his hand over the two-day black stubble on his chin.

There was no use in going back. He'd have to go through the kitchen to get to his own room upstairs and Grandma and Uncle Leonard were sitting there. As soon as he came in, the questions would start. "Where you been, Harry?" and "What you been doin', Harry?" And the minute he came back shaved and tried to get down cellar again, there'd be the inevitable "Where you goin', Harry?" Jesus Christ Almighty, you'd think he was ten years old instead of twenty-two, way they kept after him. And deaf as Grandma was, wasn't nothing the matter with her eyesight, she'd spot him having shaved, sure as hell.

Squatting on the ground back of the huge hydrangea bush, he got mad all over just thinking about it. Trying to lead some sort of life of your own, way it was, come hard. If he owned the house, it couldn't have been more trouble. Grandma old and deaf as a post, and no use to no one only to cook, and Uncle Leonard with no proper use to his legs— everything happened in this house, it had to be done by him,

185

Harry. Fix the God damn roof, fetch the food, see to the boats, mend the windows, cut and haul the wood, set traps for bait, dry the seines. Leonard was a good hand to row and fish and haul seine, but there was all there was to it. Rest of the time he just set there and ate and slept. And Grandma set there and ate and slept and talked. And in between times they'd ask questions. "Where you been, Harry? Where you goin', Harry? Harry, you been drinkin' again?"

He felt the hip pocket of his blue jeans. It had a comfortable bulge. He hadn't forgotten the pint of whiskey, anyway. Full, too, brand new. That was something. Betty might get sore at him for being unshaved, but after she had a couple pulls of this oil, she'd forget that. It didn't take more than a couple slugs to fix Betty up and then she just wanted one thing and by guy! he was the one to give it to her. Still, he wished he was shaved. Not being shaved, there'd be arguments, and more questions. "Why didn't you shave, Harry? What sort of girl you think I am to meet a boy ain't got no more respect for me than to come like this?" And maybe she'd get after him about his clothes, because he hadn't changed; say he stank of fish, or some damn foolishness like that. And all the time he'd have to try to get her to take a slug—oh, she'd take it in time—and not be able to explain.

Christ! How could you explain that a man of twenty-two had to sneak out the cellar door of his house to get to see a girl? You couldn't explain it, it made you sound too much of a sucker. You couldn't tell about Grandma and Uncle Leonard and the questions. Betty didn't live with them. She didn't know what it was like, day in, day out. "Where you been, Harry? Why don't you git the wood in, Harry? Where's the seine, Harry? What you goin' to do now, Harry?" Drove you crazy.

Well, he'd just have to go without shaving, in his old clothes. Beard or no beard, fish or no fish, he wasn't going to go back into that house. No, sir. Not this day.

What the hell, he thought, is the matter with them two old fools? Sure, it blew a gale. So what? Warn't the first gale ever blowed on that house, for God's sake. "Don't you go to leave, Harry," Uncle Leonard had said. "She's goin' to blow more before it gits less. I can tell." Ah, the hell with it! Suppose they were old and everything. Did he have to stick around that house *all* day just because a couple old fools was nervous? He had his date with Betty, didn't he? Wasn't he to have no fun?

It would be fun, too. God! Get a couple slugs into Betty, and then the fun would start. He felt the blood run up to his head and he tingled all over his body. Then he got up and walked, crouched over a little, toward the boathouse. There wasn't much chance he'd be seen.

He had meant to take the skiff and row down Naius River to the Backwater, and tie up there. Then all he'd have to do would be to cross the marsh and the field to get to the Nichols barn. He pulled out his dollar watch. It said three-thirty-five. He had an hour. Betty would reach the barn about half past four. She was usually there when she said. Yes, sir. When she wanted it, she wanted it, and she didn't waste no time. She certainly knew plenty for a girl of fourteen. She'll know more after this afternoon, he thought, and he grinned, showing his dirty, broken teeth. She'd get there ahead of him, this weather, and she'd wait in the barn, under the hayloft, as she usually did. He'd stick his head in the door and say, "You there?" and she'd giggle at him out of the dusky interior. He grinned again.

When he got to the boathouse, though, he realized he'd never get down to the Backwater by skiff. By God! It did blow! Blowed a gale. There just wasn't a chance of rowing a skiff alone against that wind. Two might make it, but not one.

He looked at the river. Never seen the tide so high, he thought. Too God damn high altogether. Water right up to the floor of the boathouse, the whole marsh to the south of him covered over, whitecaps on that protected water. Didn't see whitecaps there often, and he never remembered to have seen them so big. Warm wind, too warm. Wasn't seasonable, not from the southeast.

Well, here was more trouble. How in hell was he to cross

the river? He'd have to go by Cross Bridge, right here, or by the Iron Bridge to the south. Go by Cross Bridge and Grandma'd see him, likely, or Uncle Leonard. Go by Iron Bridge, and he'd have two miles extra, maybe three, to walk, it was that far to the southward of Nichols barn. A puzzle.

He looked eastward across Naius River. The water was right over the flat marsh there, and it was breaking against the stone ballast of the road embankment. He could get into his skiff and row right across to the road, but what'd he do with the thing when he got there? It'd just knock itself to pieces against that ballast, this wind. Maybe he could row up along this side of the river, go under the bridge, come at the roadway from the north, the lee side. If he stayed real close to the bank, the tide high the way it was, neither of them old people might see him. That's what he'd do. Walk to Iron Bridge, he'd be late now, and then maybe Betty'd be gone from the barn. It made him feel sick at the bottom of his belly to imagine that.

He shipped a lot of water getting the skiff into the river, rough the way it was and the tide so crazy high. He got his feet soaking wet, but he didn't mind that, he was too used to it, and anyway the water was as warm as soup. It came into his mind that he ought to be right here fishing, the place ought to be full of skipjacks, way the tide was, high and still flooding strongly. But he wasn't going fishing, no, sir. He'd something better to do now than fish.

The only trouble he had was to keep the boat off the shore. He didn't need to row. He had the wind behind him, the tide with him. He simply used one oar to pole the boat off the bank, and he made a jerky progress along the edge of the land. He floated under Cross Bridge's west span and, in the lee of the bridge, sculled the skiff across the river's narrow width, over the flooded marsh, along the embankment. He sculled and poled until the skiff ran aground. Then he nosed her around till the bow was against the heavy ballast, hopped out, and made the painter fast to a young wild cherry growing out of the rocks, its roots right in the water. Then he climbed up to the road and headed east. If his grandma saw him now, it would be just too bad. "Where was you goin'? Why did you leave us alone in that storm, Harry?" she'd say. Christ, he could almost hear her. Well, maybe she hadn't seen him. Or Uncle Leonard. The Nugent Family, settin' at home, by God. If they hadn't of seen him, he'd say he was working to the boathouse, fixing things up, mending the crab-car. Yep.

But Mrs. Iffley had seen him. He found that out later, and no mistake neither. She burnt the ears right off of him. "Where was you in the hurricane, you low-down good-for-nothin'?" she cried out at him. "Where was you? Whorin' around, I'll bet my bottom dollar. Drinkin' and whorin' around, while your old grandma Nugent was left alone, nobody but your uncle and him a cripple, to tend her, roof blown off, windows blown out, no one but the neighbors to save 'em. Yes, sir, you useless, drunken sot, it had to be the neighbors—her own kin had left her. And not a word. And if she dies now, you can thank yourself. And I'll remember it too. Yes, sir, I ain't one to forgit. I seen you. I watched you sneakin' acrost with the skift. I won't forgit. And no one won't forgit about Betty Gould, neither."

But that all came later. He was unaware now that anyone had seen him; he wanted so to believe no one had noticed his maneuver that he willed it to be so. He struck off for the fork, headed south there, following the river road. He walked as fast as he could against the powerful gusts of the wind, he didn't want to be late. There was something waiting for him he didn't want to miss, no, sir. Nice. Pretty and warm and cute. And wanting it. Wriggling and crying out, sometimes those little, wordless cries, sometimes the little understandable ones like "Oh, Harry, Harry!" He began to sweat in anticipation, his mouth was dry. He took out the bottle, broke the stamp, unscrewed the stopper, had a good pull. Aah! That was the stuff! Only thing was, he wished he had more. Betty would take only her two, maybe three pulls, but they'd be big ones. Might not be enough here to git real drunk on, the lovely feeling, the lighter-than-air feeling, with the God damn Nugent Family, Grandma and her by-God

189

son, forgotten just for a bit, while you thought about yourself. And Betty. But Betty for yourself, yes, sir.

It was harder and harder to walk now. The wind kept coming in fierce gusts, each one stronger. Sometimes he had to stop, bend his head, gasp for breath. It was the strongest wind he ever remembered. A full gale. Better than a gale, seems so, he thought. Between the gusts, he walked as fast as the wind would let him. There was an excitement to weather like this, it made you feel good.

As he walked, he began to wonder if Betty would come out, a day like this. It was almost a mile from Chet Gould's garage to the Nichols barn. Maybe she wouldn't of come. If she didn't come, how would he get to her? It was bad to go to the garage, Chet didn't like him there, neither did Mrs. Gould. Betty had to lie to them to see him. Or sneak off, like him. Difference was, they ordered her round on account she was only fourteen. Fourteen, hell! She acted like a growed woman, didn't she? She looked like one, too. And felt like one. I'll say! he said to himself.

The wind increased all the time, and the sound of it kept rising. He'd never heard a wind like that. For all that he was in the lee of the steep slope of Long Ridge, heavily grown with birch and maple, sumach and scrub oak, it was at moments not only impossible to walk, but even to stand erect. He'd have to crouch down in the lee of the stone wall that bordered the road, wait for the wind to subside a little, his body still shaken slightly by the force of the air.

Jesus, he thought, what'll this wind do to that old barn? Nobody'd lifted a hand to it for over ten years, not since the Nichols place burned. The roof was rotted, the doors were broken. By God, it wouldn't hardly be safe to go into it, wind like this. Damn it, he said, everything's wrong today. He wanted Betty Gould fiercely now: the more fiercely because he could foresee he might not have her. Squatting below the wall, he took another pull at his bottle. Probably no use to save it now, anyway. The liquor burned pleasantly as it went down. Well, he thought, nothing to do but git there, see if she ain't there. Then I'll scout Chet's garage. She might hang around out back, near the truck in the car dump. No use to give up yet. She usually wanted it as much as he did. If Betty warn't there, if he couldn't git her at Chet's, maybe he could git to see Annie Latchik. She might be mad he hadn't been around so long, but she might not, too. All depended on whether her folks were to home or not. Usually they warn't back till around eight, coming from Pawtucket. But Annie warn't Betty, no, sir.

It was almost four-thirty when he got to the Nichols farm, but the barn was not in sight from the road. He climbed the old barway, over the gold and salmon-colored poison ivy, walked over the little rise of land, past the blackened chimney and the weed-filled foundation of the former house, and then he saw the barn, or what was left of it. It had blown down, and its old, musty hay was scattered all over the place in drifts that moved and stirred and blew on again. The broken roof was tumbled, still quivering in the wind, against the maples at the swamp edge; and as he watched, he saw some of the maples crack and break. It was a queer thing to watch, because you couldn't hear a thing—not a God damn thing except the noise, the yelling, of that high-pitched wind. The uprights of the barn had fallen over in a horrid tangle, and some of them lay quivering on top of the hay that had fallen when the hayloft collapsed, pinning it down, though chunks of hay were seized each moment by the gusts and torn loose by forkfuls.

Christ! he thought. We can't never use that again. Never again. All the times he had lain there with Betty! It had been a wonderful place for it. Soft. Dark. Deserted. Gone now. God damn!

He walked to windward of the barn—too many bits of stuff flying off to leeward—and looked for Betty. She might be here, even so. He looked near the stone wall, near the old spring-house, which still stood intact though trembling visibly. There was no one here. You could bet he warn't going to go near that barn any, no, sir. Too dangerous. Made you feel sick just to think of it. Thing to do now was to scout Gould's garage. He was talking aloud to himself now, saying,

"Betty'd never have come in this weather, likely. Guess not. No, sir. Geez, I wanted her bad. Well, it'll probably have to be Annie now."

He walked south on the road till he came to McTavish Hill and he climbed the dirt road up to the main road on the crest of Long Ridge. The wind blew so hard there that he had to cross it on all fours and he couldn't stand at all until he got in the lee of the wall to the east of the road, his feet in the grassy gutter. Following the gutter, he went south until he could see Gould's garage ahead of him, on his side of the road, the second-storey living quarters of the grey concrete block structure sticking up above the stone wall.

Harry crossed the wall, followed along another to the east, worked his way around behind the garage to the old car-dump. It was somewhat protected from the wind by the heavy belt of maples that grew east of it, though he was shocked to see how many of the trees were already blown down. He picked his way carefully between the cars to the center of the dump and to the old, grey truck chassis where Betty and he had been used to meet. She was not there. It didn't really surprise him: it was too exposed to this crazy wind. And it was raining now. Or was it rain? He ran his tongue over the moisture on his lips and tasted salt. Jesus! Salt spray a half mile from the sea! That was something.

He walked on, crouched over a little partly as a protection against being seen, partly as a help to progress in this wind, until he came behind the little concrete-block outbuilding where Chet Gould kept his own car and his stores. Betty was not there, either. Well, she was probably indoors. The only chance he had now was to show himself, briefly, in front of this garage-shed, and hope (it had happened before) that Betty would be watching out the window for him.

He moved around the shed and stood for a moment or two in plain sight of the rear windows of the garage. He looked up at the kitchen windows, but the light was bad, he couldn't see if anyone was there at the windows or not. Then he retired behind the shed again and waited. He looked at his watch. He'd wait ten minutes—till five o'clock—and if she

192

didn't show up by then, he'd go. This wasn't a good place to be. He took a pull at his pint flask to pass the time, to give himself some courage. Then, squatted down near the ground, he lit a cigarette. It was very hard to do, it took three matches.

He was taken by surprise when Chet Gould came round the end of the shed. For all he'd anticipated that danger, he hadn't expected it. It was so surprising, that he remained squatting, his cigarette in his mouth.

"What the hell you doin' here?" Chet yelled at him. Harry could see he was yelling by the expression on his face, but the words came faintly to him over the uproar of the storm.

Harry said nothing at all.

"I told you not to come slidin' around here, didn't I?" said Chet. "I told you you wasn't wanted here, didn't I?"

Harry just avoided his eyes and looked at the ground.

"Get the hell off my place!" yelled Chet. "And stay the hell off. Or I'll bust you with this." He had a wrecking bar in his hand and he waved it.

Harry stood up and took a step toward the edge of the shed.

"Where is Betty?" shouted Chet.

Harry stopped and turned.

"Christ," he said. "I dunno."

"She sneaked out, must a been an hour or more back. Didn't tell her ma. Where is she?"

"I ain't seed her," said Harry.

"You ain't, eh?" said Chet. "Well, by God, I wisht I knew where she was, day like this. Anything happen to her, by God, I'll fix you."

"I ain't seed her," Harry repeated, his mouth sullen and angry.

"Why the hell ain't you to home?" said Chet. "Why ain't you lookin' after your old folks, storm like this? What you doin' out and around here?"

"I was just out," said Harry. "Goin' home now."

"In a pig's eye," yelled Chet, his face red now with his shouting and with anger. "Git out of here, you hear me? Git!

And don't come back around here no more, you understand?"

Harry didn't answer. He turned away quickly and slid past the edge of the shed and, bracing back hard against the wind, walked to the road. He turned south along it, following the gutter. That wasn't the way home, it was opposite to home. He looked back. He saw Chet Gould, the iron bar in his hand, watching him.

The hell with him! Harry thought. It ain't none of his God damned business where I go or when. In a moment now he was out of sight, but he didn't stop until he was a quarter-mile along the road, opposite the lane that ran down to the northeast, to the Latchik's house. Then he squatted down in the gutter and had a good drink of his whiskey. The flask was almost half empty now. Well, Annie didn't like whiskey.

He tried to think about Annie, but he got nowhere with it. He was too angry. That Chet Gould! Guy, it made you mad! What had he done? Nothin'. Not a God damn thing. Warn't as if he'd caught him with Betty, was it?

Thinking of that, he began to wonder where Betty was. She warn't to home, Chet had said. Nor by the shed, nor by the truck. Nor at the Nichols barn. Jesus, he thought, suppose she was? Suppose she'd got down there, had waited for him. Well, he'd a seen her, wouldn't he? He'd looked all around. Everywhere—but in the barn.

It gave him a queer shaky feeling to think about that. She couldn't of been in the barn. No. God, no! He hadn't seen her. No one knew that they'd met there. No one knew he'd been there. Thing to do was to git away from here. And not go near that barn. They couldn't pin anything on him. It warn't his fault if . . . anything had happened. He warn't there. Hadn't been there, anyone asked.

He went down the lane toward Annie's house. He knew now that he was doing so because he wanted to get away from Chet Gould, and away from the barn, as quickly as possible, not at all because he wished to see Annie. The idea of Annie now quite simply revolted him: he thought of her with distaste, remembering how fat she was, how soft, how she squealed and hung onto you. All the fear that was rising up in him now (and which he neither tried to define nor was capable of analyzing) centered in this distaste for Annie, the second choice, the discarded choice.

The lane was deeply cut and had high walls on both sides. It was well protected from the wind. Across it, at intervals, lay wild cherries and black ash trees and the branches of maples. They made progress very slow. When he came in sight of Annie's house, he climbed out of the lane, crossed the hayfield behind the remains of three haystacks whose tops had blown off and were streaming hay like smoke down wind. The sight of the hay disturbed him, and he hurried past, crossed into the cow pasture to the south, followed the cattle track past the spring and down the slope. When he reached the last stone wall he could see the ocean.

What really surprised him then was that the ocean was all he could see. The whole vast area of Mercy Bog, bounded on its west side by Ten Acre Creek, was under foaming water, yellow water, water that rushed around like a river gone crazy. There were queer conical waves that heaved up suddenly, and as suddenly the wind would seize them, shear them off, and they would disappear into the almost universal and stinging spray. Each time he raised his head above the protection of the wall, this spray would strike him, incessant and hurtful. Running his hand over his face, he could feel sand in the moisture. After that, he took only occasional quick looks at the water; but it was impossible not to look at all: it was too fascinating a spectacle.

Harry could feel his drink dying in him. It made him angry, it was a hell of a waste of liquor. If everything hadn't of gone wrong, he'd be a little drunk by now and he'd have been with Betty. But he didn't want to think about Betty. It made him feel sick and frightened. They couldn't pin a God damned thing on him, but ... well ... you didn't know. What would he do? Go back home? No, that was no use. Go somewhere, do something. Do something he could tell about. "All I done was go out to see the storm and then I went to so-and-so and I seen step-an'-fetchit, and we done this and that." That was what he wanted. No Annie, that you couldn't explain or talk about and anyway, who in hell wanted Annie? Women were just trouble. All you got was trouble from them. But where would he go?

There was the Twin Oak Inn up top of Olneys Ridge. He could go there, talk to Johnny Farber and any of the boys that was there. It had a good lookout over the ocean, kind of place you'd go to, to see a storm. Trouble was, to get there. Ordinary days, you'd walk along the upper edge of Mercy Bog, cross over Leckton's bridge, take the footpath back over the footbridge at the outlet to Ten Acre Pond, and follow the path along the edge of the marsh, past Tessie Barber's house and Olneys Pond, and up the hill to the Inn. But that couldn't be done now. The whole by-God marsh was under that crazy water, as far as you could see. You couldn't see very far with this spray, but if Mercy Bog was under salt water, you could be damn sure the low marsh back of Ten Acre would be.

So, you'd have to go back up the lane to the highroad, and along the road to Olneys Ridge and the Inn. Mile, mile and a half. Maybe too far? I dunno, he said to himself. I dunno. Jesus, I got to do something, I got to see somebody, have something I can tell about.

There was a momentary lull in the wind—not that it stopped blowing, but simply didn't blow so hard for a few seconds—and the spray lifted and blew past, and he could see the stump of Motherledge Lighthouse to the southward. For a moment he couldn't believe what he had seen: just the remains of the round black steel base of the light, the rest gone—the white tall shaft, the lantern, the red roof on top—all gone. Then the spray came again and even the black stump disappeared. Jesus! he thought. What sort of a blow was this cuts Motherledge down? Motherledge—it had been there all his life, it was what you set your course by, coming in to the bay. Might as well blow down Point Judith or Beavertail Light.

Curiously shaken, he squatted down out of the wind and pulled the flask out of his pocket. It was hard to pull the bottle out while you squatted, your pants held the pocket tight. But he didn't want to stand up again. When he got the flask out, he wasn't sure he wanted to drink; but he was beginning to shake in his middle, so he uncapped the bottle and drank. He had two good slugs. Right away they made him feel better. After a while, he had another pull. It didn't leave much in the bottle. He'd better save it, way things were today. If he was going to get to the Inn, he'd better get moving. It was going to take time to get there, against this wind on the highroad.

As he stood up, there was one of the lulls in the wind (they were coming with increasing frequency now) and he looked out at the water over Mercy Bog. It was just a last, casual observation, until his gaze focused on the telephone pole that was stuck through the high-bush blueberry near the water's edge, not a hundred feet off. Unless he was crazy—or the liquor was getting him—there was someone on that pole. Then the spray shut down again, the wind almost knocking his breath out, and it was too hard to look there any longer, it was dead in the wind's eye. Instinct and habit made him note that the wind had veered, it was south now, or a little west of south.

What would he do? God knew what was on that pole. Anyone floating on a pole in that weather, probably be dead by now. He didn't want to get mixed up with any dead people. But if it was a person, and was dead, how come they was still onto that pole, the waves and all? That didn't make any sense. Unless they was lashed to it. Lashed with what? The body looked to be naked or in white clothes. Didn't look to be made fast any.

If the guy was alive—well, then there he was. That's all he needed, wasn't it? Grab him off of there, haul him up to dry land, git water out of him if he had any. Then anyone said, "What was you doin'?" you had the answer. That water, rough as it was, was broke up among all them little bushes where was usually dry land, couldn't be more'n waist deep. But no one had to know that, did they? The story would be yours—unless the guy—if it was a person and not a sack of something—was conscious, and that certainly didn't seem likely. If he was conscious, what was he doin' just lyin' there, in the water? Leg broke?

Well, anyway, he was so wet now, Harry decided, he wouldn't git no wetter going down to see. If the body was dead, he'd just leave it be, go on up to Twin Oaks. If it was alive, he was fixed.

He climbed carefully over the wall and down the other side. Here the wind was so fierce, the spray so thick, that he found it hard to breathe unless he kept his head down. Keeping his head down, he couldn't see anything but the ground ahead. But even when he did look up, he couldn't see further than a few feet, the spray made him blink so. He looked, his hands making a shelter for his eyes, and he could just make out something whitish ahead in the water. That must be whatever it was, he decided.

When he got to the edge of the water, where the waves were breaking, where the water was boiling and sucking back among the bushes, full of uprooted trees and chunks of wood and other bushes floating and tossing around, he didn't want to go into it. It was terrifying. There was something terrible about that water, that wind. It hadn't seemed hard to go into it when he had stood behind the protecting wall, but it was different now. Yet if he went back, there was always the chance he wouldn't get to the Inn till late, and they'd say he was late, and then people would ask, "Where was you all that time?" Or someone—Chet Gould would start it—would say, "Where is Betty?" His whole stomach contracted in fear as he thought of that. Where *was* Betty? Jesus, he'd better do something, anything. Ahead was fear and behind was fear, and the liquor was running out of him.

With a gasp, he stepped into the water. He went down at once over his belt line, and that was so unexpected that he fell and went under. In a panic he floundered to his feet, took a couple of steps, fell again, rose, and found the water was tearing at him just above his knees, and he was clinging to a shad bush to steady himself. With his free hand he sheltered his eyes from the spray and looked ahead, his heart hammering inside his ribs so hard it hurt him. He could see the thing now, it was a body, naked, on the pole, only a few yards off.

Very carefully, staggering, sometimes falling, he walked toward it, till the water was over his waist and he could hardly control his movements any longer. The waves hit his chest, even in this oddly sheltered water. They'd rise between one bush and the next and shove forward at him or hit him from behind. It was going to be damn tough, he thought, to get that guy ashore again. How the hell would you do it?

Then he was at the telephone pole, a huge one, dark brown, creosoted. Its butt end, splintered into jagged points, lay tangled in the big blueberry. The body lay over the middle of it, arms gripping the pole, head on the arms, back and buttocks and legs going down in the dirty water at a sharp angle. As the waves hit it, the whole body would move, this way and that, as though it was swimming—although the arms were still—as if they were frozen to the pole. It was horrible and terrifying to look at, because it might be dead, and if dead, this motion was more horrible, an imitation of life.

Then Harry saw that this must be a girl. The hair was long—it hung down. Somehow that made the whole business more awful, he was being pursued by women today, women were nothing but grief and fright.

Clinging to the pole to steady himself, he finally got up the courage to touch this girl. She felt icy cold. Jesus! Dead! Well, maybe not. How did a dead girl hang on like that? How did you find out? You listened for the heart, didn't you? Well, to do that, he'd have to really touch her, take her off the pole, get her to dry land. Christ, this was an awful thing to have to do—if she proved out to be dead. Better to leave her here, let someone else find her. Here she was, naked, a woman. Maybe someone would think he had something to do with it.

He drew back from the pole, in horror, but a wave hit him and slapped him forward so that he fell against the girl's body, grasping at it for support. When he had got his feet under him again, he realized that she hadn't *felt* dead. But what did you mean by that, for God's sake? *Feel* dead? Still, if she wasn't dead, he'd have to get her ashore. Have to. There was something coming after him now, in the wind, the failing light, the storm, and this was his way out. You got to do it, he said. You got to. Maybe if he took another drink? No. He'd need it more later. And the liquor acted funny today.

Drawing in a deep breath, he took the girl's arms and lifted them. It took all his strength—either they had hardened in death on the pole, or she was still hanging on—but he got them free. Then he pulled her up and over the pole. She slid easily toward him, she was small and light. It never struck him at all that she had slid so easily over that rough pole because of the green-and-white cloth that lay under her, around the wood; he didn't notice it. Then he turned her over, put his hands under her armpits and began to drag her toward land, her body and legs floating out behind her.

It was a long process. He stumbled many times, but he was going slowly now, he never quite fell. Pretty soon he was out of the water, he lifted the girl up in his arms and carried her to the wall. There was no way to get her over, and yet he had to, he wanted to get out of that damn wind. He put her on the ground, turned to the wall, shoved stones off, one after the other, till he had a gap made. Then he lifted her and staggered through the gap, walked down the wall to a place where it was high and thick, and laid the girl on her back and squatted beside her, out of the wind.

Then for the first time he really became aware of her, realized that she was not only stark naked, but was beautiful and young.

Her coarse tawny hair lay lankly around her neck and face. Her lips, so very full and soft, were blue. Her face was white with a blue undertone to it, and yet you could see that her skin was as tawny as her hair. Her whole body was perfect, her beautiful young breasts, and it would have excited him as much as some of those pictures Johnny

Farber had showed him once if it hadn't been that maybe she was dead and that made her frightening.

With a little, nervous, semi-hysterical giggle, Harry bent down and put his ear to her left breast. After a moment or two he thought he heard her heart beat and, moving his head a little, got his ear in the right position, and heard it beating surely. It was slow, but it was steady. She was alive, then. Jesus! He felt prickles run all over him.

Now what'd he do? Take her indoors quick. Get her dried and warmed. Out here, she'd die, sure. Where to? To Annie's? No. That was the same old rat trap. What would he be doing at Annie's, with a naked girl? Even if he had saved her life. There was the Leckton house at Olneys Point, it was just as near—if he could get there. It might be closed, the old woman might have gone back to New York. Well, you could get in, somehow. That sort of a house, it always had blankets and food and stuff left in it. Maybe even liquor. That would be something.

He began to feel warmer, as though somehow the liquor was now at last taking hold. Yes, sir. That was the idea. If the house was occupied, O.K., they'd look after the girl. If it wasn't occupied, by God, there you'd be, with a girl, get her warm, get her dry. You'd be alone there. Find the liquor —give her a drink, get one yourself, by Jesus! Light a fire. Couldn't tell what would happen.

He took out his bottle, had the last drink out of it, threw it away.

No, sir, he thought, couldn't tell what would happen. He looked at the girl now with different eyes. Boy! Something to look at, too. This was shaping up good, at last.

He leaned down and picked the girl up in his arms, as you'd carry a small child. Only this warn't no small child, he thought. Though she was light, easy to carry. It never occurred to him to take off his shirt, cover her with it. Carrying her, naked and still unconscious, the heavy lashes of her closed eyes down over her cheeks, he began to walk toward Leckton's bridge.

It was a hard job, that walk. Hard to walk against the

wind, an awful job to cross the flooded water of Ten Acre Creek through the big trees that had jammed onto the bridge. But there was a satisfaction in it: you were, somehow, beating Chet Gould, you were doing something no one could say nothin' about, no one. Not so far. The house, by Jesus, it might be empty. This storm, it began to be exciting again.

It was so, in the beginning of dusk, in the wind and the spray, in the fury of the storm's voice, that Harry Frosten had brought Lucy Lagonegro to the doorstep of Miss Leckton's house.

XVI

MISS LECKTON was shaken out of her uneasy sleep by the ringing of the telephone. She had had a curious and unpleasant dream, the edges of which still remained in her mind. She had been holding a baby in her arms and the baby had become her mother and then, in a sequence that was rapid but blurred, she had been holding her sister Dora. After that, it became confused and (although she could remember no detail) horrible, except for a persistent recollection of flowers.

As she reached for the telephone, it rang again, and she knew surely if surprisingly that this was the third time it had done so. She removed the receiver and held it to her ear, wetted her lips (they were dry and her mouth felt fuzzy and tasted badly), and said, "Hello." The croaking sound she made surprised her.

A voice that seemed remote but familiar answered her.

"Hello. Is this Miss Leckton's house?"

"Yes," said Miss Leckton.

"I'd like to speak to Miss Leckton, please, if that's not inconvenient," the voice went on.

Struggling to place the voice, to put a name to it, Miss Leckton said, "This is she."

"Oh, Miss Leckton, it's Maude Cleever. I do hope I'm not interrupting you, calling at just the wrong moment?"

"Not at all," Miss Leckton said. She was surprised, and she repeated the phrase. "Not at all."

"I simply had to call you up, I've such a guilty conscience about you," Mrs. Cleever said.

"Oh?" said Miss Leckton. "Have you?" The image of the flowers she had seen in the dream brightened and faded out in her mind, like one of those half-glimpsed, half-understood thoughts that come and vanish unexpectedly, leaving the recollection of familiarity but of no comprehended connection with reality.

"Yes," Mrs. Cleever said. "I should have called you long before this. And I've thought of you every time the wind blew today, and worried about you. I'd hoped that perhaps you'd closed the house and gone to New York."

"No," Miss Leckton said. "I'm still here."

"Are you all right?" Mrs. Cleever said. "Is the house all right?"

"It is," said Miss Leckton. "It seems quite all right, thank you. The water is leaking in the windows a little, but I— we've taken precautions this time. There are no more trees, either."

"No, of course," said Mrs. Cleever. "No. That's good. I'm so glad. And I do hope you're not being swamped by people again like last time. People like me."

"No," said Miss Leckton. "Not this time. I've seen to that, this time, as far as I could. No, no one has blown in with this storm. Not yet."

"Oh, good!" Mrs. Cleever said. "That must be a relief."

"It is," said Miss Leckton. Then, almost without meaning to, she added, "Except that it would be pleasant if you were here to see the storm through with me."

"I wish I were," Mrs. Cleever said. "I wish I were there now. You, and me, and Lucy. Wouldn't that be nice? How nice of you to think it would be bearable to have us again, after all the horrible inconvenience we caused you!"

"*You* caused none," said Miss Leckton.

"I'm so glad," said Mrs. Cleever. "I feel guilty, though. I should have called you this afternoon and made you come up here to spend the night. I feel like an ingrate, not having done that."

"Very good of you to think of it," said Miss Leckton. "But I tell you, Mrs. Cleever, I shouldn't have gone, even if you had been so kind. I thought it best to stay here. Someone, someone responsible, should be in the house, to see to it, don't you think? One couldn't run off and leave it, could one?"

"Well, I don't know," Mrs. Cleever said. "After all, your life is worth more than your house, isn't it? But anyway, I'm so glad you're all right, and the house all right, too. Has the water risen?"

"No, not yet. The tide is low, this time."

"Oh, thank God for that!" Mrs. Cleever said. "Have you still got that nice Catherine with you?"

"No," Miss Leckton said. It surprised her that this question did not annoy her. "She left that same autumn, right after we got back to New York. Odd, isn't it? She'd been with me over four years. But people like that are fundamentally undependable."

"I suppose so," said Mrs. Cleever. "Though she seemed extraordinarily dependable. A tower of strength and goodwill. But they do come and go, God knows. And now, of course, it's terribly hard to find any servants."

"Yes," Miss Leckton said. She didn't in the least wish to pursue this conversation about servants any further. It seemed to her that the last thing in the world she wanted to do was to confess to Maude Cleever that she had been left alone here. There was now something shameful about it. She said the first thing that came into her head, to change the conversation.

"And Lucy is still with you?"

"Yes," said Mrs. Cleever. "Oh, yes. Indeed she is." Her voice became softer and wonderfully warm, a softness and a warmth that carried over the impersonal wires and enveloped Miss Leckton. "You wouldn't know her. She is so beautiful now, so clever. She has learnt *so* quickly. She is altogether different. She has developed wonderfully. I am still truly grateful to you for being the agent that brought her into my life. She's twenty-one now."

"She has lots of beaux, then, I suppose?" Miss Leckton said. It astonished her to find how acid her voice sounded, yet how much pleasure it gave her to ask the question.

"Yes," Mrs. Cleever said. "But she doesn't want them. Isn't that always the way? There she is, chic, lovely, such fun—and she prefers to be at home. She runs my house now. Indeed, I'm afraid she runs me. And I love it."

"And Winlock?" said Miss Leckton.

There was a very brief pause, then Mrs. Cleever said, her voice cheerful but no longer full of the warm, enfolding quality, "Oh, he's fine, thank you. Just the usual little thug. Just like all boys. Seven, and a thug already. He's very funny, he's not stupid. But a thug, just the same. They are little beasts, little boys, aren't they?"

"I know more about men than about little boys," Miss Leckton said. "More about girls. Boys are rather outside my experience."

"Well, they can be little beasts," Mrs. Cleever said. "But I mustn't keep you like this. I called up to be sure you were all right. I'm so glad you are. And I'm relieved your telephone is working. Are your lights O.K. too?"

"No," Miss Leckton said. "They went off."

"Oh, too bad! Ours are still all right. I guess we must be near the peak of the storm now. It should abate soon. Remember how soon it seemed to go down in 1938?"

"Yes," said Miss Leckton. She was wondering how Maude Cleever could have remembered the decline of the hurricane. Had she been awake then?

"So good-bye, Miss Leckton. I'm so relieved about you. We must meet soon. It's been far too long. I'm still grateful for all you did for me. And for Winlock. And for Lucy. She sends her remembrances, too. She's here with me now, she just came into the room. Would you like to say a word to her?"

Miss Leckton's impulse to avoid any such conversation with Lucy was so violent and immediate that for a moment she could only sit in astonished awareness of its violence.

Then she pulled herself together and said, "Give her my kind regards, won't you? And thank you for calling. Good-bye."

"Good-bye, Miss Leckton," said Mrs. Cleever. "It was good to hear your voice."

Miss Leckton hung up the receiver and put the telephone on the table beside her. In her mind was a vivid recollection of Maude Cleever. She could see the woman in Leah's blue dress, holding the almost naked Lucy in her arms, her lovely adult face bent down in rapt attention to the young girl; and the girl, her face radiant in spite of its blue lips, its frightening pallor beneath the tawny skin, whispering the strange words: "Remember, O most gracious Virgin Mary, that never was it known that anyone who fled to thy protection, besought thine aid, or sought thine intercession, was left unaided." The words, themselves so rich, whispered in vulgar enunciation and in that hoarse, common little voice, without the emphasis of apparent knowledge or true understanding, yet had been filled with passion, and, so very clearly, had been aimed at Maude Cleever, almost as though this young thing (past adolescence but not yet quite a woman) had seen with her reopening eyes a human being as supernatural.

Miss Leckton knew as surely as she ever knew anything that if she sat where she was a moment longer she would sink again into these recurrent recollections, that the scenes would play themselves out again. Without thinking of it, without allowing it to be expressed in word or image in her mind, she knew what the end of the scene would be, and that she greatly wished not to replay it. It was then as though all that she had gone through on this day, all the crowding and the unmanageable thoughts, fostered and bred up by the sound of the wind against her life, were leading her to this ending. All the repeated characteristics of unpleasantness, of things that lay below the surface waiting to come up in horrid and shaking forms, seemed wound now into the ending of that former storm: for all its banality, its bathos, its lack of incident (she was trying unsuccessfully to rationalize it now), it had hooked itself immutably onto the present and possibly onto the future as well. With an effort of will as great as any she had put forth that day (and with a simultaneous realization that this effort could not be indefinitely repeated, was in essence but a posponement) she turned her mind to the immediate present, shutting out the pictures of Maude Cleever and her Lucy, of all the past. The candle was burned down: the candle must be replaced.

That was a simple and mechanical act. She rose and fetched the other candle from the mantelpiece, lit it at the guttering stub of the first one, blew out the stub. As the light of the new candle flared and decreased, the sound of the storm itself, its high, menacing voice, drew closer; as the wick warmed, the wax melted and drew up to the flame, as the flame rose and created its warm light, the storm seemed more distant, less hard upon the room. There seemed to be an actual power to light itself beyond its power to illumine.

Taking the torch and the burned-out candle in its holder, she went to the kitchen. There she put a new candle in the holder, lit it, placed it on the drainboard. Watching the flame rise up to its full power, she realized that still the storm was far less menacing here than it was in the library or the dining room. The wind had not yet shifted, then. That was bad. The height of the storm must lie ahead.

It would be good, she thought, to have some more sherry, except that the sherry (while it made her sleep and so probably would have proved, in the long run, to have refreshed her) had given her some awful dream whose content was now happily forgotten. I do not want to go to sleep again, she said to herself; not until this storm is over, and I am safe.

The thing to do, then, was to make some coffee—not Sanka, now, since there was no longer need to pretend, but real coffee, hot and strong. Perhaps one could put a little brandy into it? Thus one could have the stimulus of the brandy without the fear of sleep. It surprised Miss Leckton to find herself thinking of brandy again with a real and genuine anticipation. What would brandy be like so soon on top of sherry? It didn't matter: what mattered was to have the brandy.

She got out the sterno, lit it, put the percolator on it to boil, filled the container with coffee. Then she took the torch and went to the office. In the locked cupboard—free of the blocking pictures now—was the brandy. She locked up the cupboard carefully, carried the brandy to the kitchen. The coffee would make soon. She put the brandy bottle down beside the candle. It crossed her mind that the sherry bottle still stood on the floor of the library. Well, it was out of sight— and who was there to see it? That was not pleasant to think of. She put the brandy bottle in the sink: it was a gesture against the inquisitive eyes she must invent if she could not have them. The percolator had begun to make pleasant noises. That was good. She got a cup and saucer and spoon, some sugar, from the pantry.

It was then that she heard the new noise.

There was so much noise that it was hard to separate and place this addition to it. There was the erratic scream of the wind, the continuous pound of the surf on rocks, the rattle of the windows, the creaking of the shaken house. Now there was to be heard a remote pounding, not regular, and not loud. It had a metallic quality.

Miss Leckton found herself shaking with fright; her hand (that held the lighted torch) was trembling visibly. Something had happened. Something had broken loose—and she didn't want to find out what it was, she didn't want to know; above all, she didn't want to go to discover it. She was alone, there was none to help her, she was surrounded by the dread of the loneliness that she had besought and purchased: she was afraid.

Yet it was worse, after a moment, to stand here and do nothing, to hear the pounding come to her ears, stop, begin, stop again, than it would be to go out and explore its cause. One was caught perpetually, she thought, in this recurrent dilemma: one dreaded inaction as much as one dreaded the action whose cause was beyond control; one feared to be alone, it had become an almost intolerable situation, and yet one feared as much the possible intrusion of others. Thinking this last, she saw that it was an empty thought, a shell of thinking, an attitude that no longer was valid and that she yet clung to precariously, as though to abandon it were to abandon herself to something as terrible as the storm itself and far more lasting.

With her torch lit, she went to the dining room, to the hall. As soon as she was clear of the dining-room door, she located the sound and recognized it. Someone was using the brass knocker on the front door.

She went at once to the door and put her hand on the knob to open it, sure in that first impulse that this was George Potter. But as she felt the cold metal of the knob, doubt assailed her. Suppose it were not George? Suppose a new invasion had now begun? Strangers. Frosten, even.

Acting on an impulse as deeply rooted as her fear of the solitary combat with the night and the past, she stepped to the side, shone the beam of the torch through the side-lights of the doorway. The beam disclosed two dark figures on her porch step: that was all she could discern. She stepped back, turned the torch ray to the floor.

Neither of these figures was George Potter, neither of them. Their faces had been whitish blurs. Who were they? Why had they come? If they were intent on evil, what protection had she? If they were—well—good people, what then? As she debated, the knock came again, softly now, two small knocks.

The situation, Miss Leckton felt, was once more gone out of her control: there was no way to stop these people from coming in; they would get in. They were, in a queer, uncomfortable way, already inside her house, a composite of all those others who had invaded her again this evening as they had done in 1938. The door, the locked door, was nothing: the storm had entered already, in her mind, and these people had entered, could enter, with it. She opened the front door.

The two dark figures moved into her hall, stood there, their rubber boots clearly seen in the beam of the torch she did not dare to put on their faces. They were men—she knew that at once, without the necessity of further evidence. She closed the door, and the sound of the storm diminished.

"Evening," said one of the men. "Hope we didn't scare you, Miss Leckton."

"No," she said, her voice breathless and weak.

"We're the patrol," said the man. "We been going from house to house along the shore. See if they was all right. I'm Abel Greene. This here is Jerry Coxe. I guess you got a sort of scare, us knocking so late and all."

"No," she said. Her voice came back to her. She felt a great flooding of relief sweep over her, so strong that it made her feel a little dizzy. She was swept with a sense, as sudden as it was unexpected, of happiness and well-being. Now it would be possible again to be herself, to be herself as she could only be it before some other human being. "Not at all," she said. "Very good of you to come so far."

"Everything all right?" said Greene.

"Quite all right," she said.

"We're getting near the peak of this," said Greene. "Ain't quite so bad as last time. Tide's low. We crossed your bridge all right."

"Oh?" she said. "That's good, isn't it?"

"Sure is," said Coxe, his voice very hoarse and deep.

"How are you doin' for leaks and all?" asked Greene.

"Very well," Miss Leckton said. "Of course, some water is working through the south windows, but not enough to do more than spoil the wallpaper. We got the shutters closed this time. And in time." It was remarkably pleasant to be talking to these men.

"You got a fine, stout house," said Greene. "Well built. Means a lot, this weather. Well, glad you're O.K., Miss Leckton. If there ain't anything we can do, we'll get along." He moved his feet.

The only thing Miss Leckton could think of was to prevent their going. Not yet, not yet, she cried silently.

"Oh, no," she said, the cool and civil quality of her voice surprising herself. "Do come in and sit down a moment. I'll fetch a light. I shouldn't have kept you standing here in this gloom. The lights are off, you see. A candle."

She turned swiftly and got the candle from the library and brought it back to the hall.

"There," she said. "That's better. Take off your coats and sit down a minute. You must be tired."

In the light of the candle she could now see their faces. Greene had a big square face, red, clean-shaven, a huge nose. Coxe's face was brown, and he had a sandy moustache that drooped over his lips. They wore black rubber coats and black sou'westers. They had, she thought, a wonderfully comfortable, steady, homely appearance. They must not go yet.

"Why, thank you kindly," said Greene. "We ain't tired. Not to mention. We got a good few houses yet to visit. Slow work getting around tonight. We left the car above the bridge."

"Did you?" said Miss Leckton. "That was wise. That bridge was quite flooded over the last time. The big elms, the ones from around the east of the house here, they got jammed onto the bridge. Astonishing how they got there, wasn't it?"

"Sure was," said Greene. "Funny things happen in these here hurricanes. Though there don't seem to be so many trees blowed down, this storm."

"Probably the weak ones went before," Miss Leckton said. It had seemed to her immediately necessary to produce this explanation: one could not allow—not for a moment—that this storm was not as bad as the last.

"Likely they did," Greene said. "Well, we'll just get along now. Glad you're all right. Sort of remote here, on the point and all. Good night."

"Look," she said quickly. "I've got coffee on in the kitchen. It should be ready now. Do come in there and have a cup before you go." As she spoke she had a rapid image of the bottle of brandy in the sink. It gave her a queer feeling to think of it: to think that these men would see it, if they came. But it didn't matter. The important thing was to hold them a little longer.

212

"Why, thanks," said Greene. "That's kind of you. But we just had coffee, last house we was to. Fred Latchik's house. We won't trouble you, thank you. We'll just go along now."

This time, she saw, he moved to the door. There was nothing now she could do. They were leaving her.

"Good night," said Greene.

"Night," said Coxe.

Greene's hand went to the knob of the door.

Through Miss Leckton's mind flashed the clear and precise recollection of the departure of Golotz and Leah. It was fantastically unlike this departure, except for the physical setting, and yet it was having almost as powerful an effect on her. She wanted (again) to scream at them, to tell them to go then, never come back—and at the same time prevent them from going by any means at all. But although the emotions of this passion shook her, she did not speak, did not move. She simply stood there, a sort of frozen and bitter smile on her lips, and watched them as they went out through the door and closed it carefully behind them.

They were gone. Why had they gone? Why had they not stayed, just for a little? She remembered her action at the side-lights: had the flashing of that beam upon them—so suspicious, possibly so unwelcoming a gesture—put them off? Would they have stayed, had coffee, talked to her, reassured her, comforted her, if she had at once said, "Come in!"? Would nothing in her life ever go right again? They were gone. She was alone again.

As she moved the candle back into the library, she was tempted to put it in the window: make the signal to George, bring him over. But she could not do that. Get George here to tell him the patrol had come? That everything was all right in the house? If something had broken in—something given way—how odd! She almost wished now for some sort of disaster—a minor one—something to excuse a call for George. She could not—would not—offer him coffee. If she did, he'd refuse, like those men. Only not quite like them; but a refusal, nonetheless. How difficult it was! How apparently immutable were the relationships one had established in these long years!

She put the candle on the desk and went out to the kitchen. The kitchen clock said a quarter past eleven. As she made her coffee it occurred to her that she had not yet read the barometer.

Miss Leckton poured herself a big cup of coffee, sweetened it, put in a dessert spoonful of brandy. She put the brandy bottle behind the trash basket under the sink, blew out the kitchen candle, and carried her coffee back to the library. She put the cup on the little table near her morris chair. In a moment she would sit there and drink it.

With her torch she read the barometer. It said 28.30. That was terribly low—the lowest she had ever seen, by a lot. She set the index hand. Then she sat down in her chair, the extinguished torch in her lap, reached out for her coffee.

As she did this, she knew that she didn't want to drink her coffee here. This place, this chair, bred too many recollections. They would come in upon her again, swamp her, she would be drowned in their tide. It seemed to her then that she had not the strength now to resist them, to cope with them, or to dismiss them. Not here.

She would go upstairs. Doing so, she could see to the top of the house—she could sit in the sitting room, her own as much as this, yet not now filled, perhaps, with this power to stir up the past that had become so greatly unpleasant to her? Why had it become so unpleasant? Why? It may be just fatigue, she thought. It has been a long afternoon, a long evening, so much that is upsetting in the force and the quality of the weather. It might even be that the air in the sitting room would be less oppressive. She would go there, she would drink her coffee, she would think of her mother, of the good past, the pleasant, secure past.

Lighting her torch (but leaving the candle to burn), she went up to the sitting room. She lit the two candles there, it was more cheerful. She sat on the comfortable settee. The coffee was hot and good.

This room was far more full of the sound of the storm. It was distressing to see the water leaking in small and shining rivulets from the window sills—though the newspapers were still absorbing it, it was doing little real harm. Would she do better in her bedroom? No. There was no place to sit at ease there except for the bed. If she got on that she would fall asleep; she was too tired to risk that, one did not want to fall asleep again. Some reason.

It was in this room, she remembered, that she had spent the night of that first hurricane. Here, on the settee, having given up her bed to that Mrs. Barber and the baby, Winlock. She recalled how much she had minded that: in retrospect, it seemed awfully generous of her. From this room, in the deadly stillness of the middle night—that fantastic and hushed stillness that was made deeper by the long and regular and tremendous beat of surf on rocks—she had made her tour of the house. The image of that tour came clear, and she sat up, moved, almost shook herself, to avoid falling back into that recollection. No! No! There was the deep—one did not want that. No! There had been things before, they were better. Anything was better.

Irrationally, forgetting all her earlier resolves, she sank into the remembrance of the arrival of Lucy Lagonegro.

XVII

MISS LECKTON had been in her bedroom when the front doorbell had jangled for the last time on that day. She had been planning there with Catherine and Mrs. Barber. The baby, wrapped in the dry blanket, lay on her bed, screaming at the top of its lungs.

"Now don't you worry," Mrs. Barber had said to her. "Mostly he's hungry. He's got a little temperature, but it isn't much. A hundred and a half, rectal. Miss Lovatt here, she found the thermometer. We'll make him something to eat and he'll quiet right down, you'll see. Only thing is, if you can fix it, I'd ought to stay with him for a while and I'd like to be sort of near to the bathroom. If this isn't putting you out too much?"

"Who will look after him while you're in the kitchen?" Miss Leckton asked. She did not propose to find herself maneuvered into the position of baby-watcher at this point.

"Why, I can," said Mrs. Barber. "I've told Miss Lovatt what I want, she can make it on that alcohol lamp easy enough. Can't you?"

"Yes, surely," Catherine said. "Will I go now?"

She spoke to Mrs. Barber and that annoyed Miss Leckton.

"You may do that now, Catherine," she said. "And then I expect you had better move Mrs. Barber and the baby into Miss—into the guest room."

"Yes, madam," said Catherine. She looked at the squalling

baby and her face took on a warmth that Miss Leckton had never observed in her before. "I'll go now." She left the room.

"I'm sorry to have to move you," Miss Leckton said, as a matter of form. "The other room has two beds in it, and a bathroom attached. And, after all, this is my own room, and I must have some place to go."

"Surely," Mrs. Barber said. "You been put upon enough as it is by all of us. Anywheres would do for me. I just was thinking of this fine boy here. Guess he's taken no real harm, but it won't do to be careless. Where are you going to put his mother?"

It seemed to Miss Leckton that it was really none of the woman's business what disposition she made of any of these sudden and unwanted guests.

"I shall arrange all those matters," she said. She was going to add, 'It is something you really need not concern yourself with,' when the bell had rung.

"My God!" said Miss Leckton. "It isn't possible. Why should this happen to me? Today, of all days?"

She stood frozen; it was impossible for her to move. The idea (at that instant) of going down to greet—was that the word, or was it 'repel'?—these new people, was too unpleasant to be faced. If she simply stood where she was, in silence, perhaps they would go away or, at least, someone else would have to cope with their arrival.

But this position was so at variance with her concept of herself as the responsible and sole owner (however helpless) of this house, that it could not be sustained. Her image of the avoidance of responsibility was succeeded by the picture of one of these others playing the welcoming host at her front door. That would be intolerable. Entrance there might be (since the force of the storm dictated it), but welcome there surely need not be.

As though released from a spell, she flew to the door and opened it, and ran to the stairs and descended them. Below her she could see people. In her frenzy of outrage, she could not at first separate one from the other, they were simply a mass of persons whom she did not want, whom she actively wished elsewhere. She stopped at the foot of the stairs and looked. Her vision cleared.

Mrs. Cleever stood in the very center of the hall, holding in her arms a naked young woman. The expression on Mrs. Cleever's face was remarkable: it seemed compounded of intensity and joy.

Behind Mrs. Cleever, stood the Frenchman, Birac, his trousers still rolled up, his feet bare. As she watched, she saw him strip off her raincoat, fling it to the floor, rapidly remove the awful blazer, and put it (with great gentleness) over the young woman's nakedness.

Behind Birac and near the door stood Catherine, her face working in a curious manner that betrayed only some strong emotion, but gave no clue to what that emotion was. Directly at her side stood, swaying slightly, the repulsive figure of Harry Frosten, his dirty shirt and dungarees soaking wet and dripping onto the floor, the stubble heavy and black on his face, his black hair hanging in wet yet greasy wisps over his forehead. He was grinning, and his broken, dirty teeth were exhibited in that grin.

Miss Leckton never did find out exactly how Frosten and Birac had met or by what evil chance he had brought Frosten into her house. It mattered little to her; all that mattered was that it had been done.

"Well!" she said.

As she spoke, Maude Cleever, her face still wearing the rapt look, came toward her. It was surprising, Miss Leckton thought, with what easy strength Mrs. Cleever carried the girl. She stopped a foot from Miss Leckton and opened her mouth to say something. It was at that moment that the girl stirred, opened her eyes, fixed them on Maude Cleever's face. Then, her face radiant and smiling, she had spoken the astonishing and wholly unfamiliar words: "Remember, O most gracious Virgin Mary..." When she had ceased, she closed her eyes again and laid her head against Mrs. Cleever's breast.

Mrs. Cleever looked at the girl and then she raised her eyes

218

to her hostess. Miss Leckton had never seen such an expression on any face before. It was not the same as that with which the girl had looked at her as she said her prayer, but it was like it: like it, Miss Leckton thought, as extreme opposites are so often similar—perhaps in the intensity of kind?

"Where shall I take her?" Mrs. Cleever said, her voice low and strong and full of emotion. "Where? Quickly!"

Miss Leckton was aware of the strong smell of brandy that came from Mrs. Cleever. Had she been drinking more of it while she was left alone? How much?

"I suppose it is too much to ask why these people have come to my house . . ." Miss Leckton began, but Mrs. Cleever interrupted her.

"Where shall I take her? She is cold. So cold! She must go to bed. Now!"

Miss Leckton could not answer. She felt that same sense of impotent confusion, which had hampered her so often this day, come on her now. Where? Why should this woman take anyone anywhere in her house? What room? Her room? She stood, looking at the girl in Mrs. Cleever's arms, and she bit her lips in vexation and frustration.

Before she knew what had happened, Catherine had moved into the situation.

"Right this way, madam," she said to Mrs. Cleever, as she brushed past Miss Leckton and went to the stairs. "We'll put her in Miss Leah's room. Will I help you to carry her?"

"No," said Mrs. Cleever. "Lead the way." She had turned slightly away, a curious gesture of avoidance, as Catherine had held out helpful arms toward her.

Catherine went up the stairs and Mrs. Cleever followed her. Miss Leckton, a victim of her own confusion and, she felt, her own weakness and charitableness, simply stood at the foot of the stairs and watched until they had gone out of her sight. As they disappeared she found her voice again.

"Well!" she said. "And who is *this* person?" She addressed the question to no one, although she was looking, with very obvious distaste, at Harry Frosten.

"I do not know," Birac answered her. "He was outside,

with the girl in his arms. Your man and I, we had finished with the shutters. I made him carry this girl in. I could not leave them so. He says he found her."

"Found her?" said Miss Leckton. She looked again at Frosten. "Where did you find her?"

"Found her in the water, off Mercy Bog," he said. "I seed her when the wind let up. Swum out and got her to land. I brung her here, it was the nearest."

"Oh," said Miss Leckton. It didn't seem at all a likely story to her, and she could see no reason to believe what this awful-looking person said. From where she stood, now, she could also begin to smell him. He stank of salt water and foul clothes, of fish, and (very strongly) of whiskey. "You have been drinking."

The man just stood there, still looking at his feet, which he shuffled a little.

"If you have saved the girl's life," Miss Leckton said, "that is good. Though I am not inclined to accept your story without verification. What is your name?"

"Frosten," he said.

"Well, Mr. Frosten, you can go now. I'll get in touch with you later."

"Go?" said Frosten. "I ain't goin' nowheres this weather."

"You got here," said Miss Leckton. "What will prevent your going again?"

"I ain't goin' to leave," Frosten said. His voice was loud and, she thought, full of panic. She had no key to what caused the panic, but it was wholly obvious.

"You will go," she said. "At once. I do not want you here. There is no room here."

"I do not think you can send him out now," said Birac unexpectedly. "This storm."

"My dear sir," Miss Leckton said. "This is something I shall decide."

"The weather, it has decided it," said Birac. "You live on a peninsula and the good God has now turned it temporarily into an island. I do not think you can send this man into the water that is around you now. I am sorry. I will, myself, keep an eye on him if you are worried."

"And what do I know about you?" Miss Leckton said, her voice reflecting the almost hysterical anger that was rising in her. "What do I know about any of you? Where do you come from? Why are you here? Did *I* ask you to come? Do you know what has happened to *me* today? Does anyone think, even for one moment, of what this may mean to *me*?" Her voice broke, and she felt the tears of her rage begin to pour from her eyes. Voiceless and shaken, she turned and fairly ran up the stairs.

But her own room was not her own now. Looking at the blank face of her door, it seemed again, and more intolerably than before, an outrageous exclusion. Without thinking it out, she went to the sitting room, slammed the door shut behind her, fell on the settee, and gave way to her tears.

When she had finally roused herself, Miss Leckton was aware that there had been a long passage of time. There was no way to tell how long, because the sitting room had no clock in it. It was pitch black now.

Listening to the sound of the wind, she realized that it had changed its tone: it was less fierce. The house had ceased to shake and quiver in that almost incessant pattern of alarm, though occasional gusts still shook it, and the shutters and windows rattled. Yet even there it was possible to notice a difference. The hail-like sound of water and sand blown against the panes had ceased.

There was no use in looking out the window, she decided, it was too dark now to see anything. And above all, she was not going to leave that room. It was impossible to envision herself as leaving it, going down to become once more involved in the unpleasantness of these people.

She realized that the whole matter had got so far out of hand now, and so disagreeably, that there was nothing she could do about it. Nothing, indeed, that she was required further to do. Had she not done enough? And had not all that she had wanted to do proved hideously ineffective? The very though of returning to the society of these people was repellent: somehow it constituted at once both an incitement to anger and, what was worse, an admission of defeat. Here, immured in the sitting room, she was safe from them. They had, against her will, taken over her house and her rooms. Very well, then, let them run the house, shift for themselves. Let the servants, her servants, who made so free with her unproffered hospitality, take on the burdens of caring for these people. And might God now help the one who had the temerity to invade this, her place of retirement!

She wished she had a light, but there was none in the room. She wished as well that she knew the time. Not knowing it was disturbing; her days, usually so orderly and so punctual, had conditioned her to live by the exactness of hours. This process of exile in a timeless darkness was foreign to her, was extraordinarily upsetting. It was of a piece with the rest of the day: all things being against her, she was powerless to move in her own direction, of her own will.

She was on her settee, thinking of all these things in a chagrin and discontent that bordered on anger, when there came a knock on her door.

Her first impulse was to shout at whoever was there, tell them to go away. But she was curious to know who had knocked; she wanted the satisfaction of telling this person, face to face, to go away, to get out, to leave her alone; and (deeper within her, less understood, unphrased) was the thought that it might be Maude Cleever. While she hesitated, the door opened, a gleam of wavering light came into the room, and Catherine entered, holding a tray on which were two short silver candlesticks, their candles lit with flickering flames.

"I have brought you some supper, madam," said Catherine.

All the words that had rushed up into Miss Leckton's mouth (those words of command, of strict, if polite, abuse) died and faded.

"Oh," she said. "Yes."

As the maid put the tray on a chair, Miss Leckton rose and closed the door. That was better; open, it let the house and its unwelcome contents in upon her. Then she returned to her settee.

Catherine got the small table by the fireplace, cleared it of its bric-a-brac, put it beside Miss Leckton, placed the tray on it. It had a cheerful look, the candlelight was most welcome.

Glancing about this room, whose appearance she knew so very well but which was now oddly strange enough to need a new appraisal, Miss Leckton noticed that the water was no longer coming in at the windows.

"Thank you," she said. "I see the water has stopped leaking. Has the storm abated?"

"No, madam," said Catherine. "But the wind has shifted toward the west, Mr. Birac says. It's coming over land now, mostly. None of the windows are leaking."

"That's good," said Miss Leckton. "What time is it, Catherine?"

"It's about a quarter before eight," Catherine said.

"So late?" Miss Leckton exclaimed. It surprised her. It could not have been more than a quarter past six when Mrs. Cleever had carried the girl upstairs. And she had not slept. "And the others, Catherine? Those people. What has been done with them?"

"Mrs. Barber is with the baby in your room, madam."

"And how long does she propose to remain there?" Miss Leckton asked.

"I don't know, madam," said Catherine. She was standing by the tray now.

Miss Leckton looked at the tray. There was hot tomato soup, bread and butter, some corned-beef hash, a pear. She was not exactly hungry, but she knew, as she looked at the food, that she wanted it and needed it. It crossed her mind that she wished she had the brandy bottle here, could have another small drink from it.

"I had expected her to be moved to—to the guest room," said Miss Leckton. "Why is she still there?"

"Mrs. Cleever and that girl are in Miss Leah's room," said Catherine.

"You seem to have made a great many arrangements," said Miss Leckton acidly.

Catherine's mouth drew into a thin line, and she said, "There was no one to tell me different, madam. Would you like me to move them elsewhere?"

With a slight feeling of having put herself at a disadvantage, Miss Leckton said, "No. No. That will have to do, I expect. And the others, Catherine?"

"Mr. Birac and that man," said Catherine, "are in the library. I gave him a blanket. Mr. Birac. I gave the old carriage robe to that man. Mr. Birac said to tell you that they are quite all right, that he will stay with the—with that man." Her voice changed a little, went up a tone, as she said, "He wanted to come into the kitchen. We won't have him there."

"What has he been doing?" Miss Leckton asked.

For the first time that she could remember, she heard the Irish brogue come into Catherine's voice, sounding through her patent disgust. "He has drink taken," she said.

"I thought so," said Miss Leckton. "I smelled it on him when I first saw him. And what will they do for food? I suppose they will have to be fed."

"The baby's been fed. I made it cereal. Mrs. Cleever took up a tray to the young girl. I have written her name on that piece of paper on your tray. I can't say it."

Miss Leckton picked up the paper. *Lucy Lagonegro,* Catherine had written on it. Italian. Of course, that explained the common, immigrant's voice.

"Mrs. Cleever and Mr. Birac and that man, we gave them what you have here. Mr. Birac helped Anna prepare it on the dining-room fire. We expected you down. That's why I have waited to bring you a tray."

"I see," said Miss Leckton. "And where is Mrs. Cleever now?"

"With Lucy, the one there," said Catherine, making a small gesture toward the paper in Miss Leckton's hand. "In Miss Leah's room. The other two is in the library, like I said. They are all tired out. Everyone is tired out."

224

"But of course, not I," said Miss Leckton. "*I* have had nothing to tire me. And I suppose I am expected to sleep here?"

Catherine said nothing.

"I shall stay here," Miss Leckton said. She heard her own tone of voice and its vehemence, its combative quality. "I want no one to disturb me here. Except you, of course. If anyone wants anything, let them send word to me through you."

"I am going to bed now, madam," said Catherine in a flat voice. "Anna is in her room already."

"Oh," said Miss Leckton.

"They are all put comfortable for the night," said Catherine. "Will you want anything here now?"

I am simply trapped, thought Miss Leckton. Trapped in one room of my own house. But she realized that there was nothing to be done about it unless she herself rose and did it. The idea of that was too distressing.

"You had better bring me some sort of wrap," she said. "My dressing gown. My slippers. I suppose I can still get into my own bathroom?"

"I have unlocked the door to the hall," said Catherine. "The baby is asleep now. Mrs. Barber is sitting up with him. She says she doesn't mind. She wants to do it. I can fetch you your things. Will you want a comforter, a blanket?"

"Yes," said Miss Leckton. Since she was, apparently, to be shut out of her own room, she had best have here what she would need. "And Catherine. The silver."

"I have locked it all up in the pantry," said Catherine.

"That bottle of brandy," Miss Leckton said.

"It is gone," said Catherine. "Someone has took it."

"Who took it?"

"I do not know, madam."

"Did Mrs. Cleever want it for this girl, this Lucy?"

"I do not know anything at all about it, madam," said Catherine flatly.

God knows who might *not* have taken it, thought Miss Leckton. Anna, or Birac, or Frosten. One knew nothing

225

about them. It was probably Frosten. He had been drinking. Or Mrs. Cleever? She should never have left it out. One should never leave anything like that around.

"Very well," she said. "If you will get me those things now."

"Very good," said Catherine. She left the room so swiftly, Miss Leckton thought, that it was almost as though she was escaping from something. That was, of course, ridiculous. Why should the maid wish to escape from her, the only known quantity in the house?

Miss Leckton had finished her soup and begun on her hash by the time Catherine returned, bringing with her a blanket, the comforter from her bed, her dressing gown and slippers, her nightgown. The maid put them all neatly out for her on chairs.

"Will that be all now, madam?" she said, though it was obviously not really a question, but a statement of finality.

"Yes," said Miss Leckton. "Thank you."

"Good night, madam," said Catherine, and again she left the room so very quickly and the door closed softly behind her.

XVIII

AS she recalled this now, Miss Leckton was aware of the odd similarity to the present. Once again, time seemed to have become confused, past and present were merged together; one lived an indeterminate life, experiencing the sensations of the past with a comprehension (and an unease) born of, and increased by, the passage of days to the present. Now as then, there were the two candles burning. Now as then, she was alone in this room: only, then she had been, as it were, islanded in it into aloneness, while now she was alone altogether, and to a degree by choice. There were no strangers sleeping in her beds, her rooms. No servants in her kitchen wing. No one. And now the wind racked and tore at the house, the water and its sand splattered with terrifying force and noise against the shutters and the windowpanes, the house shook and trembled in its almost incessant movement. Then, the house had been growing quieter, the sounds diminishing, the storm, past its high point of fury, had begun to let go its hold on her house, on her life. She knew now what had lain ahead of her in that night; but what lay ahead of her at this moment, she could not know, or hardly dare imagine. The future had grown to a great size of apprehension and discomfort: there seemed to her now nothing left to which she could look forward without, at the least, depression, at the most, fear.

But the past—one knew of that. Or, one knew of it, and

yet did not know of it. It grew in the remembering, showing facets never before suspected, and she did not like that. She could remember many details as secure; yet their meaning kept on developing from surprise to surprise, and the surprises were never pleasant.

She remembered eating her supper, putting the tray in a corner. Beyond that, the next hours were not altogether clear to her. She had sat on the settee, thinking about her day, about her life. To do so had roused in her the senses of frustration and anger, so that there was in such an occupation, neither peace nor rest. It was a further source of continuing annoyance that she had had no clock, no watch; that she should not have asked Catherine to fetch in the little travelling clock from her bedroom. How like everything that had happened today, that she should find herself in almost the only room in the house that had no clock in it!

Sometime later she had decided to undress. Her body felt sticky and uncomfortable, the sweat had covered it all afternoon, and she was still hot and still sweating. She undressed and put on her dressing gown and slippers, and very cautiously, a candle in her hand, she opened the door. Outside in the hall, all was deserted. The sounds of the storm had sensibly diminished and the hall semed, by contrast, almost quiet. She made her way softly to the bathroom, slipped in by the hall door. She was grateful that the door to her bedroom was closed. She locked it, with a sense both of satisfaction and relief. She did not want to see the invaders of her bedroom snugly installed there.

When she turned on the tap, although she opened it fully, there was but the smallest trickle of water. At first she was sure that the others were drawing water, particularly those in the kitchen. But after a moment she realized, with despair, that the water was running in this thin trickle because the electric pump was off, the pressure undoubtedly very low. She drew water in a tumbler for her teeth, a few inches in the basin. With this she washed.

It was not satisfactory, but it did refresh her. All the time she was washing, she thought of the awful inconvenience of the morning. No water to wash in, none of the toilets working. No water to cook with. They would have to haul water for the house from God alone knew where, and in God alone knew what, since the car was smashed. It seemed to her then that all this had happened because of these people: it was not the storm, it was the invasion; they had all, quite likely, drawn baths, flushed the toilets freely. It mattered not at all to them how low they drew the precious water in her pressure tank. It was of a piece with all the discomfort, the inconvenience, indeed the anguish, they had caused her.

She unlocked the door to the bedroom, and had just left the bathroom when the door from bedroom to hall opened and she saw Mrs. Barber standing there, fully dressed in the misfit clothes. The woman came out, closed the door behind her.

"I certainly am sorry to discommode you like this," Mrs. Barber said, in a clear whisper. "Seems just awful putting you out of your bed. If it wasn't for that baby running a little temperature, I'd never even have suggested it. He's asleep now."

"Oh, don't think about *me*," said Miss Leckton, and she could hear her own voice grow bitter. "It makes no difference at all about *me*. I'm *quite* all right."

"You want to see him?" said Mrs. Barber. "He's just a beautiful child. Would be, with that mother. He's lying there now, so lovely in his sleep."

"Oh, no," said Miss Leckton. "I wouldn't *dream* of disturbing him."

"Won't disturb him," said Mrs. Barber. "He's fast asleep now. Miss Lovatt and I, we got some orange juice and cereal into him, he ate real good, and soon's he'd eaten, he calmed right down and pretty soon he was asleep. He won't take no real harm from this. Don't you worry about him." She giggled a little. "You ought to see him," she said. "He looks so little and cute in that big bed of yours."

"I shall go and lie down," said Miss Leckton. "I am rather tired out."

"You must be," said Mrs. Barber. "Anything I can do for you?"

"No, thank you," said Miss Leckton. Then, remembering the clock, she said, "Yes, there is. Would you fetch me out the travelling clock by the bed? There is none in my sitting room."

"Surely," said Mrs. Barber. "I know just how you feel. My own watch is stopped. Water in it, I dare say, and it will need new works." She turned at once and went into the room. She returned with the little clock and handed it to Miss Leckton. "There you are," she said. "Is it wound?"

"It is wound on Sundays," Miss Leckton said coldly. "Where shall you sleep?"

"Oh, I'll set up, set in that chair by the bed. Miss Lovatt fetched me some cushions. I dassen't to sleep. I guess the baby's all right now, but if he should start something, I'd like to get after it real quick. Don't you go to worry about me. I'm used to it. Used to be a nurse, you know. It comes easy to me."

"I see," said Miss Leckton. "Very well. Thank you for my clock. Good night."

"Good night," said Mrs. Barber. "We sure are all obliged to you this night."

"I hope nothing happens in the house," Miss Leckton said. "So many people and all strangers."

"You'll be all right," Mrs. Barber said. "If it's that Frosten boy you're worrying about, why, he's no real harm. Or, all events, he won't do no harm here. He's a no-account boy, lives to Cross Bridge yonder. He knows I know who he is. He won't dast to do a thing. You rest easy."

"Rest easy," said Miss Leckton. "So simple to say! It's not *your* house invaded. Not *your* house with the rooms destroyed."

"No," said Mrs. Barber. "That's so. But my goodness, you ought to see my house now! Wind picked it up and blew it into Olneys Pond, and me right in it. I never knew what was happening, just that the house was shakin' and wobblin' and I couldn't stand up easy. Guess the wind and the water took it. Pushed it right across the pond, and she landed with a bump, sort of slanted, in the bushes clear acrost the other side. You never saw anything to beat it. House ain't hurt bad, I believe. Wasn't a bit of china broken on the kitchen shelves. Only things broke was a case of phonograph records slid off of the piano, and my father's portrait, glass broke when it fell. So much racket, you couldn't hear it fall, nor the glass break, nor anything. I took one look around, quick, and I says, 'Tessie Barber, you clear out of this house, it ain't safe. One more puff of that wind, and this whole thing, it's going to whisk right over.' No foundations, you see. Just restin' on the pasture and the bushes. Funny-looking sight it was too, and scared me. I just hope she's still upright when I get back to her. If she is, I'll swap a bit of my land with Johnny Farber and set the house up right where it is. Comical, ain't it? But I oughtn't to stand here chatterin', and you tired out. You go right along to your room and rest. You need it, goodness knows. And we all got plenty to do tomorrow. Good night."

Mrs. Barber turned at once and went back into the bedroom, and closed the door softly.

Back in her sitting room, Miss Leckton put the clock on the table. It said five minutes past nine. Although it surprised her to see how late it was, it was a distinct comfort to know the time. She put on her nightgown, spread the blanket on the settee, settled herself as flat as she could, and got the cushions into a comfortable position. All this time she was thinking about Mrs. Barber's fantastic story. It could, obviously, not be true. It was simply an exaggeration of the truth, or possibly—and far more alarmingly—a hallucination. If this woman was subject to hallucinations, was she a fit person to be looking after a baby? Was it not her duty, then, to get hold of Mrs. Cleever and warn her?

Her tiredness swept over her now in a wave of actual feeling. Her legs twitched behind the knees, her arms felt heavy, her back ached a little, there seemed no position she could assume that was really comfortable. Yet the idea of getting up, of going after Mrs. Cleever, seemed more than she could

231

do. It was something, oddly, that (in a misty way) she would like to do. Why was that?

She tried to stop thinking about this, about anything. She should go to sleep. Sleep was what she most needed. Had she not been up and about since before seven o'clock this morning? But she could not sleep. She would begin to drift off; then the recollections of the day—of Leah, of Golotz, the La Perche man and his wife, Birac, Mrs. Barber, Mrs. Cleever, the baby, Lucy Lagonegro, Frosten—would crowd in upon her and she would become angry and hot, and being so, restless and awake. Awake, yes: but in that manner where one is already not wholly awake, where the body craves sleep and will not accept it, where the mind is too active and yet neither logical nor useful. Over and over again she tried to put these thoughts, these recollections, from her mind, make it a blank, woo sleep. Sleep would not come.

Not consciously, but because of fatigue, she began to concentrate her thinking on one thing, in the unspoken hope of keeping out the others. She thought about Maude Cleever. She recalled her appearance at the door, her wet and clinging dress, the baby in her arms. The image of Mrs. Cleever holding Lucy, the girl's head falling back, at the end of the prayer, upon Mrs. Cleever's breast, was particularly clear. How beautiful she is! thought Miss Leckton. Maude. A lovely name. She said it to herself: Maude, Maude. It would be good to have her for a friend. She was someone it would be so pleasant, so—stimulating to welcome to this house. The images grew: Miss Leckton could live them now vividly, fictitious as they were, like scenes in a play, lit with sunlight and soft air, scenes played in rooms full of lovely sweet-smelling flowers. The best was the one where she heard the crisping sound of the wheels of the unvisualized car on the gravel of her drive. Out of it stepped Mrs. Cleever, she ran up the steps to Miss Leckton—beautiful, young, her splendid figure in motion and in sunlight, the flowers behind her—calling, 'Dear Carrel, how lovely to see you!' And then, Maude Cleever flung her arms around her and embraced her, kissed her. Miss Leckton could feel (with incredible reality) the sweet pressure of Maude Cleever's—Maude's—body against her own.

As she completed the image, Miss Leckton felt a sense of distant discomfort. There was something else this recalled to her, yet she could not place it at first. As she remembered it—it was the image of herself as a girl of fourteen saying a tearful good-bye to her History teacher at boarding school as she left for the holidays, held warmly and comfortingly in the teacher's arms—it seemed impossible for one thing to have reminded her of the other. She remembered that teacher now with distaste. She remembered how beautiful she had thought her, the acme of loveliness, of human excellence, and how shocked she was when, nearing forty, she had met her: a lined, dried-up little old spinster, full of a suffocating and slightly vulgar sweetness. Her mind rejected the likeness, even the likeness of dissimilarity, and, drifting back again to the imaginary arrival of Maude, she slept.

Waking, she turned her head and focused her eyes on the phosphorescent dial of the clock. Its hands stood at twenty minutes past twelve. She had a distinct sense of having been waked, and that that was somehow alarming. Lying now quite still, she listened attentively to try to discover what had waked her. Hearing nothing, it began to dawn on her mind that the silence itself was critical and unbelievable. There was no sound whatever within the house. There was no wind. Outside the house, at punctual intervals, there could be heard a very deep and solemn and hollow roar of surf breaking, followed by the grating, the almost inaudible stony whisper of the water's troubled withdrawal. With certainty Miss Leckton knew that it was this now frightening and unaccustomed silence that had roused her.

The room seemed terribly close and hot: hotter, more oppressive even than it had been during the day and its storm. It was, she felt, impossible to lie here longer and breathe—or attempt to breathe—this awful, used, sticky air. She rose from the settee, put on her slippers, made her way cautiously in the darkness toward a south window. As she approached the window, she realized that she could see the frame of it, very black, enclosing the lighter and translucent panes, and that through the panes, dimly and somewhat blurred, were stars. Stars! The sky must be clear now.

Rather timidly she felt the edges of the sash. They were damp and sticky, but there was no least draught of air coming in at the cracks. It would, she felt, be wonderful to open the window, to let the night air in: yet so powerful remained the effect of the storm on her that she hardly dared to attempt this. It was as though, on the opening of the window, the hurricane would rise again at once, strike through into her house. But these are but the alarmist thoughts of midnight, she decided. She would open the window.

It was not easy to do, it took all her strength. The sash had swelled in the wet, the sand had worked into the channels of wood. Yet it did open at last, gratingly, a noise that, it seemed to her, filled the silence of the night like a fire alarm. Trembling a little, she bent down, looked through the opening. The air came softly in, cool, fresh, clean. There was no breeze at all. One could see the reflection of the stars, in uncommon brilliance, appear and disappear in the long, smooth rolling of the ocean.

Miss Leckton drew in great deep breaths of air. It tasted wonderfully good, it was full of the old, the familiar salty flavor. Then she opened the other south window, opened the door to the hall (quietly and cautiously), to air out the room, to rid it of the dark miasma of the storm and the storm's thoughts and fears. The air flowed coldly and smoothly through the room; it was not long before she felt so cold that she put on her dressing gown gratefully. Then she sat again on the settee. In a moment she would close the door, she would get back into her makeshift bed, she would sleep. The storm was over. Her sleep could be deep and refreshing, and free of all alarm.

But could it be? What was happening in her house? What were the strangers, the invaders doing?

Listening intently, she could hear no sound from next door. She rose, walked to the connecting door to her bedroom, put her ear against it. She could hear someone snoring—it must be Mrs. Barber—gently and regularly. That was all. The baby, too, must be asleep. Let us hope so, she thought. At all events, it was not now her concern. They had seen fit to arrange this disposition of authority and comfort between them. Let them, then, assume the responsibility that went with those.

Although this formula seemed to relieve her completely and at once of any further worry about the baby and Mrs. Barber, she found her mind turning uncomfortably to the room below them. What was going forward in the library? What was Frosten doing? Mr. Birac had said he would keep an eye on him—or so she had it second-hand from Catherine—but what, indeed, did she know of Birac himself? And if Frosten was drunk, as she suspected, on his own whiskey and on her best brandy, what might not he be able to do at this hour of the night? And could Birac, with the best will in the world, control him?

Her desk was locked, thank God! There was not much he could do in the library, nor much that he would want—though it was hard to foresee the vagaries of a drunken yokel. How had he actually come by that girl? Why was she—her mind shied off the word 'naked'—undressed when he had brought her here? Was this his doing? With what intention? Had he hoped to find the house deserted? This speculation roused up such unpleasant ideas, such repulsive images in Miss Leckton's mind, that she turned her thoughts back to the material possessions downstairs. Catherine had said she had locked up the silver in the pantry. But those locks were opened but by common keys, it would be very simple to force them. Perhaps she should go and see?

She did not want to go. Not at all. This room, now, had assumed a quality of safety. It was as though the rest of the house (full of silence and strangers) no longer wholly belonged to her; as though, once she left the safe harbor of the sitting room, she would be vulnerable to new fears, new discomforts. By no difficult turn of thinking, she remembered Maude Cleever and Lucy. What had happened to them? Were they all right?

She was using the word 'they' with an effort but on purpose. It covered something, made something all right—or almost all right. But no matter about that, she should see to them, she should be sure there was nothing happening—sickness, suffering, anything—to *them*. Even though the disposition of her unwelcome (or welcome) guests was not her doing, she should assume again the responsibility of their welfare under her roof. That was one's duty, and it was not to be shirked.

Very well, then. She would go out of this room, go downstairs first. She would get the flashlight that was in the drawer of the hall table. She would see what went on in the library, police the downstairs area. Then, when that had been done—when that disagreeable duty had been done—she would come up again, she would see to Lucy and Maude Cleever, that they were all right. That was the way to do it. One did the worst of it at first, one saved the . . . one did the least bad at the end. After that, one could sleep in some peace, some security, one's obligations discharged. It would not, she felt now, be really so bad to go downstairs.

She followed her plan. With the flashlight lit in her hand, she advanced to the open door of the library. She could hear from it only a soft, heavy breathing. She raised the flashlight and swept its beam briefly but carefully around the room.

The Frenchman was asleep in her morris chair, a blanket over his knees and pulled up around his waist, the awful blazer draped around his shoulders. His head was lolled back and slightly turned to the side. On the floor beside him was a heap of cushions—her cushions—and the old carriage robe flung untidily at one side. There was no sign of Frosten.

Taking a step into the room, Miss Leckton once more swept the torch's beam around the room. There was no doubt of it, that Frosten man was not there. Where was he?

As the implications of his absence struck home to her, Miss Leckton could not restrain herself in time to prevent her from saying "Oh!" in a loud voice.

At once, with a short, gurgling snort, Birac awoke and

sprang to his feet. The blazer fell off his shoulders, the blanket dropped in a heap at his feet.

"*Qu'est-ce qui se passe?*" he said.

"He's gone," said Miss Leckton. "That man has gone. He is not here. Where is he?"

"Oh," said Birac. "Excuse me. I will make a little light." He found matches, lit the two candles on the desk. Then he turned to her.

"I am afraid I do not know," he said. "I slept. Is it very late?"

"It is almost half past twelve," Miss Leckton said. "The storm is over. That man has gone. God knows where, or what he has taken. I had understood you would keep an eye on him. Otherwise, I should not have let him remain in the house." Unconsciously she had been speaking, though intensely, in a low voice, almost a whisper, and he had followed suit. "Now he is gone," she said.

"I am sorry," Birac said. "It was too bad of me. I had not meant to sleep. I sat up not to do this. He was asleep, snoring, on the floor here. We shall go now and look, shall we not? Will you let me have the torch? Or is it that you have another one?"

"There is only this one," said Miss Leckton. "I shall keep it. I shall look around now."

"I'll come with you," said Birac.

Miss Leckton returned to the hall, her light turned here and there ahead of her. She opened the lavatory door, examined within. It was empty. She opened the door to the cellar stairs, looked down them. The beam of the light disappeared into an odd blackness there. It took her a moment to realize that what it played on was water, that her cellar was flooded. The sight was so unpleasant that she at once returned to the hall, shutting the door quickly. At all events, Frosten was not down *there*.

Moving along the hall, her light struck on the cautionary piece of paper she had pinned on the door to the living room. Could the man be there? Why should he be? But one must look everywhere.

237

"Will you see if you can open this door?" she said to Birac. "Will you try to open it silently, so as not to awaken the house?"

"Of course," said Birac.

He moved past her and opened the door. It opened easily and, except for a faint creaking of its hinges, without noise. Birac stood aside for her, and she took a step into the room. As she swung the torch around it, there was disclosed such a sequence of desolation and confusion that she wanted to weep. But wet, broken, covered with leaves and debris as it was, the room was empty of any human being.

"Close it up, close it up," she said in a quick, breathless voice, and she stepped past him into the inviolate hall.

Birac closed the door.

"My God," he said. "What a tragedy for you!"

Miss Leckton made no immediate answer. Inside herself she was saying, 'Well, perhaps he begins to realize now what *I* have been through,' and that gave her a considerable and comforting satisfaction.

But the satisfaction itself aroused in her a further sense of outrage.

"It is not only the physical damage," she said. "It is the appalling fact of having a man like this Frosten in your house at all."

"But that is something that is beyond control," said Birac. "Is it not?"

"No," she said. "I should not have let myself be persuaded by you. I should have turned him out when he first arrived. I see no reason for having to harbor his kind."

"In a moment of crisis," said Birac, "one has no choice of kind."

"What do you mean?" said Miss Leckton.

"How shall you choose the good or the bad? This storm, it has been like a war, in little. One does not rescue a wounded man, a man about to drown, a man in danger of his life, only after examination, is it not so? One does not say to him, at the moment of crisis, 'Are you a good man?

238

Is your life worth saving?' One rescues first—as you have so generously done—and then one takes steps later."

"Takes steps too late," she said. "Too late. I do not admit the analogy. If he made his way here, with that girl, he could have made his way out again—alone."

"Yet he was very exhausted," Birac said.

"He was merely drunk," she said. "I do not agree with you. I should have turned him out. Let us go ahead now, please. We have other rooms to examine."

Together they explored the dining room, the office, the pantry, the kitchen. There was no one there, everything appeared to be in order, no locked cupboard or drawer seemed to have been tampered with. Climbing the servants' stair (she went up it but a few treads, it squeaked so loudly in this new quiet of the night), Miss Leckton could hear the heavy and regular snoring of her servants. It was impossible that they should sleep so if Frosten had been there. Their obvious virtue (and patent unattractiveness) secured them, in Miss Leckton's mind, from any suspicion of harboring such a man.

In the hall outside the library, Miss Leckton spoke again. "He has gone," she said. "He has left. I can only hope he has taken nothing with him."

"I shall hope this too," said Birac. "You do not wish to look upstairs?"

"He is not there," Miss Leckton said.

As she said it, it struck her that she sounded very sure. She knew, of course, that Frosten was not in her sitting room. It was fairly obvious that he was not in her bedroom either, whence had come the soft snores of Mrs. Barber. There was nowhere else except the bathroom and the garret, and Leah's ... the guest room. She was moved, she knew, by a powerful impulse not to have Birac with her when she made the final tour of the upper house. She wished to be alone. She did not even attempt to understand why she felt this so strongly.

"He is not there," she repeated firmly. "You had better

239

settle down again, Mr. Birac, and try to get some sleep. I shall do the same."

"Thank you," he said. "You are most kind. If, in the morning, you find that anything of value is missing, I hope you will be good enough to tell me. I shall wish to be responsible for this."

"Thank you," she said. "That is quite unnecessary. Good night."

She waited for him to go past her and into the library. She stood at the foot of the stairs until he had blown out the candles; she remained there for a long time thereafter. While she waited she thought how absurd had been his offer, how empty. Where would he, an immigrant working on so small a project as the causeway across Ten Acre Pond, find the means to repay her for her valuables if they had been stolen? Absurd!

Miss Leckton never really knew how long she had stood, her torch extinguished, at the foot of those stairs, straining her eyes to hear the sound of Birac's breathing—that slow breathing which would proclaim him to have fallen asleep again. Nor did she know, or wish to know, why she so much wanted him now to go to sleep, since the question of his comfort or rest was a matter of indifference to her.

Remembering this moment, it seemed to her that she had waited until she could wait no longer: not because she was tired of standing still, for she was not conscious now of her fatigue, but because some inner compulsion drove her on. Mounting the stairs, she had made a careless examination of the empty bathroom; had opened the door to the garret, shone the torch up the stairs, seen nothing, heard nothing, closed the door again, and locked it. If Frosten was there, he could stay there. There was nothing further to postpone the final act.

Breathing in once deeply, she had crept to the door of Leah's room. It was closed. Through it she could hear no sound at all: it was as silent as though it had been empty. Then, her hand trembling slightly, she took hold of the knob

240

and turned it, very slowly, very carefully, released the catch, pushed the door open on darkness.

There was nothing to see, almost nothing to hear. Faintly, between the soft, distant sounds of the recurrent surf, she could hear gentle breathing. That was all. The air of the room was hot and moist; it smelled of human beings, so strongly that she noticed it at once, yet noticed equally that the smell was not unpleasant to her. There was also a slight smell of liquor, of brandy.

Perhaps, she thought, I should risk waking them up by opening the window? Perhaps only one would wake.

Standing in the darkness, she knew what she wanted to do, but she did not want to do it—not yet. To light the torch, to see the occupants of this room (she put it carefully in the plural), perhaps to rouse one of them, to speak with her, to ... well ... who knew? Perhaps Mrs. Cleever would come out to talk with her, so as not to waken the other. Here was, somehow, the one reward for all she had suffered. It had become, at this moment, both the justification of all her actions, and the reward of all her sufferings. It was her link with the future so dismally foreseen this short while back; but a link of happiness, of companionship?

Knowing now that she would not touch the window, that its inevitable squeak and rattle would rouse both of these women, Miss Leckton switched on the torch, its beam turned to the floor at her feet. Even so, its dim reflected radiance showed her the whiteness of the beds, the bulk of someone in the far one. Something was oddly wrong with the bed against the wall. She could not see it so clearly, the high footboard interfered, but it looked too flat, too neat.

With an absolute sense of panic, Miss Leckton raised her torch, moved its light across the near bed. It was rumpled but empty, its covers flung back. Over its edge hung a night-gown, loosely dropped there, pink, with short sleeves, ruffles, and a high neckline, one of Leah's, recognizably Leah's.

Her breath held deeply (her heart pounding now), Miss Leckton shone the torch on the other bed.

They were there—both of them. The woman and the girl.

241

The tawny head rested on the bare shoulder of the dark head. The arms and shoulders, the upper chest of the dark head, they were bare, the white skin glistened with sweat.

Immediately Miss Leckton had seen what she had seen, she turned off the torch, left the room, closed the door, softly, softly, yet swiftly. Uppermost in her mind now was the desire not to waken these two, above all not to waken them. It was of immense importance. Her breathing began again, heavy, labored, fast, as the faint click followed the removal of her hand from the doorknob, announced the door fast shut. Miss Leckton fled to her sitting room, closed the door, locked it shut. She did not know why she locked it.

Beneath the surface of her mind, held there by some sort of control she was not conscious of exercising, was a turmoil of pain, of despair, of hurt, of chagrin. Over this subsurface violence of emotion, the conscious mind was busy with the job of rationalization. How good of her! said the conscious mind. How kind, how thoughtful! To comfort, to mother that poor little, common, vulgar waif, to keep her safe, to give her sleep in security! How gentle, how sweet of Maude Cleever! She who had suffered so much lately, whose own loss ...

But as she came to that, Miss Leckton balked at it, it would not work, there was something wrong here; the hurt and the irrational grief—the capacity to be hurt by a stranger—were too near the surface. Now the fabric of her pose, the stiffening of her life, seemed damaged, softened. The invasion she had suffered had culminated wholly in discomfort and pain. This was the proper end to Leah's treachery and desertion, the storm, the importunate arrivals. Nothing that she had wanted had happened; all that she had not wanted had occurred. There was now no reward, and no justification. These people—all of them, all of them!—had, by their very coming, left her more terribly alone than she had been (not knowing it then, not caring to know it) when Leah had left her house.

In an agony of release of emotion, Miss Leckton had flung herself face down on her settee, weeping, sobbing, until,

242

from an excess of emotion and fatigue, she had fallen asleep again. When she had waked, it had been morning—summer morning, hot; still, high, cloudless blue sky; still air full of the acid scent of the fallen green oak leaves; trees bare as winter—and the sudden guests were as suddenly departing.

XIX

IT was not only the painful quality of her recollections that roused Miss Leckton now until she focused again on the present, seeing the empty coffee cup beside her, the two candles brightly burning. Her return to the present was caused as much by another of those strange, those cruelly cyclical repetitions, that had beset her and confused her all this day and night. This time, it was the sudden dropping of the wind.

It had ceased as suddenly as a radio ceases when one turns the knob. One moment it had been there, that violence of wind, shaking the house, rattling and slashing at the windows, creating an inner turmoil to match the outer one. Now, and suddenly, it had ceased, and the house stood unshaken, the windows lay quiet, all that one heard was the incessant and disorderly noise of the surf breaking in an orgy of destructive fury.

Coming to her feet, Miss Leckton wondered if the storm was really over. Could it be? So suddenly? It had not happened like that before. What time was it? She could almost have asked, 'What year is it?' There seemed so small a line to be drawn now between the actuality of 1944 and the recollected reality of 1938.

Her first nervous impulse took her to the door to the hall, although she had no idea why she was going there or where she should go from there. It was simply that she felt driven now to action, to movement, that the sitting down bred too much fear, too much discomfort and grief, shook one too much, as a storm shook and threatened the house.

But as she reached the hall, the wind began again. Once more the house was shaken, its groans and creaks and rattles took up precisely where they had left off; this had been a respite then, not a cessation. It was still to be endured.

She started for the stairs, meaning to go down to the library, but she remembered the candles and, returning to the sitting room, blew them out. The acrid smell of the extinguished wicks spread out in the hot, close air, made the room (apart from all its new associations of thought) unpleasant to her. She descended rapidly to the library.

The little clock on the desk said quarter to twelve. Was that all? She had lived a lifetime in so short a space of minutes. The barometer had fallen again. It stood at the alarming figure of 28.20. It didn't seem possible to her. She set the index hand to the reading, and again she noticed that her hand shook. It seemed to be shaking all the time now; she did not like that. Letting her hand fall to her side, she stared again at the barometer. 28.20. A ghastly figure!

Standing there, she began to realize that this room was now more quiet than it had been before. One could hear the storm, to be sure, it was omnipresent in the night, but it seemed now a little removed, less immediate. What was causing that?

Because she could not stand there forever, because she did not intend now to sit down again—not for a while, at least, since to do so would only invite further discomfiture—she wandered about the lower floors of her house, telling herself that she must do this, that it was her duty.

Holding her lighted torch, she went from room to room. In the living room, the dining room, she noticed that the water had altogether stopped leaking in at the windows. In the dining room, the pantry, the kitchen, she could hear that the noise had greatly increased, and she knew that the wind had shifted sharply to the westward. Then, following the same nervous compulsion to motion, she went upstairs, mounted to the garret. There were puddles of water on the rough floor, but it was too late to do anything about them now, and she was too tired. She went to her bedroom, to the bathroom, back to her sitting room. There was only one room left to oversee: the guest room.

But when she stood outside its closed door, she could not bring herself to enter it. She had been there too recently in her mind, it was all still too vivid. That room was peopled (as indeed the whole house was peopled, but this more intensely) by the unwanted and the wanted, the disturbers, the invaders not alone of her life, but of her way of life: the straight and wonted road she had once and for so long securely travelled. With a sense of defeat and depression, she turned away from the guest-room door. What difference did it make what happened to it? Who would use it now?

Like an uneasy ghost, Miss Leckton wandered from room to room of her empty house, looking into each room—save only that one, the guest room. She had no sense of the passage of time, knew only that she was so tired she could hardly stand on her feet; and yet was deadly afraid to sit down.

It was five minutes past twelve when she finally went back to the library. It took an effort of will to look at the barometer again. To her surprise, it had risen slightly—very slightly. Regardless of what her father had told her, she tapped it gently. The needle flickered and moved a fraction upward.

"Thank God!" she said to herself. "It has begun to rise. The storm will pass now."

Yet even if it passed, what should she do? Sit here? Go to bed? She was afraid of either. Once more she thought of setting the candle in the window, calling George over. But as she moved to the window, she saw that there was now no light in the tenement dormer, that only blackness, unmitigated and loud, lay outside the glass.

So they had gone to bed! They cared nothing now for her, or for what might happen to her. Seeing the wind shift, they concluded (George and his Ella) that the storm was over

246

and done. How little would such as they imagine that it might still be raging here, for her, alone!

For a brief moment she considered that she might put on her raincoat, her hat, go over to them. They were people, but they were not the people whose images filled each corner of this house with such discontent. As she thought of this, she dismissed it: it was impossible, and she knew it. She knew it so well that she saw (with a clarity she had never before applied to any part of her life) that she herself had locked the door against herself. How could she go? How could she face them? With what words could she ask them to let her enter, to comfort her? With what glances would they let her in, seat her, make her welcome? What worlds of the unspoken, freight of so many days, would lie behind those glances? No, no! It could not be done.

For the last time that day, Miss Leckton felt anger mounting within her. How grossly unfair it all was! That those who came to you for shelter, who did not seek your invitation, who would not accept your refusal, should remain with you and, years later and in horrible ingratitude, infest your house and your rooms and your mind, yet shut you out of their company! Was one never to discriminate? Was one to open one's heart and one's house to all the Frostens of this world? Were storms to become raging inner storms because—not of what *you* did—but because of what others imposed on you?

Suddenly and vividly, Miss Leckton saw another image, born wholly of her anger, her frustration, her despair. It was the image of Lucy Lagonegro leaving Mrs. Cleever. She could see every detail: the girl was standing in a hallway, her hand in that of a shadowy but real young man. She was saying, 'I love him, and I shall marry him. I shall go now.' She could see Maude Cleever's face, streaked with the tears of anger, pleading and threatening, telling Lucy over and over again how great was this ingratitude. Imaginary though Miss Leckton knew the scene to be, yet it was so real to her at that moment that she rejoiced in it: it was a sweet revenge.

As soon as it had come, fulfilled itself, the vision vanished.

247

It left her so weak, so let down, that she had to sit before her knees should give way. Over her began to spread the horrible, the accustomed depression; accustomed, but with a difference, for this time she felt as though she had been stitched through with an infinitely close diapering of painful thread, so that all that had ever been free within her to move and be various, had now been fastened into the single, stiff pattern of her loneliness.

She was overwhelmed with the whole, confused mass of her recollections. They took no shape at all at first, but flowed through her mind in frightening and illogical disorder, mixed now past separation with the experiences of the day. It was as though she was forced to sit, in fear and almost in despair, before the crazily edited moving picture of her days, to see again, to hear, the scenes she had remembered, but that were now in mad disorder, strung together in a montage calculated only to convince her of her own futility, to persuade her of her emptiness. Mrs. Cleever's arrival mixed with the expulsion of Grover La Perche, and in a way that gave to him and to his wife a meaning they had not had before, and the sound track of this confusion carried the voice of Birac, his accent clear and unmistakable, saying, "How shall you choose the good or the bad? One does not say to a man at a moment of crisis, 'Is your life worth saving?'" The image of Mrs. Kluger's car, the red tail-light disappearing in the night, confused with the sound of Leah's radio, the voice that said, "What we have is a rushing into a series of difficulties which may be greater than those which he hopes to avoid. Good morning." The picture of the war that still rolled over the world—as though this voice had proclaimed it against her decision—turned to the image of a crowd of people assailing her house, her privacy, her life, with importunate demands to let them in, to save them, and—more horrible than anything so far—to let them save her.

And at that moment, over the terrible sound of the hurricane, over her thoughts, the telephone rang.

Miss Leckton jumped so violently in her chair that the electric torch fell to the floor with a rattle, and she could hear it rolling over and over on the wooden floor under the desk. Then, with a shake of the head, a sharp intake of breath, she picked up the instrument, put the receiver to her ear.

"Hello," she said.

"Miss Carrel Leckton, please. Miami calling," said an operator's voice.

"This is Miss Leckton," she said.

"One moment, please. Here's your party. Go ahead, Miami."

"Aunt Carrel?" Leah's clear warm voice came again to her, but faintly now, as though its distance were reflected in its sound.

"Hello," said Miss Leckton, loudly, urgently. "Leah? Is that you, Leah?"

"Hello. Aunt Carrel?" came the distant voice. "Are you there? Are you all right? I ..."

The line went dead. The voice stopped. There was not even a humming noise now.

Miss Leckton shouted into the mouthpiece.

"Leah, Leah!" she cried. "Leah!"

It was no use. The thing was dead. It was gone. Everything was gone now.

Holding the useless, the betraying instrument in her shaking hands, Miss Leckton sat frozen in her chair. She could hear the storm in the night. But the storm—this storm—was over now, it was past its peak. There was no more danger in it. Not in the storm, itself. The house was safe, undamaged, nothing would happen to it now. The house.

Even the experiences were done and over with, played out, like the storm—these unexpectedly critical experiences of the present and of the past that she had had to relive as though they were inseparable from each other, each containing within itself both cause and effect, so that as neither could justly begin, so neither could end. They were done, she repeated, done! Yes, except as they must be experienced again within the future mind, painfully, precariously, with increasing knowledge to foster the dread of understanding.

249

Once more she lifted the telephone to her mouth, her ear. "Leah!" she said.

There was no answer: there could be none.

The storm was over. She knew herself now to be alone.

Alone, she was insufficient even to herself. Her salvation (as though that word had suddenly taken on a meaning of the most mortal importance and urgency) must depend now on her power to dispel, to abjure her aloneness: the inner storm had become more lasting than all the outer ones, it could blow on her now without hope of relief, its tide of isolating fear could rise to intolerable heights. One could not live thus—one could not live to oneself.

Yet there was still interminable night that lay ahead and any dawn would rise only as she made it to rise. Night, like this storm, was solitary. If dawn were peopled, then with whom? With whom?

I wonder, she thought, what has happened to Mrs. Barber in this storm?

The sound and meaning of the words within her mind, astonished her.